GUILTY
MOTHERS

BOOKS BY ANGELA MARSONS

GUILTY MOTHERS

Angela
MARSONS

bookouture

Published by Bookouture in 2024

An imprint of Storyfire Ltd.
Carmelite House
50 Victoria Embankment
London EC4Y 0DZ

www.bookouture.com

ISBN: 978-1-83525-527-8
eBook ISBN: 978-1-83525-526-1

This book is dedicated to all the great moms out there who feel they are never doing enough.
You're doing awesome.

ONE

Kim checked her phone for the third time.

'Anything, boss?' Stacey asked, catching her movement.

They'd all heard the radio chatter about a discovery in one of the Dudley fishing pools. The dive team had been summoned, and if the worst were to be confirmed, Keats's name would be lighting up Kim's screen any second now.

Three pairs of eyes watched.

She shook her head as their mood washed over her.

It had been a couple of months since their last major case, and although none of them wished for the appearance of a dead body, it was murder investigations that brought out the best in them, that pushed them to their limits.

Kim liked to think they gave one hundred per cent of themselves to every case that landed on their desks, but getting justice for someone whose life had been taken lit the fires in their bellies by an extra few degrees: late nights, early mornings and little other than working the case in between.

She also knew her team was waiting for her to raise a subject that none of them wanted to hear about. She supposed now was as good a time as any. This particular elephant had been sitting in the middle of the room long enough to get a parking ticket.

She moved from behind the spare desk and sat on the edge of it, signalling that she was about to address them all.

'Okay, guys, you know we've got to talk about it.'

There were groans as they all exchanged glances.

'Look, it's a talent show, for charity. One of you has to take part.'

'Us, guv – one of us,' Bryant corrected her. As her steady, pragmatic partner in crime, he always saw fit to remind her of the details.

'You really think I've got any talent that would translate well to a stage and a room full of people?' she asked.

'Good point,' he conceded.

'Come on, people, surely one of you can do something?'

Every department had been 'invited' to contribute a performance at a charity ball this coming Sunday night. She had been on the cusp of telling Woody they weren't interested when he'd asked precisely who was going to fill their three-minute spot between the traffic team and the firearms unit, making it clear that every department was doing their bit for charity.

'Surely one of you has a hidden talent that can fill three minutes,' she repeated.

'Just about but it ain't suitable for stage,' Bryant offered.

They all laughed except for Kim, who turned her attention to Penn. Surely the studious detective sergeant who never failed to amaze them with random facts about every subject on the planet had something.

'A song? A poem?'

'Ooh, yeah, I've got one,' Penn said then cleared his throat.

They all waited expectantly.

'The boy stood on the burning deck, his pocket full of crackers. A flame shot up his trouser leg and blew away his—'

'Jesus, Penn. Is that the best you've got?' Kim asked as Stacey wiped tears of laughter from her eyes.

'I was gonna say pockets,' he said, shrugging.

Kim ignored him and turned to the constable. 'How about you, Stace? Give me your best shower song.'

Catching the vibe, Stacey broke into the first few words of a famous Whitney Houston song.

All eyes were on her as they sat in stunned silence.

Kim held up her hand to end the torture after a couple of lines.

'Okay, it's a fact. We're well and truly fu—'

Her ringing phone cut off her words.

'It's Keats. We're up,' she said before pressing the answer button.

'Go ahead.'

'Blimey, Stone, it's like you were expecting my call.'

'I was.'

'Weird, but okay. I am formally requesting your presence at—'

'Hey, Keats, you sure this one's dead?' she interrupted.

She'd been waiting two months to ask him that question, following his premature pronouncement on their last case.

The silence that met her question told her that he hadn't yet reached the point of looking back on the memory with fond recollection and humour.

'Too soon?'

'Yes,' he answered tersely.

'Okay, I'm on my way.'

'To where?'

'Fishing pools at Dudley. That's why you're calling, isn't it?'

'Sorry, not a clue what's going on there. I've been tied up here at thirty-one Loudner Road, Stourbridge. Female victim, late forties.'

'Okay, Keats, on our way,' she said.

Sounded like a major case that warranted their attention. Just not the one she'd been expecting.

'And for what it's worth,' he said, lowering his voice, 'my opinion is that you won't have to look far for the culprit.'

TWO

Loudon Road was in an area of Stourbridge that bordered Stourton, part of the last clutch of roads before the A458 continued into countryside.

'How about we just carry on driving, grab us a coffee and admire the river at Bridgnorth,' Bryant suggested as he neared the left turn.

'I'm good, thanks,' Kim said. Bridgnorth was one of the many local places under a flood warning, following what experts were calling the wettest September on record.

As if on cue, the wipers kicked in as spots began to appear on the windscreen.

Not that sitting beside a river appealed to her at any time of the year, she thought as they approached the crime-scene tape. Being in the countryside didn't suit her natural disposition for being amongst noise, activity, the chaos of urban life. She saw plenty of countryside when she took her Kawasaki Ninja for a burn to blow the cobwebs away.

Seeing that there was no space beyond the cordon, Bryant pulled into a spot just feet away from the gathering crowd.

Kim groaned when she saw who was at the front of the

watching audience. Of course her arch nemesis from the *Dudley Star* was already there.

'Care to comment, Inspector?' Frost asked.

'You're an idiot.'

'On that,' the reporter said, nodding towards the house.

'On what?' Kim asked. 'I haven't even entered the cordon. And how the hell are you even here before me?' She narrowed her gaze. 'You upgraded your broomstick?'

'I have my sources. So, what's going on? Neighbours are saying—'

'Keep your gossip to yourself,' Kim said, ducking under the barrier tape. She had no wish to listen to anything any reporter had to say before she'd even seen the body.

She headed away from the tape and then turned back.

'Hey, Frost, I've got a scoop for you.'

'Go on,' Frost said suspiciously.

'It's a pretty safe bet we're gonna have some rain.'

Proving her point, the preliminary spots she'd seen on the windscreen turned into larger, heavier raindrops that spattered to the ground.

She headed straight for the tent that had been erected to cover the entrance to the property.

Keats stepped out of the tent to brief them while they donned the protective equipment.

'It's not pretty. A lot of blood. Murder weapon is right there.'

Kim pulled the overall up over her body. 'What was the cryptic bit about the killer?' she asked. 'You doing our job as well as your own?'

'In good time. Go straight through to the kitchen.'

The stench was immediate when Kim stepped into the hallway. The metallic aroma was unmistakeable as blood, and lots of it.

She walked past an upended telephone table and a broken

lamp before reaching the doorway to the kitchen. The room opened up into a sea of blood spreading away from the victim towards every corner of the room. It hardly seemed possible that this amount of blood was from one person and not an entire gladiatorial battle. How did the body contain such a vast amount? she wondered.

Bryant's intake of breath brought her back to the room, away from the hypnotic red sea.

It was only once she had taken in the bigger picture that she realised just how violent the episode had been. The woman on the ground was a petite form dressed in jeans and what was once a purple tee shirt. The front of her shirt was blood-soaked from multiple stab wounds. Her arms and hands were covered with lacerations, with even a couple on her attractive face. A scratch that hadn't broken the skin ran from her lower jaw diagonally across her neck and down beneath her dark brown hair.

Spatters of blood were evident on the kitchen counters, as were what appeared to be nicks from the knife.

There was no question that this had been a brutal attack and that the victim had fought back with every breath she had. The result was carnage, and the rage seemed out of place in this ordinary suburban home.

Kim glanced to the countertop where a knife was already sealed in a clear evidence bag. The block was one short.

'One of her own?' she asked Mitch across the breakfast bar.

'The biggest,' he said, holding up the bag. It was a carving knife around eight inches long.

Kim shuddered at the thought of plunging such a blade into someone's flesh repeatedly.

She remained outside the kitchen as Mitch and his two operatives continued to work. There was nowhere she could step without disturbing the pool of blood.

She surveyed the room and realised the radio was still playing in the background. A pile of washing had been taken from the tumble drier and placed on the table ready for folding. The faint scent of a floral fabric conditioner was trying to triumph over the smell of blood.

Two cups sat beside the kettle.

Had the woman been expecting her visitor?

Her first impressions were that the victim had been going about her business normally when maybe she'd received a call. She'd readied the cups for her visitor, but she'd been attacked just feet away from the front door, in the hallway, as though the visitor could barely get through the door before unleashing violence.

'Her name is Sheryl Hawne, aged forty-eight. No husband. One daughter named Katie,' Mitch offered. 'Phone and purse were this side of the microwave. All appears intact.'

Kim had ruled out robbery the second she'd seen the blood. Most thieves did only what they needed to do. This was too much. Way too much.

Keats appeared behind Bryant.

'Neighbour called the police after hearing screaming and shouting and then silence. She knocked the door but was too frightened to enter. Police did so and found the assailant sitting silently beside the victim, still holding the knife.'

He nodded towards the lounge.

'Who am I talking to, Keats?' she asked.

'The woman holding the knife was her daughter.'

THREE

Kim wasn't quite ready for the sight that greeted her when she entered the lounge.

Sitting on the sofa, flanked by two police officers, was a painfully thin woman in her early to mid-twenties. Her plain white tee shirt was soaked with blood, and spatters of red were present on her grey jeans, her trainers and the skin of her forearms, neck and face. There were even traces obvious in her straw-blonde hair. Her wrists were bound with handcuffs, and she sat on the edge of the sofa, staring ahead.

Kim followed her gaze to the wall, which was dotted with photos of a little blonde girl in different princess costumes, smiling for the camera.

The daughter's face was devoid of expression as she stared at the photos of herself. The woman lying butchered in the kitchen wasn't present in any of them.

Kim stepped in front of the wall, but the woman's gaze didn't falter. She stared through Kim's midriff to the images behind her.

'Katie, my name is Detective Inspector Stone. Would you like to tell us what happened here?'

No response or acknowledgement that she'd spoken.

'Can you confirm that the person in the kitchen is your mother?'

No response.

Kim kneeled down in front of her. 'Katie, what happened here?'

Nothing.

Kim raised herself back to a standing position and nodded to Bryant in the doorway.

He stepped forward and showed his identification. Given the circumstances and her refusal to speak, they had no choice but to make an immediate arrest.

'Katie Hawne, I am arresting you...'

Kim tuned out of the obligatory caution and studied the face for any change. There was nothing. She wondered if Katie was already planning her defence or if she'd talk once she was in the presence of a lawyer.

The thought of that prompted the next stage of the investigation. She turned towards the door and, as though he'd read her mind, Mitch was waiting with empty evidence bags. She took them and turned back to the woman on the sofa.

'Katie, we're going to need to take your clothing for evidence. A full search of your person will take place at the station, but now PC Murphy will assist you upstairs to change into something more suitable and bag the clothing you're wearing.'

Whether she was staying silent on purpose or in a state of shock, she would eventually realise that her clothes were stained with her mother's blood.

Kim nodded to the female constable, who touched Katie's elbow and urged her to her feet.

As Katie turned towards the door, Kim's eyes met those of the constable. She nodded that she understood the suspect was not to be left alone.

Kim indicated for the other constable to take a position at the bottom of the stairs. She didn't feel that Katie was going to make a run for it – she didn't appear present enough to attempt that – but if she took time to think about her impending future, she might be tempted.

'Bloody hell, guv,' Bryant said, letting out a long breath. 'Talk about spaced out.'

'If it's genuine,' Kim said, heading back towards the kitchen. It wouldn't be the first time a suspect had tried to feign mental health issues to avoid a life sentence.

'Anything else I need to know?' she called into the room.

'How to know when to let something go,' Keats said, narrowing his gaze in her direction.

'Unlikely, but thanks for the tip.'

Kim took one last look at the carnage that had transformed a perfectly normal kitchen into a scene from a horror movie before heading back to the front door.

There was nothing more she could do here. Her work was back at the station, questioning Katie Hawne to find out why she had taken her mother's life in such a cruel and brutal way.

With the efficiency of a well-oiled machine, she and Bryant silently removed all the protective wear beside the bin that had been provided. As she placed the last paper slipper into the bin, she heard Bryant's sharp intake of breath.

She turned and followed his gaze to the handcuffed woman coming down the stairs.

Katie had changed her clothes for sure. Gone were the bloodstained garments and in their place was a full-length sequinned magenta ballgown.

FOUR

'And she still said nothing?' Stacey asked in disbelief as Kim recounted the story.

'Not a word. She just got into the car and is now being processed downstairs,' Kim said, taking a sip of coffee.

She didn't mention the line of police officers she'd arranged into a shield to cover the short distance from the tent to the police car. The last thing they needed was that photo turning up in the national press, although she was pretty sure the story was heading that way. Cases of brutal matricide always captured the public's attention.

'Any idea why she snapped?' Penn asked.

'Nothing obvious. Home looks perfectly normal.'

'No previous calls for domestic issues or disturbances,' Stacey confirmed.

'Fancy being stabbed with your own carving knife,' Penn added. 'A kitchen utensil used every Sunday for—'

'Penn, you really do focus on the strangest things,' Bryant said, shaking his head.

Kim checked her watch. It had been twenty minutes since she'd called for the duty brief.

Despite the glazed remoteness, it was clear that Katie Hawne had killed her own mother, and Kim had to consider that the strange behaviour was part of a premeditated plan to adopt a diminished responsibility defence. She was absolutely playing this one by the book and there would be no interview without legal representation.

'Okay, guys, while we wait—'

Kim was interrupted by Bryant's internal phone.

He answered it, nodded and passed it to her.

'Stone.'

'Yeah, you might want to come downstairs,' the custody sergeant advised her.

'Brief here already?' she asked hopefully.

'Err... no. And I think you're gonna want more than the brief when you get down here.'

Kim handed the phone back to Bryant and headed to the stairs. What the hell was she being called down to? Was the prisoner holding one of the officers hostage with a hair grip she'd secreted?

She opened the door that led to the custody suite forcefully, almost hitting a constable. A further eight officers lined the corridor that led to the cells. At the far end stood Katie Hawne, still handcuffed, but something had changed. Her eyes were alive, bright, animated.

'Ah, perfect. A lady judge. Always smile at the ladies but give a little wink to the men,' Katie said in a voice that was steady and confident.

She began to walk the corridor with the poise of a supermodel, turning her head to the left then to the right, offering a dazzling smile to every officer she passed.

She reached Kim and paused.

'Take just three seconds to make eye contact with the judges, smile brightly and exit stage left,' she said, turning and swishing the ballgown behind her.

The officers looked Kim's way for guidance, but she shook her head, telling them to do nothing. Katie was cuffed in a room full of officers and was going nowhere. Kim wanted to see how this played out and was busy looking for signs of deception.

Katie sashayed to the far end of the corridor and turned again. This time her smile was childlike, hopeful.

'Did I win? Was I perfect?'

Kim tried not to let the shock register on her face.

'Katie, do you understand where you are?' she asked.

Instantly the light in her eyes vanished. She looked down at herself and a small cry of surprise sounded from her lips. She looked around at all the faces staring at her. Her expression contorted in horror.

'No, no, no, no, no,' she cried as she started to claw at the fabric of the dress. Sequins flew and seams ripped as she fought to get the material away from her skin as though it was scalding her. In the process, she'd exposed most of the upper half of her body, including a flesh-coloured bra that was now in disarray and very revealing.

Kim rushed to her side and pulled the dress back around her, shielding her from view with her own body.

'Somebody, get me some clothes,' she shouted over her shoulder. 'And the rest of you piss off.'

'On it, marm,' one of the voices called back as Katie leaned against the wall and slid to the ground.

Kim followed her down and kept her covered.

'What have I done?' Katie whispered against her arm.

Kim met her gaze, but the woman's eyes had returned to staring mode.

'Someone buzz the on-call doc,' Kim instructed. The only emotion resting on Katie's face was despair, and Kim needed no further convincing.

This woman was not putting on an act.

FIVE

'Okay, I didn't have that on my bingo card,' Stacey said, once the boss had left the room after updating them.

Kim was now on her way back to the crime scene, having left strict instructions to be informed once the doctor had examined Katie Hawne.

'I mean, surely there's got to be something wrong to kill your own mother,' Penn said, sitting back in his seat. He let out a long breath as his eyes glazed over for just a few seconds. He and his brother, Jasper, had been forced to face the loss of their mother not so long ago, and Stacey knew the woman had been very much loved by both her sons.

'There are many examples going way back,' Stacey offered. 'Cleopatra the third of Egypt was assassinated in 101 BC by order of her son. In 2005, an eighteen-year-old girl in Memphis stabbed her mom fifty times. Not everybody had the cookie-cutter childhood with a warm and nurturing mother.'

'But even so,' he said, bringing himself back into the room. 'Didn't Freud have a lot to say on the subject?'

'He was mother obsessed though, wasn't he?' Stacey asked.

'I think he believed in a pre-Oedipal phase existence which

determines mother/daughter relationships, made up of ambiva-lent feelings between love and hate from the girl to her mother, which mostly culminates in hatred.'

'Okay, Wikipenn, translated that means?'

'He's kind of saying that there's a period of time before the Oedipus complex, between the ages of three to five, when attachment to the mother predominates in both sexes. It's also generally felt that two major contributors to difficult relation-ships between mother and daughter are jealousy and expectation.'

'Isn't there a new term called "mother-blaming"?' Stacey asked, remembering something she'd read recently. 'Where every problem is blamed on something the mother did or didn't do during childhood?'

Penn shrugged. 'Not sure we're the right folks to be talking about this, Stace.'

Yeah, Stacey was with him on that one. She knew Penn had been close to his mother and that they'd shared a special bond through their devotion to Jasper. In her own case, there had never been a time in her life when Stacey had not been able to count on her mom. The woman had always represented comfort and safety, with a good measure of honesty. When Stacey made a mistake, her mom had no qualms in calling her out. As she had done when Stacey had finally confided all the events surrounding her ordeal with Terence Birch.

She had not been gentle in criticising Stacey's actions, but her anger had soon given way to concern and support.

Stacey still experienced the occasional cringe when she remembered the damage she'd done to the most important people in her life by not trusting them with the truth. But every-thing was repairing slowly and surely, and things were now approaching normality.

She had taken the boss's advice and contacted Charlotte Danks, who had also been stalked by Birch. They had met a few times, and she had experienced great relief and healing talking to someone who completely understood the level of sheer powerlessness he'd made them feel. It was after their third meeting that both of them realised that they were now keeping him alive by talking about him, and that it was time to move on with their lives.

And part of that included bringing her A game back to work.

She refreshed the system to find out if there was any progress on the incident at the lake. That would probably be their next major case, now it looked as though the brutal murder of Sheryl Hawne had already been solved.

SIX

Tiff hid her shudder as the body was placed onto the trolley.

Donkey Pool was a fishing pond on Priory Road, Dudley. Located next to a playing field, it wasn't the largest fishing spot in the area but remained popular with the locals due to a good showing of carp. It had garnered national headlines in 2019 when a prolific thief, after a car chase, fled his vehicle and swam to the island in the middle of the pond to hide. He was eventually found by a fire rescue team in a dinghy and taken to hospital suffering from hypothermia. Every police officer in the borough knew the story.

She wasn't squeamish, and it wasn't the first dead body she'd ever seen. It wasn't even the first she'd seen removed from water. But it was the first she'd seen that had been submerged in water for approximately two years.

She'd seen bodies with adipocere, the waxy formation that occurred in the right conditions. She knew that once formed it could preserve the body for years. She wasn't disturbed by the bloated, misshapen corpse that was formed into 'the drowning position', where the back is arched and the limbs appear to be reaching down. What she hadn't seen before was the presence of 'washerwoman's hands', a wrinkling and sloughing of the skin particularly on the hands and feet, common in cases of prolonged immersion.

The remaining clothing reminded her of the film *The Hulk*: the garments had been stretched and ripped in different places as they strained against the bloating.

'Wanna bet against me that's our misper from a couple of years back?' Sergeant Kendrick asked her.

'No bet, Sarge – the clothes match,' Tiff replied with a smile. Kendrick was one of the good guys and she never missed an opportunity to work with him. In some ways he reminded her of DS Bryant. He'd reached the rank of sergeant and decided that was where he wanted to stay. Only eight months away from retirement, Kendrick still treated every incident as though it was his first.

'Wouldn't be too sure of that,' he said. 'Water can discolour...'

'It's the belt, Sarge. Our misper was wearing a double looped, gold belt buckle with a lion's head.' She nodded towards the ambulance. 'Same one...'

Sergeant Kendrick nodded approvingly as two of Tiff's colleagues passed by.

'It's all right, folks. Vera's on the case. She'll have it sewn up by teatime,' said the one in front, a man she'd shared many shifts with.

Sarge heard the comment but said nothing.

She tried not to let her feelings show on her face. Thank goodness the sarge had said nothing in her defence. That would have just made everything worse.

This was how it had been ever since she'd applied for CID. She'd expected some backlash, but the root of the hurt she felt was that the snarky comments were coming from colleagues who had been her friends. She'd been drinking with both of these officers numerous times. Together they'd celebrated arrests, birthdays, promotions... but her decision to try for CID had put a wedge between her and them. Right now she was in limbo and didn't fit anywhere.

'Ignore the haters,' the sarge said, beckoning for her to walk with him. 'Your identification of the belt just earned you a prize.'

'It did?' Tiff asked. 'What do I get?'

'You get to come with me to inform the family.'

SEVEN

Kim was always surprised at how quickly a community adjusted to a major event, even a brutal murder on the doorstep.

Only an hour ago there'd barely been standing room at the cordon, but like any good show, the main event had passed. The sirens were no longer sounding, the blue lights were no longer flashing and the stars of the show had left the stage. Only a few stragglers remained to watch the crew take down the set. The rest had returned to their own priorities, which had not disappeared in the face of a brutal murder. She was pleased to note the absence of Tracy Frost. Kim was hopeful that the reporter had turned her attention to the body in the lake and was now someone else's problem.

Kim signed herself and Bryant back into the house, but didn't dress in protective clothing. Mitch had been working the scene for a couple of hours, and she had no intention of going near the kitchen. That wasn't the reason for her visit.

Although the body had been removed, the forensic techie would be inspecting every square inch. Even on a case as cut and dried as this one, forensics would be needed to support the charge in court.

No, her interest lay elsewhere. After Katie's impromptu performance at the station, Kim wanted to understand the dynamics at play. This time she was here to examine the home.

'Just about to call you,' Mitch shouted from the kitchen.

'Call me what?' Kim asked.

Mitch shook his head at her poor attempt at humour. 'First bedroom on the left. Interesting.'

Kim glanced at Bryant before heading up the stairs. As ordered, she headed for the first door on the left.

'Bloody hell,' she exclaimed as the door opened.

For a second she considered shielding her eyes.

The sun that had followed another brief shower shone through the window, lighting up a treasure trove of trophies, crowns, tiaras, sashes and rosettes. A three-tier display had been set up covered in ivory silk and arranged so that every trophy and cup could be seen. Each sash had its own hook and hung proudly from the wall above the display.

The other three walls were covered in framed photographs of a little girl wearing all kinds of sparkly, sequinned gowns. All of which Kim suspected were still hanging in the double wardrobe behind the door.

A single seat was placed beside the window.

Kim now understood that the photos downstairs weren't of a girl playing dress up but of her competing.

Katie Hawne had been a pageant child.

'Looks like they're in date order,' Bryant said, taking a look at the trophies.

'What years?' Kim asked, picking up a tiara that was made of cheap plastic and what looked like glass.

'First one I've got is Little Miss Stourbridge in 2006, and the last one was Miss Teen Black Country in 2013.'

'Seven years?' Kim queried, looking at all the trophies that had been won during that time.

'She must have been good,' Bryant said. 'Lots of first place and Supreme and Grand Supreme, which I don't understand but sounds pretty impressive.'

Kim followed his gaze. The journey wasn't hard to map. The most prestigious titles and the biggest trophies had been won during Katie's middle years.

'Is it really possible for a kid to hit their prime aged eight to eleven?' Kim asked, noting the number of second-place trophies after that age.

'Never given pageant longevity much thought. I never even knew they were a thing in this country. Laura used to love an American show called *Toddlers and Tiaras* when she was little,' Bryant said, opening the wardrobe doors and revealing dresses that appeared to span the whole seven years.

Kim took the seat by the window, which was in pole position to view the whole room. There was no musty smell and no trace of dust. Rather than being an old batch of memories, the shrine was being kept very much alive.

The question was, by Katie or her mum?

EIGHT

'I'm not convinced it was Katie reliving the experience,' Kim said as they headed down the next-door neighbour's path.

Katie no longer lived at the family home, so it was more likely the shrine was the work of a proud mother. A bit much? Perhaps, but Kim held no judgement for how people spent their free time as long as they weren't hurting anyone else. If Sheryl Hawne enjoyed reliving Katie's glory years, where was the harm?

There were few people who would envy her own happy place of the garage floor surrounded by oily bike parts, so to each their own.

They would see what made Katie tick at her flat, once they'd spoken to Sheryl's neighbour.

'Rosie Kemp?' Kim asked, holding up her ID to the woman in her early seventies who answered the door.

'Are they ready for another cuppa?' she asked, looking towards the crime scene.

'Not quite yet,' Kim answered, having been made aware that Rosie Kemp was the incident 'hen'. Every suburban crime scene had one old lady, sometimes two, who was quick to offer tea, biscuits and often sandwiches.

'Oh, okay,' Rosie said, disappointed.

Every mother hen enjoyed being useful to the attending police officers, and it was widely appreciated. Given their desire to get involved, the hen was often the most knowledgeable about the immediate environment.

'Well, come in anyway,' she said, stepping to the side.

The house was the same layout as its neighbour, and Kim headed to the kitchen. Ten or so mugs were upended on the sink drainer; returned, refreshed and ready to go again.

Kim introduced herself and Bryant. 'May we ask you a few questions about Sheryl Hawne?'

'Of course,' Rosie said, switching on the kettle, which went into boil mode almost immediately. Oh, she was a keen one. Even the kettle was on permanent standby.

'We're fine, Mrs Kemp,' Kim said, taking a seat at the table. Bryant followed suit.

'Please call me Rosie,' she said. She turned off the kettle and sat down.

'Would you mind telling me about your neighbours?'

'What would you like to know?' Rosie asked cagily.

Ah, they'd got a canny one here who wasn't going to answer open questions. The answers to those were often the most revealing.

'How long had Mrs Hawne lived here?' Kim asked, taking another route.

'I'd say about fifteen years. The wee one was six or seven when they moved in, I think.'

Kim waited for more.

Rosie waited for another question.

'Was there a Mr Hawne?'

'Not that I ever saw.'

'Did she ever mention him?' Kim asked.

'And when would she have done that?' Rosie asked, crossing her arms. For a moment, Kim forgot who was questioning who.

'Maybe over coffee, passing the time of day in the street, chatting over the garden fence?'

'Oh, I must be the first neighbour you've spoken to,' Rosie said with a knowing smile.

'Does that matter?' Bryant asked.

'Not really. I just thought you might have spoken to people with kids the same age as Katie.'

'Go on,' Kim urged.

'Well, they made more of an effort with her than we did. Our two were long out of the nest, so short of the occasional hello, me and Edmund, God rest his soul, had little to offer her. She was a young thing with a little kid so... I mean, we sent them a Christmas card but that's about all.'

'And what would the other mums in the street have told us?' Kim asked.

'That Sheryl Hawne was rude to the point of being anti-social. There's not one person in this street ever stepped foot in that house.'

'Why not?' Kim asked, realising that Rosie was a woman who needed many prompts. Although with the best will in the world, Rosie couldn't swear to the fact that Sheryl never had any visitors.

'Kept everyone at arm's-length. Some of the moms tried to arrange play dates with their kids, but she always said no. She always said Katie had lots of allergies, that she was a sickly child, but I always thought that made no sense.'

'Why's that?'

'Well, she'd have been around all them other kids at school and at the pageants. So the local young moms took the huff and stopped asking her.'

'They knew Katie did pageants?'

'Only cos I mentioned it. I'd see them out back practising,

but you'd never have known it out front. Whenever they went off to these events, Katie would be wearing normal clothes and Sheryl would have a suitcase, even if they were back the same day. She didn't like anyone knowing her business.'

So, Sheryl was secretive about a hobby they did together. Maybe Katie had been a sickly child and the mother hadn't wanted the ridicule that came with the pageants.

'Would you say they were close?' Kim asked, although the scene next door said otherwise.

'Well they were always together. I saw them out there one time when Katie was around twelve and she was giving her mom some lip. Typical pre-teen stuff. She didn't want to practise any more, but Sheryl was pushing her to get it right. Katie started to take the mickey and do it badly, which was just making Sheryl angrier. I sneezed and Sheryl caught me watching. She took Katie inside and they never practised outside again.'

'Any other issues between them that you know of?' Bryant asked.

'Oh, they sure had some rows. Loud shouting, horrible insults. I did consider calling you lot once or twice, but Edmund, God rest his soul, said that it wasn't our business to interfere. I'd had some right humdingers with my two over the years, and I wouldn't have appreciated you lot turning up every time I lost my temper and told them off.'

'Did things ever get violent between them?' Kim asked.

'I'm tempted to say no to get myself off the hook for not calling you, but honestly I wouldn't like to say. Sometimes there were noises like stuff hitting the wall... but like I say, I don't know for certain.'

Oh, for the love of the 'don't get involveders'. How many incidents could have been avoided by making one phone call? Shouting, screaming, things hitting the wall definitely warranted a welfare call to the police. Edmund, God rest his soul, had called that wrong, Kim thought.

'I'm assuming to have moved out of the home, Katie must have got herself a job. Any idea where?' Kim asked.

'I know she was out working as soon as she turned sixteen. A couple of years later she moved out. She was doing cleaning, I think. A lot of working but not much socialising.'

'You didn't see people coming to the house? Friends? A boyfriend?'

Rosie shook her head. 'Not for either of them.'

'And I assume Katie still visited after she'd left home?'

'Oh yes, she did the duty visits.'

'Duty visits?' Kim queried.

'You know the one visit each month on the same day for just a couple of hours. Duty visit. Just a coffee, a meal. Enough to maintain contact, that kind of thing.'

Every time Rosie opened her mouth, Kim became more confused.

Regardless of what had happened in her childhood, Katie had moved out of the home. She had a job, her own place, and she'd developed a routine and a level of contact that she could maintain.

So, what the hell had happened to change all that?

NINE

Tiff stood just one step behind Sergeant Kendrick as he knocked on the door of an end terrace in Netherton.

Despite the small Citroën on the drive, no one appeared to be home. Sergeant Kendrick wasn't known for taking no for an answer and knocked again – harder.

After another minute, they heard two locks being turned and a chain engaged. The door opened a crack to reveal a young man, probably early twenties, Tiff guessed.

'Is Olivia Dench home?' Kendrick asked.

'Who wants to know?'

'Police,' Kendrick answered, pointing to his uniform, which kind of gave the game away.

The chain disengaged and the door opened, giving them a better look at the man on the other side. Tiff guessed him to be around six feet tall with a muscular build but not excessively so. He wasn't a gym bunny.

'I'm her son, Logan. Can I help?' he asked, opening the door wider.

'May we come in?'

He hesitated before nodding.

They stepped inside.

'It's about the missing person report your mother filed,' Kendrick said, looking past him.

Logan waited for more detail.

'Is she here?' Kendrick repeated.

'Sorry. Yes. Of course. Mom,' he called down the hallway.

A woman appeared from the kitchen, wiping her hands on a tea towel. She was dressed in plain black trousers and a white polo-neck shirt. She wore no make-up, and her hair was short and tidy, if not particularly well styled. Her face said early to mid-forties, but her overall appearance said ten years older.

'May we sit somewhere, Mrs Dench?' Kendrick asked.

She nodded towards the lounge.

Once they'd all entered, Logan took a seat next to his mother.

'You've found him, haven't you?' she asked, looking from one to the other.

'Let them speak, Mom,' Logan snapped.

Tiff said nothing. She was here as an observer only. And as such she'd noticed the very faint expression of irritation that had crossed Olivia's face when Logan had sat down beside her.

To be fair, there was nowhere else for him to sit.

'I'm afraid to say that a body was recovered from a fishing pool in Dudley earlier today. We believe it to be James Nixon.'

A small cry escaped Olivia's mouth as Logan placed an arm around her shoulders.

'Are you sure?' she asked, turning reddened eyes on them.

'Given the description you gave us, we're reasonably certain it's the man you reported missing.'

'Oh God,' she said, dropping her head.

Logan squeezed her tighter.

'We understand you'd been seeing him for a few months. Did he have any family we can contact?' Kendrick asked.

'His only relative is a sister who lives in Italy. They're not close,' Olivia offered tremulously.

Tiff knew where this was going. They needed someone reasonably close to the man.

'We'll need someone to formally identify the body,' Kendrick said.

'I'll do it,' Logan volunteered immediately as another small cry escaped from Olivia's lips.

'Are you sure?' Kendrick asked.

'Absolutely. I can't have Mom go through that. Just let me know when and I'll do it.'

He took out his phone and recited his number.

Tiff entered it in her pocket notebook.

'And would you have a number for James's sister?'

'It's in my phone,' Olivia said.

'I'll get it,' Logan said, heading out of the room.

Tiff heard the patter of footsteps going up the stairs. Within seconds, he was back with them. He handed Kendrick the phone, already unlocked, and retook his place beside his mother.

'Her name is Esther,' Olivia offered.

Kendrick scrolled down and clicked on the contact number, which Tiff also logged in her notebook. The sarge handed the phone back to Olivia, who put it in her pocket.

'May I ask where he was found?' Logan asked.

'Donkey Pool,' Kendrick told him. 'There'll be a post-mortem to determine a cause of death and potentially an investigation, but that will be handled by CID.'

'You don't think someone could have hurt him?' Olivia asked.

'Not our area, I'm afraid,' Kendrick said, placing his palms on his knees as though to stand.

Tiff had seen a pensive expression flit across Logan's face. She was here as an observer only and wasn't sure what to do.

Sarge hadn't noticed, and she didn't want to step on any toes, but she resolved that she'd rather be bollocked for something she did rather than didn't do.

'Logan, are you okay?' she asked, leaning forward.

'Yes, yes, I'm fine. It's probably nothing.'

'Tell us, lad,' Kendrick urged, retaking control.

'Well, it's just that I'm not surprised you found him there. It was his favourite place to fish. He loved it. And...' He looked towards his mum uncomfortably.

'Go on, Logan.'

'Well, he was suffering from depression.'

Olivia's head snapped towards her son.

'Sorry, Mom, but he didn't want you to know. He knew you'd want to try and fix him and that you'd feel bad if you couldn't.' Logan turned towards them again. 'He didn't want Mom thinking she wasn't enough for him, that she wasn't worth living for. He just wanted to deal with the dark thoughts in his own way.'

'Had he talked about taking his own life?' Kendrick asked.

'He hadn't said those exact words, but he'd said he wanted peace, to escape his own head,' Logan said, tapping his temple.

'Okay, thanks. Be sure to pass that on to the person investigating his death. Mrs Dench, we're very sorry for your loss.'

'Thank you,' Olivia said, without meeting their gaze.

'We'll see ourselves out.'

'It's okay,' Logan said, rising. 'I'll lock the door.'

They said their goodbyes on the doorstep.

Tiff followed Kendrick up the path and heard the locks click. She had an odd feeling in her stomach that she couldn't place, but her mind kept going to the tea towel that Olivia Dench had been holding. Throughout the entire conversation when they had informed her that her boyfriend's body had been recovered, she hadn't let go of it once.

TEN

Olivia stood at the sink as Logan locked the front door.

She removed the tea towel from her hands and ran them under the tap. The cool water soothed the burns immediately, but right now she didn't know which pain to focus on first, her hands or her heart.

Deep down, a part of her had known that James was dead, even though Logan had tried to convince her he'd just upped and left her for someone else.

She'd never believed that. They had clicked the minute they'd met. To some it had seemed a little soon after the loss of her husband, Logan's father, but she had known Joe's passing was coming, had been allowed to prepare for it. Following the grief, self-preservation had kicked in. She hadn't been looking for love, but she had wanted to laugh again, to dance, to go out to dinner with someone who wasn't slipping away day by day. She and Joe had made the most of those last few months, but every smile, laugh or moment of intimacy had been grasped under the shadow of death.

Just four months after his death she'd met James, a confirmed bachelor who loved working for himself as an odd-

job man and spent his free time fishing or travelling or sometimes both.

Despite his confirmed singledom, something had been
growing between them. Their nights out had been increasing,
and there had been more than a few occasions of staying over at
each other's homes.

The only negative had been Logan, who had taken an
instant dislike to James.

Standing here now, it was hard to remember the time when
it really had felt that simple and Logan's animosity had just
seemed like an obstacle, but oh, how her life had changed in the
two years since James had disappeared.

Hot, angry tears burned in her throat, but she knew better
than to let them out.

Had James been depressed and she hadn't known it? But
why would he have shared that with Logan when they could
barely stand the sight of each other?

Instinctively, she felt her son's presence somewhere behind
her. Her body tensed.

'Well done, Mom. You behaved impeccably.'

She relaxed only slightly as he closed the distance between
them. She felt the heat of his body even though they weren't
touching. Despite her best efforts, her knees began to tremble.

'But haven't you forgotten something?' he asked, as though
talking to a child.

'N-N-No,' she said, turning to face him.

He'd already said she'd behaved well. She had done nothing
to raise suspicion.

He held out his hand. 'Your phone. You know you're not
allowed to have it.'

'Logan, let me—'

The punch to her stomach forced her back against the sink.
The same sink where Logan had held her hands under the hot
tap just an hour earlier. Nausea rose inside her.

'Don't make me ask again,' he said, opening his palm, flexing his fingers and then making another fist.

Experience told her that the next blow would be even worse.

Shame warmed her cheeks as she handed him the phone.

ELEVEN

Katie Hawne's home was just a few miles away from Lye on the outskirts of Pedmore.

Stacey had phoned ahead to the landlord, who was waiting outside the premises.

It still amazed Kim how quickly the detective constable had bounced back. Only a couple of months ago she'd been a shell of her former self after her ordeal at the hands of Terence Birch. There was no question that she had returned to her previous level of performance, and Kim's trust in her had been restored.

'DI Stone and DS Bryant,' Kim said, showing her ID.

'Derek Hudson, owner and landlord,' he responded, leading them into a small corridor. There were three doors, and he paused at the one on the left.

'What's happened?' he asked before putting the key in the lock, as though entry was dependent on information.

'Not at liberty to share right now, Mr Hudson,' Kim said, nodding towards the door.

'Is she dead?'

'Any reason you'd ask that?' Kim shot back, growing impatient.

'Rent's due in two days, that's all.'

Kim said nothing and continued to stare at the door.

He opened it and went inside.

'Good tenant?' Bryant asked, following him in.

'Ideal, to be fair. No noise, no complaints, no late-night visitors.'

'And you'd know that how?' Kim asked.

He pointed across the hall. 'My place.'

Kim was unsure if she found that reassuring or ominous.

'Not my type, so you can get that out of your head. She's a nice girl, but I prefer a bit more meat on the bones and miles on the clock. I run a decent place.'

For some reason Kim found herself believing him as he pushed the door to the living room open.

At first glance, the apartment looked clean and well decorated.

'How long has she lived here?' Kim asked.

'Just over two years. Pays her rent on time. Called me once about a faulty boiler. I sorted it the same day, and other than small talk in passing that's pretty much it.'

'Okay, thanks, Mr Hudson. We'll give you a knock once we're done. We know where to find you.'

He took the hint gracefully and left them alone.

'All pretty normal,' Bryant observed as they moved further into Katie Hawne's home.

'Yep, it's almost like she never stabbed her mother to death,' Kim observed.

'The flat, not the situation,' he clarified.

'Hmm... not really,' she said, taking a good look around the living room.

A comfortable and functional sofa, a fashionable minimalistic coffee table, a plastic plant in the corner, a smart TV, candles, scatter cushions, a matching throw.

'Guv, you're seeing stuff that isn't there.'

'Accurate assessment exactly. What you got on your fire-place at home?'

'Holiday photo of me, Jenny and Laura taken about seven years ago.'

'What you got on the walls?'

'Currently pictures of the Highland cows that Jenny loves.'

'How about your coffee table?'

'Some weird crystal and pebble thing Laura bought us from — Oh, got it.'

'Two years she's lived here, and I can't see one personal item.'

'But that aside, what exactly are we hoping to find?' Bryant asked. 'Some kind of confession that backs up the knife in her hand and the blood-soaked clothing? I mean, do we really need anything else?'

'A reason. Whatever their relationship was like, it endured for twenty-five years, so why did it end today?'

Bryant shrugged as they headed into the kitchen. The room was small and boxy, but the space had been used wisely with drawers and cupboard space in every available spot.

'Same in here,' he observed.

No fridge magnets, no silly ornaments and no keepsakes. It was more understandable in a small space where there was less inclination to clutter, but it just compounded what they'd already seen.

'Maybe the bedroom?' Bryant suggested, stepping across the hallway.

The situation was exactly the same there. A double bed was made with a tartan quilt set. Only one bedside cabinet with a lamp and an alarm clock on it. The wardrobes and drawers revealed tasteful, stylish clothes with little variation. After checking them all, Kim deduced there was not one sequin in sight.

'You don't find it strange that she took nothing of her

achievements from her childhood home? Not one crown or sash or award?'

Bryant shrugged. 'I got a certificate for winning first place in the egg and spoon race when I was eight, but I didn't take it when I left home.'

'First of all, why do you insist on telling me these things knowing I'm gonna use them against you? And secondly, can you really compare your bean bag race—?'

'Egg and spoon,' he clarified, like it mattered.

'Tragic that you felt the need to correct me, but what I'm saying is that unlike yours her achievements were notable. You wouldn't want to take any reminders of that with you? It's a part of who you are.'

And right now, Kim was struggling to get any idea of who Katie Hawne was. Her home was attractive and stylish, but it wasn't personal.

'Back to the kitchen,' she said, marching across the hall. 'I want to find the drawer.'

'Oh yeah, we all have one,' Bryant said.

Kim's 'it' drawer contained screws, tape, scissors, a broken old doorbell, bulldog clips and all kinds of other things that she had no intention of using but hadn't yet thrown away.

She started opening drawers as Bryant headed for the cupboards.

'Ah, got it,' Kim said, although it wasn't overly impressive.

It was half empty except for a couple of recent utility bills.

Underneath was a business card. Kim picked it up and frowned, turning it over. The only information on it read *Girls' Club*, above a phone number.

'Bryant,' she said, passing it to her colleague.

He shrugged and handed it back. 'Maybe it's a group that offers advice on how to make a meal out of three ingredients,' he said, looking in the fridge.

She took the card back and put it in her pocket.

'Not everyone has a wife they don't deserve who fills the cupboards and freezer.'

'Guv, I'm not talking forgot to go to the shops and fill up. I'm talking nothing to cobble together for a snack.'

Kim double-checked. He was right. She didn't eat that much herself, but she always had the ingredients to throw a quick meal together.

Kim recalled the image of Katie's protruding collarbone, even more pronounced in the ballgown, and wondered if they were dealing with a bigger issue than an aversion to cooking.

'Okay, there's nothing more to see here,' she said, heading towards the exit.

She crossed the hall and knocked on the landlord's door.

He answered almost immediately.

'Okay, we're done. You can lock up, and don't reopen to anyone who isn't carrying a badge.'

He opened his mouth.

'We'll keep you in the loop, but just do as we ask for now.'

'Will do.'

'One last thing though,' Kim said, desperate to find out something about Katie Hawne. 'Are you saying that in the two years Katie lived here, you never saw any visitors come to her door? Not even her mother?'

His eyes widened in surprise. 'Well, that would have been a shocker. Katie told me her mother was dead.'

TWELVE

Tiff took another gulp of tea and paused in writing her report. The statement was to be passed to Dudley CID as a record of the conversation with Olivia and Logan Dench.

It was meant to be objective and factual, but Tiff kept wanting to add in her own senses, her own unease. Despite her training, she wanted to start each sentence with 'I feel' or 'I think'.

'Look lively, Tiff,' Sergeant Kendrick said from behind as he entered the canteen. 'Your shift's nearly over.'

'Sorry, Sarge. I'll be done in a minute. Just trying to put stuff into words.'

He paused his journey to the counter and took a seat. 'Why, what's up? You do these every day.'

She shrugged. She was wondering the same thing herself. But the meeting with Olivia Dench and her son just kept playing over in her mind. She had felt a tension in the house from the moment she'd walked in. Nothing that had taken place afterwards had changed that.

'Just record the facts, Tiff. We did our job. It's up to CID now. Although I'm not sure when they're gonna fit in the identification of the body. Our lot are busy with the murder of the woman in Stourbridge, and Dudley are tied up in court for the next few days on that big armed robbery case. It'll probably be sent over to—'

'I can do it,' Tiff said quickly. 'I'm off shift in fifteen minutes. I'll do it on my own time. Just to help out. Is that against any rules?' she asked, not wanting to end her CID career before it had even begun.

Kendrick frowned, and Tiff could see that his first instinct was to refuse, but then he shrugged.

'It does need doing quickly, and CID will end up going over our tracks anyway. It'll be one job less for them.' He smacked the table before getting up. 'Okay, give that Logan kid a call. Show him the body and then do up your report before shift in the morning.'

'Thanks, Sarge,' she said, taking out her phone.

'Don't mention it. Happy to let you take on extra jobs any time. Eventually, CID will be lucky to have you.'

Tiff smiled her appreciation. She certainly hoped so.

THIRTEEN

'What's the verdict from the FME?' Stacey asked Penn.

The Force Medical Examiner was a GP from a rota of local on-call practitioners who assisted the police with situations like assessing suspects claiming excessive force, taking blood samples of suspected drink-drivers and providing official medical opinions.

'He's with her now. The duty brief kept tapping his watch at me as if I can get the answer any sooner.'

'Okay, so while you're sitting here doing nothing, I'm gonna pick your brains. I've been looking at all these pageants that Katie entered.'

'Yeah,' he said, tapping his fingers on the desk.

'Well, she entered loads over the years: Little Miss Halesowen, Little Miss Stourbridge, Little Miss Gornal, Little Miss Sunshine in Walsall, Little Rascals in Wombourne, but never anything bigger.'

'I've never heard of any of them,' Penn admitted.

'Well, they don't really make the news. Most are only reported in the local free papers, but she was clearly very good so why not go for the bigger ones? There are county pageants and nationals, even internationals, so why didn't she enter them?'

'Does it matter?' he asked, scrunching up his face.

Stacey hid her smile. Typical Penn. There was no puzzle to solve here. They had their victim, and they had their killer, so his attention span was like the dipped beam of a headlight.

As ever, though, the boss was on full beam and wanted to uncover everything, not least a motive.

Stacey had to agree with the boss. How could anyone not want to understand every detail of why Katie Hawne had walked into her mother's home and viciously butchered her? Katie was not known to them and didn't appear to have suffered any prior violent episodes.

'You're not at all intrigued?' Stacey asked.

Penn shook his head.

'It's her mother,' Stacey exclaimed. 'I'm sure Freud has a lot to say on the subject, but from a layman's point of view, our mothers are everything. We're dependent on them from conception. They house us, they feed us for nine months and then we're completely reliant on them once we pop out. It's the most nurturing bond in existence. How does that transform into those crime-scene photos we saw earlier?'

'It doesn't endure,' Penn said after a minute's thought. 'We don't consciously recall the supplying and nurturing, so as we grow up, we become immersed in our own emotions. And there's always some kind of emotion involved in taking a life, whether it's anger, hatred, jealousy – or, for the really depraved, joy.

'There are hundreds of examples. Remember the film *Heavenly Creatures*? That was based on Pauline Parker and Juliet Hulme, who bludgeoned Pauline's mother because they didn't want to be separated. Did you ever see *Savage Grace*?'

Stacey shook her head. She had yet to discuss any subject with Penn where she didn't learn something.

'It's about Antony Baekeland, who murdered his mother in 1972 at their luxurious London apartment. It was said that she'd raped him to cure him of his homosexuality.'

'Jeez, even Freud would have his work cut out with that one,' she said.

'Susan Cabot, an actress in the fifties, was beaten to death by her son in 1986. Doctor Kathleen Hagen, a prominent urologist, killed her mother and father in 2000 and was acquitted on the grounds of insanity. Jennifer Pan staged a home invasion that led to the murder of her mother in 2010. Dee Dee Blanchard was murdered by her nineteen-year-old daughter, Gypsy-Rose, in 2015. Then there's—'

'Hang on,' Stacey interrupted. 'Although I can't reel off countless cases of matricide cos, like, I'm not a freak, even I know that some of those cases are extreme. Didn't Dee Dee Blanchard terrorise Gypsy-Rose for years due to Munchausen syndrome by proxy?'

'Exactly. Killing a parent, especially a mother, would require some intense emotion of some kind.' He shrugged. 'Maybe Sheryl was the critical type and she just said the wrong thing over coffee.'

'But the drinks weren't touched,' Stacey offered. 'The boss said the cups were still by the kettle. It didn't look like Sheryl had much chance to say anything. Doesn't sound like a sudden fit of rage over elevenses, does it?'

'You think it was premeditated, like Katie already had the plan in her head on the way over?' Penn asked.

'It sure looks that way. Almost like she discovered something and came to confront her mother.'

'Well, if she doesn't speak, we're likely never gonna know,' he said, looking at his watch. 'And on that note I'm off back downstairs for the doctor's verdict. Let's just hope it's the one the boss wants.'

Stacey's head was still spinning with information when Penn left the room, but now another question was uppermost in her mind.

What intense emotion had propelled Katie?

FOURTEEN

'Shit, shit, shit,' Kim said after ending the call from Penn. She was annoyed but relieved at the same time.

She had known to proceed with caution after Katie's performance in the custody suite, and it appeared the on-call doc agreed with her.

There were exceptions in the regs that allowed an interview to take place even when someone was under the influence of alcohol and drugs, or when someone had a mental disorder or disability, but to get permission she had criteria to prove. And that was a struggle here.

Katie was unable to interfere with evidence. She couldn't interfere with other people; she couldn't harm others or lose or damage property, confer with co-conspirators or delay recovery of property connected to the offence. There was no reason to question her urgently.

Kim understood the reasons for the protection. In England and Wales, a person could be convicted of a crime solely on confessional evidence, meaning that any interview was admissible.

'So, what now?' Bryant asked, taking the motorway island and heading towards Oldbury.

'She'll be transferred to Bushey Fields pending a full mental health assessment.'

Bushey Fields was a psychiatric hospital attached to Russells Hall Hospital. Within the facility was a suite where the police could place anyone with suspected mental disorders. The unit was secure but separate from other patients. During the seventy-two hours they were authorised to hold her, Katie would be assigned a team of professionals including a psychiatrist.

'All I know is she's now off limits. Can't ask her anything. Not even why she lied to her landlord about her mum being dead. We need to get our information elsewhere, and let's hope this is a good place to start,' she said as Bryant parked the car in a road behind the Sainsbury's superstore.

The woman who had answered the number they'd found at Katie's had been very cagey about who she was until Kim had given her a brief rundown of why she had the card.

The woman had given them her address and stated she was free for the rest of the day. Free from what Kim had no idea.

The property was a two-storey detached Victorian terrace. There was no sign at the front door to indicate the occupant was practising her profession at home.

Kim's curiosity was increasing as she rapped on the stained-glass window.

The door was answered by a plump woman in socks, jogging bottoms and an incredibly tight sports top.

Kim held up her ID. 'DI Stone. We spoke earlier. This is my colleague DS Bryant.'

'Please come in. I'm just through there.'

Kim headed to the back of the house and into a spacious kitchen that looked out onto a small tidy space. A number of strategically placed red robin bushes offered both privacy and shade. The bifold door was open despite the threat of rain, and the exercise bike was pointed towards the garden.

'Makes me feel like I'm actually riding somewhere,' the woman said, approaching a state-of-the-art coffee machine that wouldn't have looked out of place at Costa. 'What's your pleasure?'

'We're good, thanks,' Kim said, taking a seat.

'Oh, please don't make me feel guilty for the extra-shot double-froth cappuccino I'm going to have.'

'Okay, an espresso,' Kim said.

'Whatever you're having,' Bryant told her.

'With chocolate?'

He hesitated, and Kim felt sure an image of Jenny's wagging finger passed before his eyes.

'Best not.'

'Okay, why all the secrecy?' the woman asked.

'Ironic, given we don't even know your name,' Kim countered.

She slapped her own forehead, 'Sorry, Judith Palmer. Call me Jude – everyone does.'

'And what is the Girls' Club?' Kim asked as Jude put an espresso in front of her.

'Don't you owe me the answer to a question now?'

'Maybe, if we weren't actual police officers investigating a very serious crime.'

'Fair enough. One sec,' she said, focussing her attention on the milk frother that was blowing into Bryant's cup.

Kim took a sip of her own drink. It was excellent, but she wasn't going to be seduced by good coffee.

'Jude, if you could just give us a clue what it is that you do.'

'I offer support,' she said, placing Bryant's cup before him.

'You're a psychologist?'

'No.'

'A trained counsellor?'

'No.'

Unable to compete with the volume of the frother, Kim took another sip of her drink and remained silent while Jude continued to fix her own cappuccino.

'You offer advice without training?' Kim asked dubiously, once Jude sat down.

'I didn't say advice. I offer support.'

'To whom?'

'Girls who need it.'

'Based on what?'

'Experience.'

'Hang on,' Kim said. 'You charge people for counsel without any type of accreditation?'

Jude regarded her with interest. 'Wow, two assumptions in one sentence. Pretty good. Are you always this judgemental?'

'Yes, she is,' Bryant said, clearly enjoying his cappuccino and probably hoping for a refill by sucking up to the barista.

'I don't offer counsel and I don't charge. I offer support.'

'Yes, you've said. Did you offer support to Katie Hawne?'

'I did indeed.'

'May we see your records?'

'I don't keep them.'

'We could get a court order,' Kim said.

'That won't make them suddenly exist. People come here. They have coffee like you're doing now. We talk and then they go away again.'

'Why?'

'Cos I don't want them moving in,' Judith joked.

Kim took a sip of her drink.

'All right, not funny. They contact me because of my blog.'

'Which is about what?' Kim asked, trying not to lose her patience. The woman was forcing her to ask many questions for very little information.

'Mommy issues. Katie has issues with her mother.'

No kidding, Kim thought, picturing the scene at Sheryl's house.

'How serious are her issues?' Kim asked, interested in this woman's perspective.

'Debilitating,' Judith answered.

'Interesting word, meaning that she was unable to function normally. She's an adult.'

'I'm going to assume you didn't have a narcissistic parent, Inspector.'

Kim idly wondered if admitting to having a schizophrenic mother who had constantly tried to kill her and her twin would gain her entry to the club.

'Care to expand?' she asked Judith instead.

'No. Katie came to me in confidence, and I won't break that, but I will talk generally and use myself as an example. It's all on my blog if you'd prefer.'

'No, please continue.'

'Okay, if you didn't have a narcissistic mother, it would be impossible for you to understand. Generally, narcissists have a grandiose sense of self-importance. They exaggerate achievements and talents so they can be recognised as superior. They are preoccupied with fantasies of unlimited success, power, brilliance, beauty. They require excessive admiration. They have a sense of entitlement, an expectation of favourable treatment. They lack empathy and are unwilling or unable to recognise or identify with the feelings or needs of others. They are often arrogant and have the mindset "I am the best; I can't be wrong, and you should be like me".'

Sounded like most of Kim's bosses over the years.

'Narcissistic mothers exist on a spectrum from neglectful to tyrannical and will begin the ongoing damage by labelling her children as one of three types.'

Judith paused, and Kim nodded for her to continue. There was something about this woman's knowledge that had drawn Katie here for advice, and she had to find out what it was.

'Firstly, you have the golden child. This child is worshipped. They are a reflection of everything the mother wants for herself. This one has to fulfil the mother's emotional emptiness and give her attention. This is the trophy child.'

Kim briefly considered Katie's achievements. Was that the label Sheryl had given her?

'Next, we have the scapegoat child. This one gets blamed for the family's problems. Narcissistic mothers are threatened by them as they tend to click to what's going on in the home. The mother uses unpredictable mood swings and bullying to keep this child in line. The mother takes credit for everything good, and the child takes the blame for everything bad. The child's achievements will always be minimised.'

As Katie was an only child, Kim guessed this wasn't the case for their murderer.

'And finally, we have the lost child. This one is quiet and causes no trouble and is good in school. They are prone to depression, as being a low-value child carries over into being a low-value adult.'

'You said narcissists exist on a spectrum,' Bryant said, mirroring her own thoughts. Although speaking generally, Judith was telling them that Sheryl had been one. It was safe to assume that having had no siblings, Katie had been the golden child and had therefore been responsible for her mother's emotional state. But how had Sheryl's emotional dependence manifested itself?

'Severe narcissistic mothers will lock kids in their rooms. They're completely neglectful and happy for the streets to raise their kids. They simply don't care.'

They both knew immediately that didn't apply to Katie.

'An enmeshed mother is harder to spot but no less deadly. She applies emotional handcuffs and never lets go. She may seem perfect, but she's turning her kids into lifelong infants. She'll never allow them to grow up. She'll make them feel unsafe outside the home. She'll punish them for being self-sufficient. If they're a boy, she'll turn them into a surrogate husband and suffocate them. She'll ruin them for every other woman in their life.'

'And if they're a girl?' Kim asked.

'Phew, now we're really getting to it. The relationship between a narcissistic mother and her daughter is one of the most complex bonds that exists. Remember, this isn't the case for all mothers and daughters. Only the narcissistic ones.'

Judith paused as though to ensure this was understood.

Kim nodded for her to continue. It was insight they desperately needed.

'The relationship revolves around manipulation and control. Mother is constantly making daughter feel guilty about something. The manipulation is always about guilt. She will pretend to care deeply, maybe by buying things, and then start the guilt trips which are designed to control the daughter's emotions and therefore her behaviour. She will control by withholding affection and giving them the silent treatment. Mothers can go weeks or even months without speaking to their child.

'The mother will gossip to family members, undermine the child and project their dissatisfaction. She'll play the victim and ignore any suffering as she is unable to show empathy or compassion. Everything is about her. She will attempt to live through her daughter and won't even realise there's a problem.'

'Physical abuse?' Bryant asked.

Judith shook her head. 'Abuse is rarely physical. It's verbal, dismissive, with constant analysis and criticism, shouting and swearing, insults, disparaging jokes, steady prodding about weight, body type, denying embraces, disregarding, threatening, confining. The list goes on. She'll use guilt trips and fear or obligation. She'll gaslight and shame her daughter.'

'And what are the long-lasting effects?' Kim asked, again picturing the scenes she'd witnessed this morning.

'What's happened?' Judith asked.

'I can't say, but if you check the news later, I'm sure you'll work it out. For now, I need you to answer the question.'

A pensive expression rested on Judith's face as she collected the cups together.

Clearly the answer to this one called for another drink.

FIFTEEN

Tiff found herself a dry spot underneath the canopy of the crematorium.

Sandwell Valley in West Bromwich had been one of the first locations to offer digital post-mortems, and this was where the body of James Nixon had been brought. The process was less invasive than a physical autopsy, with imaging scans used to develop three-dimensional images for a virtual exploration of a human body.

Logan came into sight about thirty feet away. He offered her a wave and a wide smile. The gesture felt a little odd, under the circumstances, but she supposed he was just relieved to see someone familiar given the gruesomeness of the task.

'Sorry, I'm not late, am I?' he asked,

as though they were meeting for lunch.

'No, not at all,' she said, turning towards the entrance.

'I was hoping it would be you,' he said, falling into step beside her with his hands in his pockets.

'I'm happy to help. It's a difficult process to—'

'I don't even know your name,' he interrupted.

'Tiffany,' she said automatically and then questioned her response. Maybe she should have given her last name or told him to call her constable, but she was off shift and out of uniform so such instructions didn't come naturally.

'You look much younger in your own clothes,' he remarked without looking at her.

Maybe she should have kept the uniform on. Neither his manner nor his words were offensive, but she couldn't help wondering if he'd be saying the same things if she had still been dressed as a police officer.

'Is your mom doing okay?'

He nodded as they turned into the corridor. 'Yeah, she's handling it well.'

'Must have been quite the shock for her.'

'It's a shock for anyone,' Logan answered. 'But it's not like they were really serious. Mom hadn't long lost Dad. She wasn't really over him. James was an all right guy, not deeply intelligent, but he was just a distraction anyway. He made her laugh, but it wasn't going anywhere. He didn't challenge her, and it would have fizzled out.'

'But she reported him missing,' Tiff said. The report she'd read stated that the two of them had been seeing each other for around seven months. Seemed a bit more than casual to her.

'Yeah, because she hadn't heard from him in a couple of weeks. They were hardly heading up the aisle. You're making more of it than there was,' he said, annoyance creeping into his tone. 'It was no great love affair. We were just the last ones to see him alive due to Esther living so far away.'

'Okay. Understood. Now I have to warn you that this might be difficult for you,' she said, buzzing for admittance. 'I'm assuming it's your first dead body?'

'It's fine. Honestly. I'm not easily shocked,' he said as the affable smile returned. Whether he'd been close to James or not, she'd expected a more sombre demeanour.

'Good of you to save your mom from doing it.'

'Yeah, yeah, is he in there?' Logan asked, nodding towards a closed door.

'Yes, the door will open in—' She stopped speaking as the door did as she'd predicted.

An assistant appeared and held it open.

'I'll be right there with you,' she said, gesturing at the door.

Tiff had a feeling that his youthful nonchalance might be challenged when presented with the actual body of someone he had known.

No body viewing was a pleasant experience, but corpses removed from water were probably the worst.

The bloating, waxy appearance could distort the facial features to a grotesque parody of their former selves.

Logan appeared to take a deep breath and ready himself as the doors opened and the trolley came into view.

Tiff allowed him to remain in silence as they made their way back to the entrance.

As she'd anticipated, upon seeing the body, the easy smile had disappeared and had been replaced with a blank expression. Adopted, she suspected, to prevent the true horror from showing on his face.

They stepped outside.

Tiff had never done this before and had no idea how much support she was obliged to offer.

'Again, I'm sorry for your loss, and—'

'Wanna grab a coffee?' he asked, flashing her a wide smile.

'Excuse me?' she asked, unsure she'd heard correctly.

'Or a meal – maybe a movie? I dunno, both?'

Hadn't he just been in the same room as her, looking at the disfigured, bloated, grotesque form of someone who at the very least had been a family friend? And now he was hitting on her?

'That wouldn't be appropriate, Logan, but thanks for the offer, and give your mom my regards.'

She turned and walked away before the flesh actually crawled off her body.

SIXTEEN

'Okay,' Judith said after making them all a second coffee.

Kim had seen Bryant's eyes glaze over at times while Judith was talking. She knew he'd grown up in a poor but stable environment with hard-working parents who had encouraged him to be whatever he wanted to be. Not everyone was quite that lucky though. And in the absence of an interview with Katie Hawne, they were going to have to put some of the pieces together themselves.

'It's important to understand that we are afraid of our mothers being disappointed in us,' Judith said.

Oh yeah, her own mother had been really disappointed every time she'd thwarted the woman's attempts to kill her and her brother.

'In the ancient part of our little-girl brains, we unconsciously believe that if she's disappointed in us, we will die. When we're children, even well into our early twenties, our prefrontal cortex – the part of our brain that is able to reason and think more objectively – isn't fully developed, so we have a tendency to take everything personally. It's normal for even adult daughters to seek their mothers' approval. Your mother's beliefs are the basis for your own, and it's helpful to look at your mother's relationship with her own mother to see—'

'But can't cycles be broken?' Bryant asked, showing Kim he was paying full attention now. 'Like cycles of abuse?'

'Yes, that's exactly what we're talking about. It is abusive, and the cycle can be broken if the abuse is recognised.'

'So how do mother issues show?' Kim asked.

'Shame, blame, guilt, desperation. There's a fear of failure, even a fear of success. You accept bad behaviour in others. You're constantly seeking approval, validation, by being a people pleaser and being afraid to say no. You take on other people's problems and think you have to fix them. You'll try and control the uncontrollable. There'll be chronic worry and anxiety. You'll believe it's selfish to put yourself first as your own desires don't matter. You have no sense of self or what you want. You'll have weak or non-existent boundaries, and you'll be afraid to speak your truth.'

'Surely there are others around who can prevent it from happening?' Kim asked. It was impossible to imagine loving fathers, like the man sitting beside her, allowing such treatment.

'They're called enablers and that's exactly what they do. They're not malicious but will often just say stuff like "forgive your mother" or "she doesn't mean it". They're conditioned to believe the behaviour is okay. In some cases, an enabler becomes frightened and won't protect the children. It does them no good in the long run as a relationship with a narcissist is the same as with an infant. It's one-sided.'

'Even if all this were true in Katie's case, can't she recover as an adult?' Kim asked.

'Somewhat, but any meaningful recovery begins with one unalterable first step.'

Kim held up her hand to pause Judith as her phone rang. Her heart leaped when she saw the name of the caller.

'Stone,' she said, standing and moving away from the table.

'I'm at the morgue,' Keats offered quickly.

'Okey-dokey. Is that news I need?'

'I'm not ringing for the good of my health. There's something here you need to see.'

'You can't just tell me about it?'

'I'd rather you see it for yourself. I've never seen anything quite like this before.'

From a man who had been doing the job for more than thirty years, it was a rare admission.

'On my way,' she said, ending the call.

She sighed and turned back to Judith as Bryant moved away from the table.

'So, what is it?' Kim asked.

'What?'

'The one thing that a damaged child must do to heal?'

'The child has to permanently and irrevocably remove the narcissistic mother from their life.'

Well, Katie Hawne had definitely managed to do that.

SEVENTEEN

Tiff found herself drinking a cup of coffee at Costa but very definitely not with the young man who had invited her.

If she returned home now, her mum would start in on her immediately. The woman had the power to know her every mood swing, but Tiff was also aware she hadn't done a good job of developing a decent poker face.

Her mum hadn't been keen on the idea of her trying out for CID, feeling that her shifts were long enough without the extra pressure of studying around a full-time job.

Tiff suspected that her concern was only half baked, though, and that she was more concerned that the time studying was keeping her further away from finding the man she would eventually marry and produce grandchildren with.

Her mum wanted her out socialising, actively trying to ensnare some poor unsuspecting male. Unfortunately, studying wasn't the only element affecting her dwindling social life.

Since joining the police force, many of her civilian friends had drifted away after countless refusals or cancellations due to shift working. Eventually the invitations had dried up. And now many of her police friends were distancing themselves from her too.

So, here she was, hitting her mid-twenties with no boyfriend, hardly any friends and still living at home with her mum. And yet none of these facts were responsible for the need to stop for coffee and gather her thoughts.

There was a feeling in her stomach. She could only liken it to a mixture of anger and despair. She felt like a child being led in the wrong direction, knowing it was the wrong direction and not being able to stop it because her fingers were clamped firmly in someone else's hand. It was panic, resistance, and she'd never felt it before.

The meeting with Logan had been unsettling. She told herself she didn't blame him at all for his odd behaviour during the identification. There was no right or wrong way to act under unique and unexpected circumstances. *Yes, but there is a normal way*, a small voice whispered inside her. Normally the viewer didn't ask if they could see the whole body. They didn't ask if they could touch the skin or stare studiously as though memorising the details.

At first, part of her had believed he was holding stuff in for the sake of his mother. That he'd taken on the task of identification to spare her feelings and the trauma of seeing the man she'd been dating in such a state. But his recent behaviour was causing her to question her initial thoughts.

She sighed heavily, knowing she had to shake off the alien feeling inside. Her job was done, and tomorrow she'd be back in uniform and under other instructions. You couldn't like everyone you were forced to deal with.

And that was part of the problem, Tiff realised. She didn't actually like Logan Dench, but she had no idea why. He'd been polite and respectful. Yes, he'd overstepped the mark asking her for coffee, but she could have read too much into that. It could just have been a casual 'wanna get coffee so I don't have to go report back to my mom quite yet' kind of thing. He wouldn't relish having to relive the experience if his mom insisted on detail.

To put her feelings to bed, she decided to focus on the fact that Logan was trying very hard to take care of his mom.

She drained the last of her coffee as her phone sounded from her satchel.

It was an international number that looked vaguely familiar.

'Hello,' she answered.

'Is that Tiffany Moore?'

The woman's voice was tremulous, and Tiff knew exactly who was calling.

'It is. I assume you got my message.'

'I did,' James's sister, Esther Nixon, said. 'And thank you for leaving your number. Is it definitely him?'

'We have a positive identification from one of the last people to see him alive,' Tiff said gently.

She heard a small sob on the other end of the phone.

'Did he suffer?'

'I'm sorry, I can't share a lot with you until an investigation team takes over the case. I can only tell you that he was found in a fishing lake, and it appears he'd been there some time. I'm so sorry for your loss.'

'I knew it. When he didn't call after a couple of months, I knew he was dead. Really, I knew straight away. He'd never have run out on Olivia like that. He was head over heels. He wouldn't have—'

'Really?' Tiff asked. 'I thought it was more of a casual thing.'

'Not on his part. He told me he'd never met anyone like her, that when they were together all they did was laugh. He was almost in tears when he told me about how she'd taken care of her late husband. After all those years, I really thought he'd found the one. He was the happiest he'd ever been.'

'Despite the depression?' Tiff asked.

'What depression?'

Tiff grimaced, feeling like she'd said too much. If he'd been hiding it from his girlfriend, it wasn't much of a stretch to believe he'd hidden it from his sister.

'You're saying James didn't suffer from depression?'

'Well, maybe occasionally, but not for a long time.'

Tiff tried to be as tactful as possible. 'So he could have been depressed?'

'Well, I suppose. I mean, there's a chance, but he would never have taken his own life.'

'No one is saying that. He could have fallen into the water after being unwell. We won't know anything for sure until after the post-mortem.'

Suddenly Tiff was beginning to feel out of her depth. She had no place in this conversation. She was just the officer at the scene.

'Look, I promise that a member of CID will be in touch as soon as there's more detail available.'

'Okay, thank you. Can I ask how Olivia handled the identification? It couldn't have been pleasant for her.'

'She was spared the ordeal. Logan offered to do it in her place.'

The line went silent.

'Esther?'

'I'm sorry. I just had the irrational thought that James wouldn't have liked that at all. But of course he wouldn't have known.'

'Why's that?' Tiff asked in spite of herself.

'Because he hated the sight of that boy.'

Tiff said her goodbyes and wasn't surprised to find that once again her stomach was in knots.

EIGHTEEN

'You thinking that was Katie's motive?' Bryant asked as they got out of the car at Russells Hall Hospital.

'Well, Judith did say that if the daughter wanted to heal, the relationship had to be forcefully and permanently ended, with no further contact possible. That's a given now. Whatever the relationship between Katie and her mum, it was complex enough that she was seeking advice on how to deal with it. Think about Katie's home, well, where she lived – it was hardly the space of someone well rounded and stable. It's almost like she was waiting to develop into the person she's going to be.'

'And only murdering her mother could accomplish it?' Bryant asked doubtfully.

'It's a theory,' she said as they entered the hospital.

'You really want to know why, eh, guv?'

'Me and a jury of twelve,' she answered. Despite the evidence, a conviction of a woman in her mid-twenties for such a brutal murder was a tough sell if they couldn't explain why.

'Okay, Keats, this had better be good,' Kim said as they entered the morgue anteroom.

Jimmy was wheeling the body of Sheryl Hawne back to cold storage, and Keats was cleaning down.

'Well, if someone from your team had been here to witness the process, you'd have had the information immediately.'

Kim leaned against the counter and folded her arms. 'Keats, did you get enough attention as a boy?'

He offered a sideways glance.

She continued. 'I know you enjoy performing for Penn, whose fascination perplexes me, but it was unnecessary. We know the where, the who, the how, and all we're missing is the why.'

'And you think there's nothing I can offer to assist in answering that last question?' he asked, shaking his hands before pulling paper towels from the dispenser.

'Is that a trick question?' Kim asked. Never before had Keats had any involvement in establishing the why. 'And to be fair, it wasn't long ago that you weren't sure you could establish the "if" at the crime scene.'

Bryant hid his chuckle behind a cough.

Keats pinned her with his best haughty stare. 'Is that the last? Are we done?'

Fine, he'd suffered long enough. 'We're done.'

'Okay, follow me,' he said, shaking his head.

He held open the door into the autopsy room and strode to the small desk he kept in the corner. Despite the fact the procedure was now finished, the smell of death hung in the air. He passed her the form he'd completed ahead of the full report and began speaking even as she read.

'Our victim was in perfect health. Her weight and BMI were within healthy parameters. Her internal organs were strong and functioning well. No signs of smoking or excessive drinking. No obvious surgeries or major health conditions and no reason for her not to live well into old age.'

Kim handed the sheet back to him. 'So she took care of herself. How does that help us?'

'It doesn't. I'm just giving you background.'

'Keats,' she warned, looking pointedly at her watch. Her time would be much better spent talking to the doctors at Bushey Fields to establish when they could have another crack at Katie.

With an early confirmation of her well-being from a mental-health professional, she could have this case wrapped up by suppertime, which was fast approaching, she realised.

'Oh, Stone, I remember when you were more fun than this,' Keats said, reaching for an evidence bag.

'Liar, I was never— Jesus Christ, what the hell is that?' she asked, taking the bag.

Inside was what looked like an upper denture, a full bridge of bright white teeth but in miniature.

'Lodged in her throat,' Keats explained, enjoying her bewilderment.

'It couldn't have been hers,' Bryant said, stating the obvious.

'It's called a flipper,' Keats said, nodding towards his computer, indicating that was where he'd found the information. 'Fake teeth used for performing arts and pageants to hide any break or defect in someone's smile. They're used to hide missing teeth or to cover up marks. Gives any kid the perfect smile.'

'Where is it from?' Kim asked, looking at it from every angle.

'They're custom made and the cost depends on the material used. This is a good one and would have cost a few hundred.'

Kim tried to picture the item being forced into someone's throat. She found herself swallowing in response.

'Okay, Freud, give us the why,' she said, handing the piece back to him.

'Obvious, even to you. Katie Hawne is resentful of the

pageants and is angry. Maybe she was forced into doing them and the presence of the flipper is symbolic. It's been rammed down her mother's throat.'

All that from the pathologist without the added insight from Judith, which totally backed up his theory.

'Okay, thanks, Keats,' she said, heading for the door.

His assessment did mirror her own thoughts and did answer some of her questions. It was already clear that pageants had played a huge part in Katie's childhood, but only now were they discovering the negative impact that might have had. The flipper being forced down the throat was a powerful message, but Katie had left the pageant world years ago.

So now they knew the why, but they also needed to know the 'why right now'.

NINETEEN

'Honest to God, Mom, you should have seen it,' Logan said through a mouthful of burger. 'I almost asked if I could take photos to show you, but that might have seemed strange.'

Such an ordinary scene, she thought. Mother and son sharing a meal while mother listened to son recounting his day. No one would have known that the scene he was describing was viewing the dead body of the man she'd loved, or that she'd been allowed out of a locked room for him to regale her with the details.

The filet-o-fish sat untouched before her, but Logan didn't seem to have noticed, so fixed was he on sharing every element of what he'd seen. She'd switched off, not wanting to picture James in any form of decay. She'd hoped that he had left her, that he was out there having adventures, living the life they'd talked about. But all the time he'd been dead.

She pushed away any thoughts of him. The memories were good, but they didn't serve her well. They only reminded her of a time when she hadn't been a fear-filled shell.

Looking back, she could see how gradually the change had taken place. Logan had been their only child and had been spoiled. He had demanded attention from both her and Joe, and they had been happy to give it. They had adored the spirited and confident little boy.

Maybe they had looked the other way when he'd occasionally patted the dog too hard when it wouldn't sit or when he'd come back from school with bruises.

His expulsion at the age of fourteen for consistent bullying had confirmed to her and Joe that he needed one-on-one tutoring. Hers was the lower-paid job so they had decided she would leave it to take over Logan's education.

Her child had thrived under the one-to-one instruction and had excelled in all his subjects.

College had been a trial, but with perseverance she and Joe had got him the qualifications to get onto the media course at Loughborough University.

And then Joe had fallen ill and had eventually been diagnosed with brain cancer.

She now knew that during that time a subtle shift had taken place. She had allowed Logan more control in just about everything that didn't concern taking care of Joe.

He took control of the house and her debit card. Suddenly the cupboards were full of everything Logan liked to eat. The energy provider had been changed to get a better price and put in Logan's name. She didn't care. He had maxed out the credit cards to get cash should they need it.

He managed everything so that she could focus only on Joe.

What she hadn't noticed was that he had also taken her phone and was responding to concerned text messages from her old friends and colleagues with short sharp notes. Their calls went unanswered and eventually stopped.

On the morning of Joe's funeral, an outfit had been laid out on her bed. She gratefully accepted the decision. She was fighting with her grief and was unable to make any choices for herself.

And every day after that when she had her morning shower, an outfit was waiting for her.

One day, wanting a touch of colour, she had gone to her closet in search of a yellow silk blouse Joe had loved. Her clothes had been replaced. Gone were the figure-hugging jeans and V-neck tee shirts. Her special-occasion dresses had vanished, and in their place were A-line skirts and smart trousers.

When she'd questioned Logan over breakfast, he'd happily admitted to 'updating' her wardrobe with clothing more appropriate to a mother in her late forties.

It wasn't only the clothes. He had remained in control of their finances, sorting the life insurance that meant neither was forced to work for the time being. She had signed the papers he had slid before her at the breakfast table willingly, relieved that he was taking care of issues she felt unable to address herself.

The thing that still surprised her now was how readily she'd accepted the reversal of their roles, but she'd since realised that she'd done so thinking that she had a choice. That she could choose her own clothes when she was up to it. That she would take back control of the home and finances when she was stronger.

It was during this period she'd met James. The point at which she was being controlled and hadn't really known it. When every action from Logan had seemed designed to remove the stress from her day and every instruction had been cloaked as a well-meaning suggestion. After spending a little time at the house, James had mentioned Logan's influence on her, but she had defended him, explained how he had taken care of her when she'd been unable to do so herself. James had accepted her explanation, and she had firmly believed it herself until a week or so after he had disappeared.

The backhander across the face had come from nowhere after asking Logan to load the dishwasher. Somehow the balance had shifted between them. Her compliance had been read as permission, authority to control every aspect of her life. From that point on, the threat of violence became yet another form of control.

'You're not even listening,' Logan said, throwing her untouched meal at her.

Too late, she realised that he'd eaten his burger and his attention had all been on her. Most of the meal landed on her shirt, but some of the lettuce hit her face.

The fear was already swirling in her stomach. Logan didn't like to be ignored.

To her surprise, he burst out laughing. He reached for his phone.

'Do you have any idea how ridiculous you look?' he said, taking a photo. 'You're pathetic sitting there with salad on your face.'

The laughter was short-lived, despite the fact he'd been laughing at her not with her.

She moved to push her chair back.

'Not yet,' he said, reaching for his drink. 'I haven't finished telling you.'

Olivia felt shame warm her cheeks. The soggy lettuce was stuck firmly to her chin.

She raised her hand.

'Leave it. Next time you'll eat the meal I bring you. You're going to be very hungry later. Anyway, Tiffany was lovely out of uniform. She is a babe. I invited her for coffee, but I think she had something else on. I'll get a date with her. You just watch. You always told me I was irresistible.'

When she didn't smile in response, his face darkened.

'Okay, you're boring me now. You can go to bed.'

He stood and pulled out her chair. 'Come on – up you go,' he said, walking her to the stairs.

He followed closely behind and all but pushed her into the room.

'Night, night, and I'll see you in the morning.'

He presented his cheek for his goodnight kiss, which she knew better than to refuse.

The door closed and locked behind her.

She dutifully reached beneath her pillow for her nightdress.

It wasn't even seven o'clock.

TWENTY

It was 7.15 p.m. when Kim entered the squad room.

Bryant followed her in and headed for the coffee machine. Kim shook her head. She didn't intend to hang around long enough to drink it. The day had grown long, and she planned on dispatching her team imminently.

'Anything from the shrink?' she asked. Katie had been at Bushey Fields for a few hours.

Stacey shook her head. 'After my third call he refused to speak to me.'

Some hope of getting done by suppertime. If Katie hadn't been assessed by now, they weren't getting an answer on whether they could even question her until the morning.

'Okay, I'll draw up a battle plan for tomorrow but tonight — Hey, Tink,' she said, seeing the familiar face in the doorway.

'Hey, boss, got a minute?'

'Of course,' she said, pointing towards the Bowl. 'You need me...?'

'No, no,' she said, closing the door behind her. 'I don't mind you telling me I'm overreacting in front of everyone.'

'Oookay,' Kim said as Tink took a seat at the spare desk.

'I was there today,' she said, twisting her fingers together. 'At Donkey Pool when they brought the body out of the water.'

'Okay,' Kim said, still unsure what was going on. She'd heard there had been developments, but Keats had got to her first and saddled her with an open and shut case. 'Your first dead body?' Was she traumatised? Did she need to talk? Did she need comfort, and if so what the hell was she doing here?

Tiff shook her head.

'We were waiting for the call,' Penn said.

'I wish you'd got it.'

Kim folded her arms. 'We were assigned another case. Why, what's up?'

Tiff's troubled expression didn't look like she'd suffered personal trauma.

'Something doesn't feel right. The guy's been missing for almost two years, and the last folks to see him are acting a bit weird. A woman and her son in his early twenties. She was upset; he wasn't bothered. He identified the body and then asked me out.'

'After being in the morgue with Keats?' Stacey asked, raising an eyebrow.

'Not Keats. Body is over at West Brom. Post-mortem is tomorrow.'

'Likely to be sent to Wolvo then,' Bryant offered.

'Yeah, Dudley's stuck on a court case. I feel like this is gonna be passed around until it falls through the cracks,' Tiff said. 'There's probably nothing forensically viable due to the time in the water, and no one is really fussed in chasing a result. His only relative lives abroad and they weren't particularly close.'

'So what exactly is your problem?' Kim asked.

'Something feels off with the partner and her son. There was a tension in the air. It was like I wasn't getting a truthful reaction, emotionally, from either of them.'

'You think they're responsible?' Kim asked.

'Yes. No. I don't know. I just didn't know what to do.'

'So what do you want us to do?' Kim asked, not unkindly.

'Investigate?' Tiff asked hopefully.

Kim understood the girl's frustration. She was in the process of making the transition from officer to detective. She'd come across a situation that didn't smell right, and she knew this case was going to fall by the wayside. It was a frustration Kim understood. Throughout her career, she had always done her utmost to ensure no one got left behind.

Problem was they had their own major investigation. They had their own victim in Sheryl Hawne. And although they might have some of the answers, they didn't yet have them all.

'No,' Kim said.

Tiff's face dropped. 'You won't investigate?'

Kim shook her head. 'No, we won't. You will. Penn will help, and you'll work it together. I'll clear it with Inspector Plant and square it with Woody.'

Because Tiff was in training it would officially be Penn's case, and she would be assisting as she had done on other occasions.

There was not one time they had gone to this girl for help and been refused. She had a hunch, and they had a responsibility to help her either prove or disprove it.

'Okay, briefing at seven, including you, Tink. Now get lost, the bloody lot of you.'

TWENTY-ONE

It was after midnight when Kim took Barney outside for his last walk, and she still hadn't been able to shake off the memories of Katie Hawne.

That look of bewilderment while sitting on the sofa. The lost, childlike expression as she was being put in the car. But the image that wouldn't get out of Kim's head was the bright, infectious sparkle that had been present while she'd been doing her impromptu performance in the holding cells. She felt as though she'd met three different Katies in the space of one day, and she still wasn't sure which one was real.

'Park tonight, boy,' she said, having already gauged the weather.

There'd been a dry spell about an hour ago, and she suspected that most of the dog walkers would have taken the opportunity to get their last walk in before the rain.

Neither she nor Barney minded the rain, and both were happy to weather it for an empty park.

She was pleased to see the small car park empty and after a cursory glance around established that only the two of them were stupid enough to be out in the wet.

She leaned down and unhooked his collar.

He ran off fifty feet ahead and then came back. It was a process he repeated until she put the lead back on him. It was as though he liked that taste of freedom but not too much. He could also smell the apple in her pocket that she brought for recall emergencies.

As she watched her dog's ritual, her mind returned to Katie Hawne. She hoped for a call early tomorrow from the doctor to say that she'd been faking and she was perfectly fit for interview. Yet a small voice inside insisted that wasn't going to happen.

Her thoughts were interrupted by the ringing of her phone. It sounded loudly in the silence of the empty park.

She reached to take it out, and Barney hurtled back towards her.

'Wrong pocket, buddy,' she said before seeing the name.

'Stone,' she answered as her heartbeat increased.

'Let me first confirm that earlier today we were in agreement?' Keats said.

'About what?' she answered. It was a bit late at night for an 'I told you so' call.

'The reason why Katie Hawne killed her mother.'

'Not sure why we're having this conversation at midnight, but yes, I could see your point. Why?'

'Because it turns out we were both wrong. We've got another one. Early hours of the morning.'

Kim stopped walking as her whole case crashed to the ground. A moment ago, she'd had one victim and one killer, and their time was being spent filling in the details. At no point had she considered the idea that Katie Hawne had not brutally killed her mother. But if Keats was correct and this crime mirrored the first, Katie could not have been responsible and they were already a good twelve to fifteen hours behind their killer.

'Fuck. Text me the address,' she said, reattaching the lead to Barney's collar.

'Already done,' he said before ending the call.

Her phone tinged receipt of a message as she put Barney in the car. She considered calling Bryant but decided against it.

'Okay, buddy. You're gonna be my partner in crime tonight.'

TWENTY-TWO

The house in Bromsgrove was a semi-detached property in a small cul-de-sac about a mile away from the motorway island.

Ten pairs of houses looked onto a small green that was also used as a turning circle, and right now it was a meeting point for most of the residents watching the flashing blue lights illuminating the sky.

'Don't go anywhere,' she said to Barney as she lowered her window just an inch.

She pushed through the crowd and ducked under the cordon as Mitch's van pulled up.

Keats was already waiting.

'Andrea Shaw, aged forty-seven, stabbed multiple times, found by her daughter, Toyah, twenty-two, who lives at home and had returned after a night out.'

Kim was already donning protective equipment while Keats talked.

'The body is in the living room, and the daughter is hysterical in the kitchen.'

Kim entered the home and immediately saw evidence of a

struggle. Cushions had been thrown from the sofa, a small book-case had been pulled over and ornaments littered the floor.

The woman on the ground lay amid a pool of blood. Her nightgown was stained red from the breastbone down to the lower stomach.

'Woken from her sleep for this,' Keats said from behind.

'She wouldn't have been properly sleeping. Not if her daughter was still out. Likely why she answered the door in her nightie, thinking the kid had forgotten her key.'

'You're the expert?' he mocked.

'Keats, I can't go to sleep if I don't know exactly where my dog is, so it's a pretty safe bet I'm right.'

'Ah yes, that brave, fearless dog who will get all the honours when he—'

'How long since the murder?' she snapped. It wasn't something she gave thought to. Unlike any other dog, Barney was going to live forever.

'No more than an hour.'

'Jesus, her daughter probably just missed the killer.'

'Wouldn't have been long,' Keats confirmed.

'Anything on her clothes?' Kim asked.

'Not a drop. Still got her clubbing clothes on, and they're as clean as a whistle.'

Kim walked to the top of the body, taking care to avoid the blood. From this angle of the room, she could picture clearly what had happened.

Andrea Shaw had come down the stairs sometime around ten thirty to let in who she thought was her daughter having forgotten her key. The door had been forced open. Andrea had backed into the lounge, pulling down the bookcase to block the intruder, but in effect had trapped herself.

The killer had crossed the room and started stabbing. Kim counted more than a dozen defensive wounds on the hands and arms.

She stood above the victim and looked down into a face that would have been attractive just a few hours ago. Her hazel eyes were framed by shapely brows, and her full lips bore the imprint of recently removed make-up.

She looked closer at the mouth and then at Keats.

'Anything in there?'

'I think so, but I'm going to wait until I have her back at the—'

'Why aren't you trying to save her?' screamed a voice from the hallway.

A constable grabbed the girl from behind before she entered, looking apologetically in Kim's direction.

Kim made it to the other side of the room and removed the protective clothing before following the constable and the girl.

She found them sitting at the kitchen table. The girl was bent forward, sobbing uncontrollably into a circle made by her arms.

Kim took a seat and nodded for the constable to remove his hand from the girl's shoulder.

'Toyah, isn't it?' Kim asked, leaning forward.

Toyah nodded as she raised her head. Her face was a reddened mess of tears, mascara and mucus.

Kim held out her hand for a roll of kitchen towel. She ripped off two squares and passed them to the girl, who was heavily made-up, with a shock of short green hair. Unlike her mum, her eyes were a deep blue beneath the panda smudges. She appeared much younger than Katie, even though there was only a couple of years' difference.

'Why aren't you trying to save her?' she asked again.

'She's gone, Toyah,' Kim said gently. 'And you knew that when you found her, which is why you didn't touch her.'

'I didn't want to hurt her,' she said as the tears fell from her eyes. 'But I should have tried. If I'd have known what to do, I could have saved her.'

Kim shook her head, 'She was gone and there was nothing you could have done.'

'I shouldn't have been out. This wouldn't have happened if I'd been here.'

Kim wondered how many different ways the girl was going to blame herself.

'You don't know that. You could have been a victim too,' Kim reasoned.

Toyah's phone sounded and lit up on the table. The name *Tony* flashed on the screen.

Toyah answered it. 'Where are you?'

'Outside. They won't let me in,' Kim heard.

'He's my brother; I called him,' she wailed. 'I need him.'

Kim nodded to the constable, who keyed his radio with the instruction to allow the man to enter.

'Does he know what's happened?' Kim asked, assuming that Andrea was Tony's mum too.

'I told him. He lives in Romsley, just a few miles—'

'Toyah, Toyah,' a male voice called from the hallway.

'In here,' the girl croaked.

Kim guessed Tony to be a little older, maybe mid-twenties, but the likeness was unmistakeable. Kim felt sure they were full siblings.

'Where is she?' Tony asked, looking Kim's way while still holding his sobbing sister.

'She's in the lounge, but you can't go in there,' Kim advised.

He looked as though he wanted to argue.

'Don't do it, Tony,' Toyah snuffled against his chest. 'Don't put that picture in your head. It's awful.'

'But what's happened?' he asked, setting his sister slightly away so he could see her face.

'Mom was murdered, stabbed. She's dead, Tony. She's gone.'

Tony pulled his sister to him again as she cried tears that seemed like they were never going to stop.

'I called Dad; he's on his way back from Glasgow. You're coming home with me.'

Tony looked at Kim over the top of his sister's head. He appeared calm and in control, and there was no evidence of tears.

'Can I pack her a bag and get her out of here?'

There were questions that Kim wanted to ask, but as the sound of Toyah's sobbing increased, she knew the girl was in no fit state to answer right now.

She nodded. 'We'll speak to you tomorrow.'

Toyah had walked in on a scene so horrific it would haunt her dreams for years. Right now, she needed to leave and be comforted by family.

Kim went ahead and stood close to the lounge door to block the view. Tony bundled past her and up the stairs. All credit to him, he didn't even try to look. His sole focus was on his sister.

'You still here?' Keats asked, joining her in the doorway.

'Where else would I be at almost two in the morning?'

'That's our theory up in smoke,' he said, watching Mitch closely.

'Yep. I'm pretty sure Katie is still safely confined at Bushey Fields, so we ain't pinning this one on her.'

'We're about to start the process of moving the body.'

'Five minutes, Keats. Let's just let her kids get out of here first.'

'Understood,' he said, moving back towards the forensic techie.

Within minutes, Tony and Toyah reappeared with an overnight bag.

'Try and get some rest and we'll talk later,' Kim said as Tony guided his sister out the door.

Once they were out of sight, Kim gave Keats the thumbs up for removal before heading upstairs.

The first door on the left was clearly the master bedroom. A quick glance around confirmed it to be the room of the deceased.

There was a small television as well as a large bookcase and a reading nook in the corner. The single bedside cabinet held a lamp, a couple of books, reading glasses and a phone.

The covers were thrown back and the pillows piled on one side, indicating that Andrea had most likely been sitting up, reading and waiting for Toyah to come home.

A small en-suite bathroom was tidy and functional.

The next room was filled with a desk and shelves holding boxes of crafting materials. On the worktop were stickers, a guillotine, crafting wire and paints. There were models and card-making projects at every stage of the journey scattered around. Although crowded, it looked organised and well used.

The next room was clearly Toyah's.

Perfume bottles and make-up cases cluttered the dressing table, and stuff had been slid, hid and wedged into every available spot, giving the impression of a clutter-free zone unless you looked too closely.

It was a room being outgrown, Kim thought. Toyah was in her early twenties and she had accumulated a lot of stuff in that time that she didn't seem eager to part with.

Kim closed the door behind her and smiled at the sign.

Entry by Appointment Only Unless You Bring Food.

So far it looked like a perfectly normal household. A mother who had her own interests and hobbies, a daughter who was on the cusp of grasping her own independence.

She opened the last door. The junk room. The space filled with boxes and bags of things that were no longer needed but hadn't yet made it to the tip either because of time, motivation or emotional attachment.

Such boxes revealed the whole history of a family.

Kim started opening the lids of boxes that hadn't been disturbed in years. The ones at the back held wedding memorabilia and photos, packed away when the marriage had ended presumably, baby clothes, books, toys, shawls, blankets, stuffed toys. It was a history lesson of their past, an era represented in each area of the room.

Kim had the sudden thought of Andrea's boxes coming to join them. Hours ago, she had been a vital, busy woman, living and enjoying life, and now in the not too distant future she would be consigned to a box, a selection of worldly possessions chosen as a representation of her life.

Kim shook away the maudlin thoughts, knowing they had gathered because this death was untimely. Andrea shouldn't have been joining the family history for decades.

Just a couple of boxes remained, nestled between board games, old school uniforms and certificates.

Kim opened them, wondering what on earth was left.

'Aww... shit,' she said as she flipped back the lids.

The crowns and sashes were just stuffed inside. This was nothing like the shrine at Katie's old house.

This was a memory box of a time that had come and gone. It wasn't worshipped or relived or even remembered, as Kim had seen no clue anywhere else around the house.

Kim closed the box and left the room.

With a second murder linked to the world of pageantry, this case had just got a hell of a lot bigger than she'd first thought.

TWENTY-THREE

The rest of her team filed into the office within a minute of each other.

They all looked to the board, which had been updated since they'd last seen it the night before.

By the time she'd returned home, it was almost four and not worth the extra steps to the bedroom. She and Barney had napped on the sofa together for a couple of hours before the early morning walk and breakfast routine had kicked in. Given the disturbance to his sleep routine, Barney would be out for the count until Charlie collected him at lunchtime.

'Boss?' Stacey asked, putting her satchel under her desk.

'Yep, we got another one.'

'You're joking,' Penn said.

There had been no doubt in anyone's mind that Katie had been the killer. And they had all been wrong.

'I wasn't laughing when I was called out in the middle of the night,' Kim answered.

'You attended a crime scene without me?' Bryant asked, feigning hurt.

'Yeah, I took Barney with me. Far more use at two in the morning.'

'Fair point,' he admitted.

'Sorry I'm late,' Tiff said, sliding into the seat at the spare desk.

'You're not, but just cool your heels while we get out of the blocks on this one. It's changed since last night.'

'Got it, boss,' she said, removing her coat.

Kim continued. 'Our second victim's name is Andrea Shaw. She was forty-seven years of age and worked as a doctor's receptionist.'

'Motive discovered,' Bryant offered.

Kim gave him a look before continuing.

'Phone indicates she socialised with friends a couple of times a month and filled her down time with crafting and reading. Divorced amicably some years ago and has two grown children, a boy and a girl.'

She paused while they took it in.

'Anyone want to take a guess at the link between the two women?'

'Both worked administrative roles?' Penn asked.

She shook her head.

'Both women home alone?' Bryant asked.

'Nope.'

'Pageants?' Stacey asked.

'Jeez, guys,' she said, looking from Bryant to Penn. 'Don't know why you even bother trying when Stace is in the room. It is indeed pageants.'

Only Stacey had, in a few seconds, put together what they'd found in Sheryl's throat and that their second victim also had a daughter.

'Same kind of shrine?' Bryant asked.

'No. Total opposite. The tiaras were packed away with the old karate suits and cricket bats.'

Tiff held up her hand and nodded towards the door. 'Boss, do you want me to...?'

Penn looked disappointed.

'No, I said we'd help and we will, but if we need to pull Penn off to assist...'

'Of course, of course.'

Kim turned to Stacey. 'Bryant and I have a couple of calls to make, so your top priority is the pageants. Were the daughters on the circuit at the same time? Were there any issues, any enemies, any fights, any scandal?'

'Got it, boss.'

'Look at the family members of both victims too. Start with Sheryl, as relatives seem to be a bit thin on the ground. Check other areas to see if there's anything similar happening elsewhere. That should be enough to keep you going for now.'

'On it, boss.'

Kim headed to the Bowl for her jacket.

Here they were again. Finding out that what they'd been presented with had been an illusion. It was not as cut and dried as their first assessment had seemed. One victim and one suspect. They had thought it was an isolated incident and that no one else was at risk. With a second victim already in the morgue, she knew they were behind the clock, and she prayed they could catch up before anyone else lost their life.

The puzzle board had been placed on the table and they knew the subject matter, but they were waiting for the pieces to fall so they could be arranged into a cohesive, sensible picture.

The first piece was currently under lock and key at Bushey Fields.

Before their second victim, pageants had been no more than a detail to examine while unpicking what appeared to be a complex and toxic relationship between a mother and her daughter.

With the discovery of a second pageant mum found dead,

Kim was forced to wonder exactly what these two mums had done to deserve such punishment. What did they have in common? Were pageants to blame for the hostility between Katie and Sheryl? And what exactly had life as a pageant girl been like?

TWENTY-FOUR

I look down at the plate and the tears sting my eyes. Three lettuce leaves and a tomato cut in half. I can see the rip marks at the edge of the lettuce where the brown bits have been torn away. The skin of the tomato looks soft and saggy, no longer firm and fresh. My stomach grumbles in protest. It's five o'clock and I've eaten nothing since a single Weetabix smashed with thin, watery milk for breakfast.

'Don't even think about complaining. You've put on a pound since last week's weigh-in. Just a few days and you'll be back to normal or even thinner, if possible. We all have to make sacrifices. It's just a BLT without the bacon or bread. It's that or nothing.'

'Okay, Mommy,' I say, knowing it'll do me no good to complain.

'Come on. Eat up,' she says, tapping her watch. 'Back to practise in three minutes.'

She watches me as I eat what tastes like a plate of water. All too soon it's gone and I feel like I've eaten nothing.

'Okay, get dressed and come to the lounge,' she says before heading out of the room to fix herself a drink.

I remove my clothes and slip the new pink dress over my head. I'm willing and praying for it to feel looser so that I can have something to eat, but as I slide it over my body, I know it's still pulling at the seams. If Mom sees this, I might not even get a Weetabix in the morning.

The sequins around the neckline scratch at my face as I lower the dress and put my arms through the sleeves. As it comes to rest, it's as though each sequin finds the exact spot it rubbed earlier.

I pull on the shoes. They're new and stiff. The hard leather made the skin on my heel look like a prune before the skin disappeared altogether and left behind a raw circle. Each time I put them back on, the soreness is worse than before, but I know that I have to wear them.

I make my way into the lounge, trying to walk as normally as possible. I know what she'll say if I show the pain.

I see the books and the oranges and know it's going to be a long night. The fuzzy feeling comes into my tummy.

'Mommy, I have homework,' I breathe. I have to draw and name all seven continents.

'Don't be ridiculous. What important homework could a seven-year-old have? Teachers are just trying to palm off their jobs. I'll send a note.'

I recognise the steel in her voice. There's no point protesting. She'll ignore me. If I tell her that I don't like the look of disapproval Miss Hichins gives me, she'll laugh. If I explain that I get funny looks from my classmates because I never hand in anything to be marked, she'll sneer.

'We'll do your walk first,' she says, putting a book on my head.

I know to stand perfectly still until she has returned to her chair to observe me. She sits and nods.

I move slowly at first. If I move too quickly straight away, the book will fall down my back. I see the frustration in her eyes at my speed, but I've learned that the irritation comes much quicker if she has to keep getting up to replace the book.

'Ten lengths and we'll move on to the oranges.'

I don't let the panic show on my face. Ten lengths of the living room is much further than the distance I walk on the stage. If I drop the book once, we start again from the beginning. I've only ever managed ten lengths once before, and I didn't have new shoes then. I want to point this out, but I know better. If I argue, she'll increase the lengths to twelve.

'And speed up. I'm not going to start counting until you're moving faster than that.'

I feel my bottom lip begin to tremble, but I bite down to force the tears away. They have no effect on my mom and normally just enrage her more.

I speed up and before I've completed two lengths, the book has fallen. Every step is agony on my heels, and now I have to start all over again. All those steps wasted. The extra rubbing on my flesh for nothing.

I start again – four lengths.

And again – seven lengths.

And again – five lengths.

As I walk, I know I'm wincing with the pain. I can't stop myself. Every time the new leather moves against it, it feels like it's rubbing straight through to the bone.

'Come on – try again,' my mom says. 'No pain no gain.'

I feel sick. My legs ache, and I can feel blood running from the back of my heels into my new shoes.

I reach down to pick up the book to start again, and the motion of bending brings flashes of light darting across my eyes. The room starts to spin around me. The sickness rises up to my throat. The world tilts and then turns black.

My eyes open.

What happened?

Why am I on the floor?

Why is she standing above me?

'Mommy?' I ask.

'Do you have any idea how useless you are? All you have to do is walk nicely and throw a few oranges in the air. You can't even do that. You have no skill, no talent and now you're a little porker as well. Look, you're bursting out of your dress.'

My eyes are stinging, but I try not to cry.

'Get out of my sight. You're so disgusting I can't even look at you.'

I hobble to the bathroom and wipe the blood from my feet.

However hard I try to stop them, now that I'm alone, the tears roll over my cheeks.

TWENTY-FIVE

No matter how many flower beds were planted to soften the buildings that made up Bushey Fields, your mind knew that no amount of marigolds were going to help the people inside.

Mental illness didn't respond to well-cut borders or manicured lawns, and all efforts to the contrary were designed to assure onlookers and visitors that care was taken both inside and out.

A nurse buzzed them through the first set of doors into what Kim always termed a decontamination chamber. He checked both of their IDs and then tapped a few keys.

'Who referred her?' he asked.

'I did,' she answered.

'Date and time?'

She understood the need for security. They had never met before and a decent-looking fake ID wasn't that hard to come by.

These were basic questions that only the genuine officers would know.

'Yesterday afternoon around five p.m.'

'Reason?'

'Unusual behaviour following arrest.'

'For?'

'Murder.'

'Thanks for your patience, Inspector. Wait there and I'll have someone escort you to her room.'

'No, bring her out. We'll sit at that table over there,' she said, pointing beyond the second set of doors.

'No problem,' he said, buzzing the door open.

The nurse spoke to another member of staff and then approached them. 'She'll be with you soon.'

'How's she been?' Kim asked.

'Hasn't left her room. Hasn't spoken. Hasn't eaten or even drunk a glass of water.'

'Okay, thanks,' she said, taking a seat.

'Why out here?' Bryant asked, sitting beside her.

'Her world is alien right now. Her only safe space is that room down there, and we're not going to take it away from her.'

'Got it,' he said.

'You know what else you've got? Or will have once you've fetched them from that vending machine over there?'

'What?' he asked, following her gaze.

'Three bottles of water.'

'You don't drink bottled—'

'Just get 'em,' she said as Katie appeared from the corridor.

She was pleased to see that more suitable clothing had been found for her, even if the jeans were a bit big and the cardigan sleeves too short. It was neither a ballgown nor a boiler suit, so she finally looked the age she was.

As the nurse guided Katie to the remaining chair, Kim caught her eye. 'Any meds?'

'Light sedative last night.'

Kim thanked her as Bryant returned to the table with three bottles of water.

'How are you feeling?' Kim asked.

Katie said nothing and stared at her fingertips.

Still the silent treatment, which was confusing. She could understand it when Katie thought she might say something to incriminate herself, but now Kim knew that she hadn't murdered her mother, and Katie had known that all along.

'Why didn't you just tell us that you didn't kill your mother?'

Katie's head shot up. Kim was stunned by the confusion on her face. What the hell was going on?

'I didn't kill her?' Katie asked disbelievingly.

'Do you remember killing her?'

Katie frowned and stared at the table. 'I remember wanting to. I really, really wanted to.' She shook her head. 'No, I don't believe you. I must have killed her.'

'Tell us what you recall, and remember we're not here to trip you up.'

'No, you're trying to trick me. You're trying to get me to say something you can use against me.'

'I swear I'm not. You have no legal representation, you're not under caution and you've been deemed unfit for interview. You could tell me you murdered a house full of folks and I wouldn't be able to do much about it.'

Katie looked to Bryant, who nodded his agreement.

'But I must have done it. I was angry. I went to the house...' She paused, and the frown deepened. 'I was on the floor, covered in blood, with the knife in my hand. I killed her.'

And there it was: the confession she'd been after for almost twenty-four hours. Except it wasn't true.

'Katie, you blacked out. Your mother was already dead. You saw that and it was too traumatic to process. You blacked out and lost time, but you didn't kill your mother.'

'Oh God,' she said as her head fell into her hands. 'I didn't kill her. It wasn't me.' The relief in her voice was obvious.

'You're sure?' she asked, lifting her head before reaching for a bottle of water. As Kim had suspected: guilt-induced self-denial. She hadn't eaten or drunk anything for hours.

'We're sure,' Kim said as Katie chugged half the bottle in one go. 'We know you had serious issues with your mum, Katie. You spoke to Judith Palmer about it.'

'She helped me understand that it wasn't my fault, that my mother was a narcissist who held me in a twenty-five-year guilt trip.'

'Go on,' Kim urged.

Katie finished off the first bottle of water, and Kim pushed another towards her.

'Nothing I did was ever good enough. Every day she would tell me of the sacrifices she'd made for me. Her love was conditional on how hard I practised my walk or how well I smiled. She would mark my practise performances out of ten. Anything below an eight got a scowl and twenty-four hours of silent treatment. Above an eight I got cuddles and toys.'

'Did you want to do the pageants?' Bryant asked.

'At first, when I thought it would be fun to dress up in sparkly dresses, but that soon wore off. I was weighed nightly and even a few ounces over was starved off me. I had no friends because I couldn't play out. God forbid I'd get a bruise or a scratch that would mar my perfect appearance.

'My mother controlled everything. She wouldn't allow me to do anything. She was still cutting the fat off my bacon when I was nineteen years old,' she said, staring off into the distance.

Kim coughed to regain her attention. She wanted Katie to remember it but not relive it.

'She had no boundaries. She would walk into the bathroom while I was showering to check that I'd shaved my pubic hair.'

'But you got out,' Kim said, hiding her shock and trying to remind Katie of her own strength.

'Yes, eventually, with Judith's help, but the problem was that I didn't know how to act. I found myself in my own home without knowing how to do anything. I'd never even cooked myself a meal.'

The empty cupboards were beginning to make more sense.

'I've found cafés that cook the meals I've got used to. I don't know how to do anything for myself. I'm useless. I don't know how to make friends or make small talk, and now the only person that knows me is dead.'

The tears began to fall from her eyes, and Kim started to understand the complexities that had existed in this relationship. Only moments ago, she'd admitted to wanting the woman dead.

'Did Judith advise you to cut your mother off completely?' Kim asked.

Katie nodded. 'She said it was the only way to heal.'

Either that or make it feel like being cast adrift in the ocean in a dinghy, Kim thought.

'And yet you were going to see her, despite Judith's advice,' Kim noted.

'I was angry,' she said, glancing at the wall above Kim's head.

'About what?' Kim asked, sensing the walls were going back up.

'Just stuff. The things I was just talking about.'

'But those things were in the past. Why choose that day to confront your mum about them?'

Katie's expression was closed as she took a sip from the second bottle of water. 'Am I free to go now?'

Legally they had no reason to detain her. She'd committed no crime, she wasn't in any trouble, she wasn't a suicide risk, no family member had expressed a fear for her or their own safety, and other than some eccentric behaviour, she was able to function and hold a perfectly coherent conversation. Kim knew that few of the residents of this facility were able to claim the same thing.

'You do know that you gave us quite the performance in the holding cells yesterday?' Kim asked.

Her face showed nothing. 'Just a bit of light entertainment, some role-play to lighten the mood. Nothing you can keep me here for.'

'Katie, I think you need help,' Kim said honestly. How many times had those same words been said to her? And how many times had she chosen to ignore them?

'Am I free to leave?' Katie persisted.

'I think you should stay for a while and learn how to manage—'

'Inspector, am I free to leave?'

'Yes, except for a bit of paperwork, you're free to leave,' Kim answered, defeated. Any other response could result in a lawsuit.

'Thank you,' Katie said, pushing back her chair before leaving.

A quick glance at Bryant confirmed he was as bewildered as she was.

This visit was supposed to have cleared Katie of murder, and it had, but she was still lying about something. It was more than rage about her past that had driven Katie to her mother's house yesterday morning.

'Inspector Stone, I assume,' said a voice from above.

She ignored the outstretched hand as the man introduced himself.

'Doctor Michaels. I'm about to assess your prisoner.'

'Good luck on that – she's probably halfway out the door.'

'Ahh, I see. There's not enough to hold her so I assume you're hoping my examination will conclude that she is fit for interview so you can extract a confession.'

'You're a bit behind the times, Doc. What I really want is

for you to take your time, diagnose her and then make her better. But unfortunately, I don't think you're going to get that chance.'

TWENTY-SIX

Stacey tried to be kind to the environment where she could and work purely from electronic devices, but sometimes she needed to look at good old-fashioned printouts. Nevertheless, an internal groan sounded inside her every time the printer kicked into life.

Once Penn and Tiff had left for the post-mortem of James Nixon, she'd taken a minute to think about how best to try and cross-reference the mass of information that was available in different places.

It was clearly no coincidence that two pageant moms had been brutally murdered in the space of twenty-four hours, but to find links between the kids, moms, organisers, judges, make-up artists and dressmakers was going to take a lot of work. Finding just one event that both victims had attended was not going to help her. It needed to be condensed. And the only way she could think to do it was a grid system.

She'd narrowed it down to the seven most local events. To go national and international would include too much data, given that she had to record it across multiple years. Katie had only ever done the local pageants, so that was the logical place to begin her analysis.

According to the entrant rosters for the competitions, Katie had done all seven pageants from the years 2006 to 2013.

Stacey entered her name on the left-hand side and filled the grid square with her placement in each pageant. She moved on to the next line and entered the data for Toyah, who had started a year later and ended a year before Katie. Any squares for pageants Toyah hadn't attended were blacked out to show non-attendance.

Stacey allowed the smile to show on her face. She loved many aspects of her role, but her favourite was data analysis. Using numbers to paint a picture.

From just two lines of data, she could see that Katie had taken the whole thing more seriously. Her rankings were solid whereas Toyah's were haphazard. Sometimes she was top three, sometimes nowhere and sometimes not even attending.

If she could pinpoint every person who had been around the two mothers, would she eventually have a list that included their killer?

She grabbed the next pile of printouts and began adding to the list.

The ringing of the internal phone startled her.

'Wood,' she answered.

'Got a call for you,' Jack said before the line silenced for a second.

She introduced herself and gave her title.

'Hello, it's Doctor Michaels from Bushey Fields. May I speak to Inspector Stone?'

'No, but I can get a message to her.'

'It's about Katie Hawne. I have an update on her situation.'

Stacey listened with a growing sense of dread.

This was not going to thrill the boss one little bit.

TWENTY-SEVEN

'Shit,' Kim said in response to Stacey's news. 'How the hell did that happen?

'She refused the assessment, gathered her things and signed herself out. They tried to persuade her to stay and she threatened them with legal action for false imprisonment, so they had no choice but to let her go.'

'All right, Stace. Thanks for the update,' Kim said before ending the call.

'Damn it,' she growled, even though the hospital had done nothing wrong. 'And where the hell is this house?' she snapped.

'Deliberately hiding just to piss you off,' Bryant quipped. 'And we're about two minutes away, which is nowhere near long enough for you to shake off your irritation that somebody didn't do what you told them to do.'

'You don't think it was the right thing to suggest?' she asked. How could he possibly think Katie was stable enough to have been released?

'Doesn't matter. She didn't want the help, and she'd done nothing wrong except a bit of a performance in the holding cells. And after chucking-out time on a Friday night, any one of our overnight guests might do that just as well.'

'Hmm...'

'I know you're not convinced, but there's nothing more you could have done short of inventing outright lies to keep her there. I'm sure that crossed your mind, but luckily you just let that bright idea sail along.'

'But I'm right,' she insisted.

'Are you ever anything else? And anyway, she obviously trusts Judith.'

'A woman without one single qualification is advising impressionable people making serious decisions. Don't open people's boxes if you're not qualified to deal with what you find inside.'

'And on that note, I'm gonna pull up right behind that Lexus.'

Kim hadn't realised that they'd turned onto a lane where the land was measured in acres rather than feet. The gate to the property was open, and beside the Lexus was a mid-range Ford.

There was no doubt Toyah's father's house was bigger than the one she lived in with her mum.

Kim had the strangest idea of the kids being divided equally in the divorce settlement, but she said nothing as they headed for the front door.

It was answered by Tony before they'd had a chance to knock.

'We're all in the kitchen,' he said, opening the door wider to let them in.

She stood inside, not knowing where the kitchen was.

'Sorry, follow me,' he said.

The smell of bacon and scrambled eggs hung in the air, but the three plates on the table looked barely touched.

'Sorry to intrude,' Kim said, looking from one family member to the other.

'No, please, come in,' said the man she hadn't yet met. 'I'm Ben, Ben Shaw, Toyah's dad.'

Bryant shook his hand and introduced them properly, but Kim's attention was on Toyah. Her pale face, now devoid of any make-up beneath the shock of green hair, gave her a ghostly appearance.

'I came back as soon as I heard the terrible news. Please tell us you've made progress.'

'There's little I can add at the minute, Mr Shaw, but we do need to ask Toyah some questions. May we?'

'Of course. What am I thinking? Please sit. Can I get you anything?'

She shook her head as Tony sat down beside his sister.

Toyah turned and gave them her full attention.

Kim's heart ached. The girl was exhausted, and she had the face of someone physically unable to cry any more tears.

'We really are very sorry to intrude, Toyah, but can you think back to anything suspicious lately? Any unexpected phone calls your mum might have mentioned?'

Toyah shook her head.

'Anything at all about anyone following her or any strange things happening when she was out?'

'Nothing. Surely it was just some kind of psychopath who broke in and—' She stopped speaking, unable to say anything that would make the current situation too real.

'We think that's unlikely.'

She didn't want to use words like brutal or frenzied, but the attack was clearly targeted.

'You think the killer knew Andrea?' Ben asked, horrified.

'It's often the case.'

'What about the kids? If this was personal, are they in any danger?'

Kim considered all the information she had that Ben did not. Their other victim was also a mother, but there'd been no opportunity to kill Katie as she'd been taken into custody immediately. Right now, she couldn't say anything for certain.

'I don't think so, but I wouldn't let them too far out of your sight for a little while.'

'But who could have wanted to hurt mom like this?' Toyah asked. 'She was so sweet to everyone she met. She must have been terrified. Oh God, I can't even think about it. Please just ask me your questions.'

'Did your mom keep in touch with anyone from your old pageant days?'

'My old— Are you joking?' The question had taken Toyah by surprise. She clearly hadn't thought about those days in a long time. 'Why would you ask that? It was years ago.'

'It's just an avenue we're exploring.'

Great, now the whole room was looking at her like she'd lost her mind. The minute she left, Ben Shaw would be ringing the station to ask for a competent officer to replace her.

'We have our reasons for asking. Was she still in touch with anyone?'

Toyah shook her head. 'I can't imagine that she would be. It was so long ago, and I'm sure she would have mentioned it.'

'Did you keep in touch with any of the other girls?'

'No. It wasn't like that. You were there to win. The other girls were your competition so you didn't make proper friends. I mean you saw many of the same faces at each pageant and you'd wave and smile, but your team was you and your mom.'

'Did you enjoy it?' Kim asked.

'God, yes. Me and Mom had loads of fun. We'd go shopping for dresses and jewellery and shoes. We'd practise a few times each week during pageant season. Mom would do the walk with me, and she'd exaggerate it and we'd collapse on the floor laughing and tickling each other.'

Tony stiffened, and Toyah bit back the laugh that had come out of her mouth as though it had no right being there.

'It's okay, Toyah. They were good times for you and your mom. Cherish those memories. What made you stop doing the pageants?'

Toyah shrugged and broke eye contact. 'Got bored, I suppose. It was great fun, but eventually when pageant season came around, I wanted to be out with my school friends, having sleepovers and stuff.'

'And your mom didn't mind when you stopped?'

'Wh-Why would she? Mom never tried to make me do anything I didn't want to do.'

'You're sure?' Kim asked. Tension seemed to have been injected into both siblings.

'Of course she's sure,' Tony offered, breaking free of Toyah's grip and putting his hands into his lap.

'Got it,' Kim said. 'Did it ever bother you that these pageants get a bad rap and a lot of criticism?'

'No, cos I disagree. You get tiaras, crowns, sashes, bouquets, sceptres. I got savings bonds and prize money. Mom put it all in an account and it bought my first car.'

'Do you feel it harmed you at all?' Kim asked.

'How could it harm me? It was good fun. It was exciting. It was a laugh, but I learned loads. My confidence grew, I was comfortable on stage and I got better at public speaking, which had terrified me before I did pageants. I suppose I also learned how to be a good sportsman and lose gracefully.'

'Okay, thanks for—'

'I also learned how to be respectful to adults. I learned manners. How could any of that be negative?'

It seemed to Kim that Toyah could talk about the enjoyment of the events with far more eloquence than her reasons for stepping away.

'Okay, thanks for sharing your experience, Toyah,' Kim said, getting to her feet. 'One last thing. Did you ever meet a woman named Judith Palmer?'

The girl thought before shaking her head. 'The name isn't familiar. Is she a judge or something?'

'Never mind,' Kim said, satisfied that Judith Palmer wasn't linked to both girls.

'I'll see you out,' Ben said, crossing the room.

It was on the tip of Kim's tongue to refuse, but often there was a reason for the offer.

Her suspicions were proved correct when he closed the front door behind him.

'For the record, I didn't like the pageant thing, and it wasn't quite as rosy as Toyah makes out. I only mention it because you did.'

'Please continue,' Kim said.

'Well, it's fair to say that Andrea took it a bit more seriously than Toyah did.' He rubbed his hand through his hair. 'God, I feel awful for saying this.'

'The loss of a person doesn't change the facts,' Bryant offered.

'Toyah is being truthful when she says it was a laugh. It started out that way. Andrea loved Tony very much, but she'd always wanted a girl she could dress up. Oh dear, I don't know if this is coming out right. She got fully into it. Buying the dresses gave way to having them custom made. The list of accessories grew, the entrance fees got larger, the hotel rooms, a make-up artist. It all spiralled because Andrea wanted Toyah to do well. She didn't want her confidence battered due to not competing on the same level as the other girls. Luckily, we could afford it, but it was no cheap hobby.

'What started as fun dress up with a bit of make-up and a sparkly dress turned into emails to organisers about rules and age ranges, arguments with dress designers who didn't deliver. Over time, the fun aspect was replaced with rivalry and the desire to win. It took up more and more time.' He paused. 'Other things suffered.'

'Tony?' she asked.

He nodded. 'It wasn't something he could join in with. Distance grew between him and his mom.'

'Ben, may I ask if it was the reason for the divorce?' Kim asked, hoping she wasn't overstepping the mark, but he'd been fairly candid himself.

'It would be easy to say yes, but that would put all the blame on Andrea, which isn't fair. Still, us growing apart was certainly a factor.'

'You couldn't find a way to get involved, to spend some of that time together?'

'I had no wish to see my little girl parading on stage like a small adult. Those years were short enough as it was.'

'Okay, Ben, thanks for being open. We'll be in touch,' she said, heading for the car.

She couldn't help wondering how two people could have such opposing views of the same period in time.

'Ooh,' she said as her phone vibrated in her pocket. 'Text from Keats.'

She read his message and then looked at the attached photo.

'Jeez,' she said.

'What?' Bryant asked, glancing over her shoulder.

'The foreign body found in Andrea's throat. Eyelashes,' she said, holding the phone towards him. 'A pair of false bloody eyelashes.'

TWENTY-EIGHT

It was the first time Penn had ever visited Sandwell Valley crematorium.

The hexagonal building was fashioned from cream-coloured brick, and it had a distinctive red-tiled roof.

'This way,' Tiff said, guiding him towards a dour grey-brick building that was attached to the crematorium and which looked as though it had been tacked on from somewhere else.

A woman in her mid-thirties, wearing a pale blue suit, happened to be walking past the doors as they entered. After showing their IDs, she pleasantly guided them to a side room beyond a cafeteria area which was used for wakes. Before closing the door, she assured them that Doctor Connor would be along shortly.

A call ahead had secured them a ten-minute slot with the pathologist responsible for James Nixon. He wondered if the man would be equally as keen to share his expertise as Keats.

Despite the unexpected turn in the case of Sheryl Hawne, Penn was still happy to be working alongside Tiff. She was a police officer and she'd had a hunch that needed further exploration. A feeling he knew well.

In his early days as a constable, he'd been tasked with over-seeing the removal of a five-year-old boy from an alcoholic mother. His only job was to ensure that the situation didn't get heated or violent during the removal. The mother had been completely co-operative, and the boy had been taken away for assessment. Two weeks later, he learned that the child had been returned and something hadn't sat well in his gut. After replaying the incident in his mind many times, he'd finally realised the cause of his unease lay in the little boy's expression when he was being removed. Although scared, he had also appeared relieved.

After a five-minute contemplation of risk versus reward, he had taken action.

There had been a possibility that child services would get annoyed at his involvement, but the reward of them listening and acting had been well worth it. After pleading with them to do a spot-check follow-up, the boy had been found with a black eye and a sprained wrist. He'd been removed immediately, and Penn had learned never to ignore his gut feelings.

'You ever met this guy before?' Tiff asked while they waited.

He shook his head. He'd only dealt with Keats since being back at West Mids and, as grizzly as the pathologist could be, Penn enjoyed and respected him.

The door opened, and the doorway was filled with a bear of a man. His white coat strained at the upper arms and had no chance of ever meeting in the middle.

Penn had the sudden vision of this man in the dark, clad in blood-covered overalls, wielding a meat cleaver.

'Doctor Connor, thank you for seeing us,' he said, shaking away the thought and standing.

Doctor Connor waved him back down. 'Always happy to help our friends in the Dudley borough. What do you need?'

Penn wasn't sure if there was an edge to his voice or not. What he did suspect was that with this man, ten minutes meant ten minutes. As if to prove that point, the pathologist looked at his watch.

Never had Penn been so conscious of how short ten minutes was.

'We're here about the body of James Nixon. We're assessing whether there are any suspicious circumstances around his death.'

'You looking for extra work, Sergeant?'

'Just answers,' Penn replied.

'After a cursory physical exam, I'm leaning towards an accidental death. I remain open to being proved wrong, but I see nothing obvious on his body to suggest violence.'

After two years in the water, that was hardly a surprise.

'I think it most likely he either had too much to drink or he stood too quickly and had a dizzy spell which caused him to fall in the water.'

All this from a cursory glance at the body. They sure did things differently over here in Sandwell.

'Can you tell if he definitely drowned?' Tiff asked.

'It's a safe bet, love,' he said indulgently, and Penn felt the hairs stand up on his neck. 'But I will be conducting a digital post-mortem later today, which I expect will confirm my suspicions.'

The problem with having a preconceived idea was that it left little opportunity for further development. Instead of looking at everything, you tended to look only for facts that supported the theory you'd formed.

'But if he was pushed?' Penn asked.

'No pathologist would attest to such a theory after two years without video evidence or a sworn confession.' He looked at his watch again. Clearly the ten minutes he'd allowed included travelling time. 'To be honest, Sergeant, I'm not sure exactly what you were hoping to achieve with this meeting. There's really nothing more I can do to help you.'

'Will you send me the report?' Penn persisted, unwilling to let go quite so easily.

Before the pathologist refused, Penn took out his notebook and pen. He quickly scribbled down his email address and pushed it across the desk.

Doctor Connor folded it into his top pocket as he stood up.

They both thanked him and left the room.

Tiff waited until they were outside before speaking.

'Sorry for wasting your time, Penn. I suppose that leaves us with nowhere—'

'Hey, us Dudley lot don't give up quite that easily. Come on – let's get out of here.'

'To go where?' she asked, following closely behind.

'To where it all began.'

TWENTY-NINE

Stacey sat back and took an eye-break from the grid that was almost complete.

Every girl and every local pageant had been logged, along with the placement results. In total there were 127 names on the grid. The bottom fifty-seven names belonged to girls who had done the odd pageant here or there during that seven-year period.

The middle section consisted of around forty girls who had been consistently attending but only for a portion of the years that Katie had been active. That left a core group of thirty girls at the top, the most prolific at that time.

Stacey was now working her way down the list, searching for criminal records or scandal. She seriously hoped she was going to find something before having to go through all their social media accounts looking for clues.

So far, she'd found two drug addicts, one deceased and one incarcerated, and a prolific shoplifter with no form for violence.

On the other hand, she'd found a couple of models, one swimwear, one editorial, plus two doctors, an army recruit and a bakery owner.

After everything she'd read, she still wasn't sure of her opinion on pageants and wondered at the ratio of successes and failures compared to other early endeavours. Was pageantry more or less likely to have adverse effects in the future? Were there any detrimental long-lasting effects of taking up kick-boxing, or netball or football? Was participating in pageantry as a child any more harmful than any other hobby? But that was a whole new set of data, she thought, typing in the next name.

No criminal convictions, no form, not even known to them.

Ah, Carly Spencer had followed the profession and was now a pageant director herself, working out of an office in Hagley.

'Hang on,' Stacey said, scrolling further down to a tiny search result from the local news. Yes, she'd definitely got it right.

Stacey picked up the phone and called the boss.

THIRTY

The office of Carly Spencer didn't give the greatest first impression.

A cheap sign above the door read *Spencer and Co*, giving no indication of the nature of the business. It certainly wasn't trying to appeal to passing trade.

A piece of hastily applied board covered a crack in the top-right corner of the main window. Weeds and moss grew out from the gaps between the slabs on the pavement, reducing the kerb appeal even further.

Looking around, it wasn't a bad spot at the top end of Hagley High Street. Plenty of footfall but no clue given about what was going on inside.

'Is she in there?' Bryant asked as they approached the door.

Kim was unsure herself until she saw a single bulb shining within.

She tried the door. It was locked. She knocked and heard footsteps approach immediately. The door opened, and for a second Kim was stunned. The woman before them bore no resemblance to the building she occupied.

Long chestnut hair fell silkily over her shoulders. Brown eyes were accentuated by the perfect amount of eyeshadow and mascara. Her face had been contoured with professional skill. There was no question that this woman turned heads wherever she went.

'May I help?' she asked with a smile that displayed perfectly even white teeth. Although casual, her jeans and white shirt were impeccable too.

'Carly Spencer?'

'If she's won something, yes; for anything else, I'll check if she's available.'

Kim smiled and held up her ID.

'Never heard of her,' Carly joked, stepping aside for them to enter.

The space was small and contained a few chairs, a desk and a lot of boxes.

Expensive perfume filled the air and covered any smell of musty paperwork.

She turned to move a box from an office chair. 'Excuse the mess and take a seat wherever you can find one. I'm not sure why they sent you lot. It's no great mystery, and I know it's a minor thing, but I do appreciate you—'

'Ms Spencer, why do you think we're here?' Kim asked.

'Carly, please. My broken window – the vandalism? I called it in this morning.'

'I'm afraid that has nothing to do with our visit. We're investigating a major incident, and your name has come up.'

'Oh, damn, what's Petra done now? Where's she been caught?' she asked, rolling her eyes.

'Petra?'

'My Porsche. We tend to get noticed on all kinds of cameras.'

'You have a Porsche?' Bryant asked.

Kim knew it was her colleague's fantasy car.

'Don't get excited,' Carly said with a smile. 'She's an old bird. It was my dad's. He left it to me when he died.'

'No, nothing like that,' Kim said before Bryant could take the Porsche conversation any further. 'We understand that your mother died recently.'

'She was buried two weeks ago, but why would that interest you?'

'The obituary didn't mention the cause of death,' Kim said.

'Breast cancer. She'd been fighting it for three years.'

'I'm sorry for your loss,' Kim said, now aware that they were wasting their time. Although she'd known there had been no brutal stabbing, she had wondered if the woman had met her demise in suspicious circumstances. But even their killer couldn't orchestrate terminal illness.

'Thank you. I'm still trying to navigate the world without her.'

'You used to do pageants together?' Kim asked.

Carly looked puzzled. 'Why would you know that?'

'It's come up in our current investigation. Were they good years?'

'Good enough that I got into the business myself,' she said, sweeping her hand around the boxes.

'You enjoyed it?'

'Of course. It was fun. I made lots of friends. Many of us did the same events every year. It was like meeting up with old buddies again every time. We'd run around the venues doing cartwheels and handstands. We'd compare dresses and jewellery.'

Carly's account was in complete contrast to Toyah's recollection.

'No jealously or rivalry?' Kim asked.

'We were kids. It was dress up for a few hours. It wasn't life-changing stuff. We were having a great time. I think maybe some of the parents took it a bit more seriously, but to us it was a few minutes doing what we'd practised and the rest of the time just messing around.'

Kim had a sudden thought. 'Any particular girls you hung around with?'

'Blimey. Loads. But can I ask why you're interested in my old pageant days?'

'I can't really elaborate further. Was Katie Hawne one of your friends?'

She frowned while thinking. 'Katie... Katie... Oh God, no. Never Katie. Her mom wasn't having any of that kind of nonsense.'

'Nonsense?'

'Having fun,' Carly clarified. 'Even between rounds, Katie wasn't allowed to leave her mother's side.'

'How about a girl named Toyah?' Kim asked, thinking the first name was probably enough.

'Oh, Toyah was hilarious, at first. We had a lot of laughs, but she started to take it a bit more seriously towards the end. Sorry, I have to ask, are they okay?'

'They're fine,' Kim lied. 'So, why the move?' she asked, nodding towards the stacks of boxes.

'I'm not moving. I've closed the business. It's not what it used to be.'

'How come?'

'My mom loved the pageant business, so we started our own a few years ago. It wasn't a major event, but it was growing in popularity. I've not got the heart for it any more though. It's hard to keep defending it, and the repercussions are getting worse.'

'Go on,' Kim said, sitting forward.

'Well, at first it was just trolling online, then emails and now bricks being thrown at the window. That's why I thought you were here. It's the pageant haters growing bolder by the day, the insults, the threats. I'm over it.'

'Is there any way of finding out where it's coming from?' Bryant asked.

'Oh, I know exactly where it's coming from. I can even give you the address.'

THIRTY-ONE

'Bloody hell,' Stacey said, looking at the webpage of a group called the ERA.

She could see that the initials stood for Equal Rights Activists but wondered if the similarity to the Irish terror group was more than a coincidence. Unlike the IRA, this group seemed to hate everyone: at least everyone who didn't fight for the cause of battling men.

At first look, the website was like an assault on the eyes. Headlines screaming words like 'rape', 'subjugation', 'inferior', 'objectification' were plastered everywhere. Drop-down menus led to itemised reports of sexism, domestic violence, misogyny, pay scales. There were lists of patriarchal companies, places and events to boycott due to poor gender balance.

It didn't take long for Stacey to realise it was a very angry website. Every article was an attack on someone or something. Finger-pointing in every direction. Just reading it was exhausting and not a little depressing. Spend too much time here and you'd grab a gun and shoot every man on the face of the earth.

She continued surfing until she found a drop-down menu

called 'female fails'. Under the heading were exotic dancers, glamour models and beauty pageants.

Stacey browsed the articles and found the group was equally as angry towards the competitors and the organisers.

'Oh,' she exclaimed as she scrolled through the photos.

Right there was a photo of a cracked window with the headline: *'Oh dear, Pretty Pageants has had another unfortunate act of violence'* followed by a laughing-face emoji.

Okay, so this group had no problem acting on their disapproval, and it appeared they had no trouble shouting about it.

But just how loud were they prepared to shout?

THIRTY-TWO

It was almost lunchtime when Penn parked the car at Donkey Pool. At the last minute, he grabbed a Twix from the meal deals they'd bought on their way.

'It's gonna come again,' Tiff said, looking towards the clouds that were likely to end the short dry spell.

He opened the packet and offered her one of the fingers. She took it, and they ate silently as they walked.

'So, whereabouts was he fished out?' Penn asked as they approached the lake.

'Right here,' Tiff said, standing just to the right of a bunch of bulrushes.

Penn looked around and saw a man at a spot directly opposite.

'Come with me,' he said, heading towards the lone figure.

As he neared, he noted the gear. Three rods, deck chair, cooler box, flask, umbrella.

Perfect.

'Hey there,' Penn called out. 'How are you doing?'

'My doings are fine, thanks for asking.'

Penn introduced them both and then waited.

'Harry Guestford, Lower Gornal. Son of Thelma and Stan. Stop me once I'm boring you.'

'You know about what happened here yesterday?' Penn asked, getting right to it.

'Hell, yeah, it was the talk of my local last night. Half expected to get turned away by your lot this morning but nope. I'm all set for the day.'

Yeah, seemed like the search team hadn't spent too much time investigating.

'Did you know him?' Penn asked.

'Not really. We all have our favourite spots. His was over there. Mine's over here. I'd see him and wave, but he was a different fisherman to me,' Harry offered.

'How so?' Penn asked. Surely fishing was fishing.

'I get a steady stream of bites over here. Nothing huge but not tiddlers either. I ain't got no need to pose for pictures for folks on Bookface. Most of 'em know what a fish looks like. I get a bite, reel him in, land him, thank him and throw him back.'

'You thank the fish?' Tiff asked.

'Yeah, I've just put a hole in his mouth for sport so the least I can do is show my appreciation. That suits me. I don't need the big 'uns over there.'

Penn said nothing, hoping he'd continue, and he was happy to.

'Some folks sit over there to cast out wide after the biggest fish in the lake. Wait all day and catch nothing. Where's the fun in that?'

Penn failed to see the fun in any of it, but horses for courses. 'Why over there?' he asked.

'There's a ledge that slopes down off the bank, maybe five or six feet out. Beyond that it goes deep pretty quickly, maybe to twenty feet. That's where the big fish live.'

'So there's a ledge?' Penn clarified.

'Yep, the little buggers hide underneath it.'

It was now making sense to Penn how James Nixon had remained submerged for so long, but it raised another question.

'Harry, where does that ledge run from?'

'It starts just by the rushes and goes about ninety feet to the right.'

'Got it. One last thing. If I head back over there, will you give me the thumbs up when I'm in the area where James used to sit?'

'Can't see why not. You're brightening my day no end.'

'Cheers, mate.'

'What are you thinking?' Tiff asked as they headed back around the lake.

'You tell me,' Penn said, marching ahead.

He stood to the left of the bulrushes and waved at the fisherman. He moved crab-like along the bank one foot at a time until the guy raised his hand.

Penn turned to Tiff. 'Tell me what we've learned?'

If she was going to join CID, this was how she was going to have to start thinking.

She walked around, took a look and then stood beside him.

'We know that he most likely drowned and there's no obvious evidence of foul play but...' She started tapping her chin thoughtfully. 'If the pathologist is correct and our guy had some kind of episode, he'd have fallen. Even with a stagger he'd have landed in the shallow part of the water on the ledge.'

'So?'

'He could only have made it to the deeper water if he'd been pushed and then his body got caught on the underside of the ledge.'

'Absolutely,' Penn said, heading back towards the car. 'Now we may well have ourselves a case.'

It took him a few seconds to realise that Tiff hadn't heard, as she hadn't yet caught up with him. He turned to find her still standing at the water's edge with a puzzled expression.

'Hey, what is it?'

'The man was here fishing. He fell in or was pushed. He got stuck under the ledge after drowning.'

'Yeah, we got that, Tiff,' Penn said.

'So what happened to his stuff?'

Penn felt the smile tug at his lips. Honestly, he hadn't given that a thought.

In this particular instance, two heads were definitely working better than one.

THIRTY-THREE

The premises of the ERA were in a small office suite in a building at the end of Brierley Hill High Street.

The door was answered by a woman in her mid-twenties, wearing denim dungarees with half of the front flapping open. The tee shirt beneath was pink and sported a one-finger salute.

Kim held up her ID and asked if they could come in.

'How can I refuse a woman in charge?' she said, stepping aside. 'And I'm Bobbi, Bobbi Carter, chief volunteer of all that you survey,' she went on, making a sweeping motion with her hand.

What she surveyed was small but impressive. Four glass desks butted up to each other in the middle of the room. Each desk held a large screen and a keyboard-and-mouse combination. The chairs were identical. The fun stuff was against the walls. She saw two fruit machines, pinball, a dart board and a flatscreen TV.

'We're volunteers, funded by people who support our cause but don't have a lot of time,' Bobbi explained, following Kim's gaze. 'Gotta have a bit of fun while doing our good work.'

Kim wondered if this was how the Google offices had looked in the early days.

'And what work do you do?' she asked, pulling out one of the seats.

'Education, primarily,' Bobbi said, taking a seat but rolling herself away from the desks. 'Equality is a constant fight. The suffragettes started it, and we have a huge responsibility to continue it. We can't allow the momentum to slow. Women are battling the patriarchy in every—'

'Not all women,' Bryant said, nodding Kim's way.

'What, you think you're a hero cos you have a female boss and you don't make a fuss about it? Fuck, give the man a medal. Thanks for allowing the little woman to do her—'

'I'm only saying that we're not all bad,' Bryant defended himself.

Bobbi slapped her own head. 'Lord save me. I bet any money you're part of the "all lives matter" crew. Am I right?' she asked in a direct challenge.

'They do,' Bryant answered.

'So, when you donate your fiver to the hurricane victims of the Philippines, do you send a fiver to every other charity in the world?'

'Well, no.'

'Exactly, but they all matter too. At that moment, your focus goes to who needs the help most. A catch-all doesn't cut it. You telling me you're one of the good guys doesn't help me one bit unless you're prepared to call out the bad ones. It's like—'

'Bobbi,' Kim said, refocussing her attention. As entertaining as it was watching Bryant get schooled, it wasn't the purpose of the visit. Although she'd be happy to set up another appointment for it to continue. 'We understand you've been trying to educate Carly Spencer on pageants.'

'Absolutely. It's our duty.'

'To intimidate, abuse and induce fear in another woman?'

Bobbi shrugged. 'You can't make an omelette without cracking eggs. Some women need to be educated about their obligation to fight the system, not play into it.'

'Is it your obligation to put a brick through her window?'

'Of which you have proof?' Bobbi demanded.

'I have the photo on your website,' Kim countered.

'I took a photo of the damage as I passed it on my way in this morning,' Bobbi returned.

'Seems a natural progression from the emails and the messages.'

'Or an indication that other people feel as strongly about that abhorrent industry as we do.'

'So you won't be too disappointed to learn that she's decided to wrap up the business?' Kim asked to gauge her reaction.

'Yessssss,' she cried with a fist pump. 'I'm happy to count that as a win.' She looked delighted and triumphant.

Kim couldn't help the irritation that gnawed at her stomach. 'I don't think you can take all the credit, but I do think harassment and aggravation on top of the recent loss of her mother may have been a bit much.'

'Hey, I'm happy to be the straw that broke the camel's back as long as the camel's back is broken. Not literally, of course, I love animals, but I'm not going to pretend I'm unhappy that there's one pageant less in the world. I mean, as a woman, do you have any idea of the damage they do?'

'Go on,' Kim said, happy to let her preach. Not only would she discover the depths of the passion but also how far she was willing to go to make her point.

'Let's start with the pressure on women to conform to conventional beauty standards – the fashion, make-up, hair styling, cosmetic surgery and diet to the point of starvation. The fact that beauty is scored out of ten. The total objectification and the need to attain perfection.

'I'm sure you'll recall that the delightful Donald Trump

owned the Miss Universe competition for almost twenty years. He joked about being forced to sleep with every contestant. He also said that when the bathing suits got smaller and the heels got higher, the ratings went up.'

'So there's a market for it?' Kim said.

'There's a market for foie gras. Does that make it right to force-feed a goose until its liver explodes? The whole spectacle is debasing. One year, Miss Venezuela was humiliated by being forced to exercise in front of a group of reporters after she gained weight during her reign. Other contestants have lost their titles for putting on a few pounds. You think that's a healthy industry?'

'Many professions require sacrifice,' Kim said, playing devil's advocate.

Bobbi offered her a look of disgust before continuing. 'Pageant popularity grows each year. They perpetuate the idea that women are just bodies to be rated from one to ten, that the best we have to offer is our appearance, and if that message is being taught early...'

'You mean child pageants, like what Carly manages?'

'They should be outlawed. Do you have any idea of the harm they do?'

Kim thought of Toyah's enjoyment of the whole process. 'But isn't it just dress up?'

Bobbi rolled her eyes in frustration. 'Dress up is when you put on your mom's shoes and stagger around her bedroom. Pageants teach little girls they need improvements to their image to compete. We're talking flippers, hair extensions, acrylic nails, make-up, spray tans. Eventually young girls can feel ugly without all that stuff, and that poor self-image lasts into adulthood. Natural developments like acne and other body changes hit hard.

'It's not just dress up having little girls being sexualised for attention. The kids are being taught to act older. It's obscene to teach a six-year-old to pose like a model in her twenties.

'One pageant had a child smoking a fake cigarette, another was dressed as a prostitute, another wore fake breasts. If you're not horrified by these things, then there's nothing I can tell you.'

'You're saying pageants damage every child who takes part?' Kim asked.

'Who knows? All I know is that it isn't healthy to wax and thread a child's facial and body hair to give them a glowing appearance on stage. These kids learn that they gain attention and status when being sexualised and that their sexuality is a means to an end. It doesn't take a genius to work out that it can lead to premature sexual activity.'

'Don't they also give kids confidence?' Kim asked, remembering Toyah's words.

'Many parents believe the pageants boost their kid's self-esteem, but data shows that later problems include depression, low self-esteem and eating disorders.'

'We've spoken to girls who loved it,' Kim defended.

'They're either the exception or they're liars. In 2013, France became the first country to ban child pageants for the under thirteens. You have to understand that it takes hours and hours of learning how to pose, walk straight and fake smile. Most of these pageants are more for the parent than the child.'

'Doesn't that translate though?' Kim asked, again thinking of Toyah. 'If it's just a bit of fun for the mom, won't that carry down to the child?'

'The beliefs the pageants create become ingrained in the child. Kids feel as if they've let their parents down if they don't win. Ultimately, you're still transforming a typical child into a desirable woman. The sexualisation of children is a contributing factor in reports of kids being sexually abused. It's a foul industry that is hyper fixated on achieving professional adult aesthetics at a young age. Sexuality is imposed by parents without consent.'

'So, what are you campaigning for?' Bryant asked.

'A total ban on beauty pageants. Never gonna happen, but it won't stop us trying. Failing that, remove the beauty standards, end the sexualisation. As a start, Miss Teen USA replaced swimsuit with athletic wear. It's a step in the right direction, but much more needs to be done.'

'And your methods?' Kim asked, thinking about Carly having been driven out of business.

'I'm going to do whatever works,' Bobbi said without apology.

Kim thanked her for her time and stepped out of the building, exhausted by Bobbi's passion.

It was clear how strongly she felt about getting the events banned, and Kim couldn't help wondering if there was any line the woman wouldn't cross.

THIRTY-FOUR

Tiff tried to understand her feeling of foreboding as they knocked on Olivia and Logan Dench's door.

She'd been riding a strange wave of misplaced euphoria since leaving the lake. Inappropriate because a man was dead, but no less real. Penn agreed with her that something wasn't right. The feeling in her stomach hadn't been due to an overindulgence of dairy.

But Tiff was starting to realise how immersive it all was. When she was in uniform, she reported for duty and she followed instructions. She finished her shift, and although there were people still on her mind once she got home, they were not her responsibility. She had done her job, handed over and entrusted the incident to people much higher on the food chain.

But she'd been unable to un-grip this case from her mind once she got home. It was as though she'd taken responsibility for it, that it was hers and that she'd never rest until it was solved. Did the rest of the team feel that way about every case? she wondered as Penn looked at her questioningly.

She nodded as he knocked again. It had taken the same

amount of time for someone to answer the door the previous day.

They heard the sound of locks and chains being opened.

'Hello again,' Logan said, offering her a wide smile before looking curiously at Penn.

'A colleague of mine,' Tiff explained as Penn showed his identification.

'Ooh, CID,' he said, looking Penn up and down. Tiff could swear she saw a dismissive glint in his eye. 'Sorry for the delay. I had headphones on, and Mom had the radio on loud in the kitchen. Do you want to come in?'

'If you don't mind,' Penn said, crossing the threshold.

'Mom's in here,' he said, pointing to the lounge.

He followed them in.

Olivia sat in a single chair close to the fireplace. She nodded a greeting, and Tiff sensed an unnatural stiffness in her posture.

Penn took a seat on the sofa, and Tiff sat beside him.

'CID, Mom. Must be something important,' Logan said, closing the door before taking the other single armchair.

'Just a few questions, if you don't mind,' Penn said.

'Of course,' Olivia said, nodding.

'I'm not sure what else we can tell you,' Logan offered. 'But if you can tell us when the funeral—'

'We can't release the body quite yet. There are still questions around his death.'

'What kind of questions?' Logan asked.

Tiff realised that although Penn had initially been talking to Olivia, Logan had steered the conversation so that all eyes were now on him.

'We're not convinced his death was an accident,' Penn said.

Logan nodded. 'Yeah, I think it was suicide too.'

'Not the line we're going down either,' Penn responded evenly.

'But I told you he was depressed,' Logan said, and Tiff

wondered if she'd imagined the note of petulance that had crept into his voice.

'Depression doesn't always lead to suicide, and his sister didn't think he was depressed. In fact, Esther thought he was the happiest he'd been in years, especially since meeting Olivia. He talked of a bright future between them.'

A small cry escaped from Olivia's lips as her eyes filled with tears.

'How would she know? They barely spoke. We were closer to him than anyone.'

'Well, actually, she didn't agree with you on that either. She said the two of you didn't get on.'

'That proves my point exactly. We didn't get on at first. I was probably a bit overprotective of my mom, recently widowed, vulnerable. It didn't take long for me to see he was genuine. I really liked the guy, didn't I, Mom?'

'Yes, yes, that's right.'

Tiff turned towards Olivia. 'Had James been in any kind of trouble that you know of?'

'How would she know that?' Logan asked.

Tiff ignored him and waited for the woman to answer.

Olivia shook her head.

'Did he mention any arguments with anyone?'

Before shaking her head, Olivia offered the briefest of glances at her son.

Tiff turned to Logan. 'I'm a bit dry. Any chance of a glass of water?'

'Sorry, water's off. Burst main half a mile away.'

Tiff hid her frustration. This kid was not going to let them speak to his mother alone for even a minute.

'Had James received any strange phone calls or visits?' Penn asked.

'Nothing while he was here,' Logan answered.

'Logan, I'd really like your mom to answer.'

Olivia shook her head before Logan stood up abruptly.

'And I'd really like you both to leave. Mom is upset and grieving, and your presence is intrusive.'

Tiff looked to Olivia, but she said nothing and cast her gaze to the ground.

As they reached the front door, which Logan was holding open for them, Penn paused.

'If your mom needs any help or support, we have people—'

'Mom is fine. She has everything she needs.'

Tiff swore as the door closed firmly in their faces.

'What?'

'I messed that up,' she said.

'Not really. As soon as you directed a question to his mom, he was looking for a reason to throw us out. Despite appearances, he's uncomfortable with our presence and doesn't like his opinion on James's death questioned. Pretty sure he thinks we should have just accepted his word about the depression and left it well alone.'

So Penn had caught that too. But she still felt as though she'd messed it up.

'But I've antagonised him now. He's never going to let us back in that house.'

'He probably wasn't going to anyway, and to be honest, we have no cause to return. Let's head back to the station and regroup.'

Tiff took a last look around and then paused.

'Okay, Penn, but just give me a minute. There's one more place I'd like to go.'

THIRTY-FIVE

'Okay, pull in,' Kim said as they approached a Costa drive-thru.

'Your usual?' Bryant asked, approaching the window.

She nodded. He gave the order, which was more words than he'd spoken in the twenty minutes since leaving the ERA office.

She waited until they were parked before speaking.

'Okay, spit it out,' she said, removing the lid and blowing on her coffee. 'Something's narked you.'

He sighed heavily. 'Well, she's right, isn't she? I am part of the problem. I think I'm a decent kind of guy, but what's the point if I don't call out the shit heads?'

'You spend your day dealing with shit heads.'

'You did a good job of avoiding my point there, guv.'

'You really wanna do this?' she asked, to be sure.

He nodded.

'Okay. It's not enough, any more, to just be a good guy and proud of it. You don't get gold stars for doing the right thing or being a nice person. That's like taking an exam and getting a pass. No extra credit and no distinction.'

'What more can I do?' he asked, and she felt for him. Being twelve years her senior, he had grown up on a staple diet of comedies full of racism, sexism and offensive content. He'd adapted since, and his strong moral compass guided him well.

'I'm not gonna preach at you, buddy, but as an example, have you ever entered the locker room and seen a bunch of coppers looking at photos of naked girls?'

'Of course,' he said, and then his face registered the penny dropping.

'Exactly. See how easily you acknowledge that as normal behaviour? It's just the guys, doing guy stuff.'

He started to nod slowly.

'It's not enough to not take part. You wanna see change, call them on it. Remind them that's someone's daughter, sister, whatever.'

Kim felt a stab of relief when her phone started to ring. Bryant was a good guy, but Bobbi had a point, and although it wasn't her job to school him, she knew she'd made him think.

'Go ahead, Stace.'

'Boss, I'm just working on my second matrix.'

'Well done, Neo,' she quipped.

Stacey's laugh on the other end clearly came because she was the boss and not because she was amused. Jeez, she didn't know why she bothered.

'Anyway, my second spreadsheet is detailing organisers, judges, etcetera, just to see who was around the scene frequently, and there's a dressmaker's name that's coming up a lot.'

'Okay, shoot.'

'Kelvin Hobbs, owns a small shop in Bewdley called Sew Cute, get it?'

'I'm assuming by your jovial tone that's spelled with a double U.'

'Yeah, boss. I'm easily amused. Back to it,' she said before ending the call.

Something somewhere in the pageant world linked their

victims. Had they been involved in something then that had come back to haunt them now? If so, what had they done ten years ago that would revisit them now? Was it something to do with their daughters? Someone else's child? The competition? Rivalry?

With those questions in mind, it made sense to start talking to some of the people who had likely dealt with their victims back then.

THIRTY-SIX

A bell tinged above them as they entered the premises of Sew Cute in Bewdley.

A man sat side on to them in front of a top-of-the-range Singer sewing machine. It appeared that the shop space was divided into two halves. To the left were small garments with sales tags on, and to the right were garments which looked like alterations hanging on a long rack.

'Kelvin Hobbs?' Kim asked, taking a step forward. There was no reception or desk, so it was unclear where shop space and workspace divided.

'I am he,' he said, standing.

'Got time for a chat?' she asked, holding up her ID.

'Oh my, about what?'

'Our current investigation.'

'Well, of course. Do you prefer downstairs or up there?' he asked, pointing out back.

Kim looked past him. 'Why, what's up there?'

'My flat.'

'Down here is fine,' she said, looking towards the front door.

She didn't want their chat to be constantly disturbed by the tinging of that bell.

'Almost the end of the day anyway,' he said, walking past her. He turned the sign to closed and locked the door.

She guessed him to be mid-forties from his face but a bald patch that he was valiantly trying to cover aged him by a further ten years. He was wearing knee-length shorts and a colourful tee shirt.

'Bear with me,' he said, heading out back. He returned with a couple of metal chairs. 'There, that's better.'

'We understand you're well connected in the pageant world,' she said, taking a seat.

'Oh, not any more. Ten years ago maybe.'

'You may still be able to help us, Mr Hobbs.'

'Kelvin, please,' he said, holding up his hand. 'The only Mr Hobbs I know disowned me when I made my first dress, but that is a whole other story.'

'Okay, Kelvin, we understand that you were chief dress-maker to the pageant girls back in the day.'

'I was indeed,' he said proudly before letting out a long sigh. 'I was very much in demand. Couldn't keep up with orders. I was turning people away,' he finished wistfully.

'Do you miss it?' Bryant asked.

'Sometimes. I got to meet such a lot of lovely little girls. Not all of them. Some were brats; proper spoiled little madams.'

'What about the mums?' Kim asked.

'Oh, all of them were brats,' he said and laughed, leaving Kim to wonder if he was serious or not.

'What drew you towards the industry?' Kim asked, wondering how exactly that happened. Was it a detour from another career or what he had always dreamed of doing?

'Oh, I'd loved reading about pageants since learning of the medieval May Day celebrations.'

'The what?' Kim asked.

'That's where they date back to. A May queen would be chosen from a procession. Beauty contests became more respectable with the first modern Miss America in 1921. They developed over the years, but the majority were for young, unmarried women. I used to watch all of the big four: Miss Universe, Miss World, Miss International, Miss Earth. The smaller ones that feed into these aren't normally televised, but the big ones are quite the visual spectacle.'

'How about child pageants?' she asked.

'Well, the modern child beauty pageant emerged in the sixties in Miami. I think the first Little Miss America began at an amusement park in New Jersey, but that was for the thirteen-to-seventeen age range.'

'How many ranges are there?'

'However many the organisers can include to make as much money as possible.'

'Explain,' Kim said. She hadn't known it was that complicated. She figured kids turned up, put on their sparkles, got judged and went home.

'I've been at pageants where they have as many as eight age ranges, the youngest being zero to eleven months and the oldest being sixteen to eighteen.'

'How does that make the organisers more money?' Bryant asked. 'Surely it's the same number of competitions?'

Kelvin shook his head. 'The ranges are announced ahead of time. Parents see less competition for their child if there are many age ranges. Imagine if you had one-year-olds competing with four-year-old kids. Then when you add up the entrance fees for each category...'

'Hang on. Don't you just pay to enter the competition?' Kim asked, starting to wonder just how much money was involved.

'Ha, no chance. Each category is usually a separate entrance fee, so there's talent, outfit of choice, sportswear, theme wear, evening wear, decade wear. They all cost money to enter, and you can't get the big prize unless you enter them all.'

Kim said nothing, indicating he should continue.

'The supreme titles are only available to girls who have entered every category and then a Grand Supreme is crowned. That's the title with the money, big prizes, scholarships. All the things that help to make the investment worth it.'

'Investment?' she asked, making no attempt to hide her incredulity. That was a word that belonged in sentences with houses, savings schemes, jewellery, perhaps *Star Wars* collections but certainly not beauty contests.

'Of course. Many parents feel the expenditure will be recouped and multiplied in the future, from modelling contracts, acting or even presenting work. Pageants are raking it in from parents who want to give their children the best chance of a bright future, but so are all the subsidiary services. In America alone they have over two hundred and fifty thousand pageants and the industry is worth twenty billion dollars. We don't have the same numbers here, but it's growing in the UK every year.'

'What's an average spend per pageant?'

He laughed. 'Oh my goodness, there are too many variables. A lot depends on whether it's glitz or natural.'

Her blank expression earned her a dramatic eyeroll.

'Natural only allows lip gloss and mascara.'

How natural was lip gloss and mascara on a six-year-old? Kim wondered.

'But the money is in the glitz. You're looking at the cost of hotel rooms, professional make-up artists, coaching fees. A good pageant dress can cost up to eight thousand pounds.'

Kim balked. Her entire wardrobe wasn't worth that.

'There are families that have gone into debt, even lost their homes chasing the big prizes. Don't get me wrong, the kids deserve it. Training includes long hours and strict daily routines. Some are pushed beyond their limits and denied necessary rest. There are private coaches and pageant schools popping up around the country. It's a growing economy.'

'I'm waiting to hear about the fun,' Kim said.

'Hmm... it's not really about that. It often starts that way, but the attitude of the child is often dictated by the parents.'

Again, Kim found herself thinking of Toyah, who had been having a great old time. Kim didn't doubt that for a minute. When she'd spoken of those times, a natural joy had appeared to spread over her face. She'd said she'd loved it all, and Kim believed her. What she wasn't as sold on was the girl's reason for leaving. There was more to that story than she'd been told.

The dressmaker continued. 'I've been at pageants where contestants have put itching powder in their rival's dress. I've seen girls distraught because their dress has been cut up. I've seen clothing and underwear missing, basic bullying.'

'Sounds pretty toxic,' Bryant observed.

'It can be. It all depends on the parents. Some have been known to send presents to the judges to curry favour. Many moms target the biggest competitors with gossip and criticism. Kids have been disqualified due to the behaviour of their parents, but few people take it as far as Wanda Holloway.'

Kim shrugged to indicate she had no clue.

'Wanda Holloway was a Texan woman who, in 1991, hired a hitman to kill the mother of her daughter's rival for the cheer-leading squad. I know that's not quite the same but...'

Close enough, Kim thought.

'Why not try and kill the kid though?' Bryant asked.

'Ooh, it takes a seriously sick person to kill kids. The death of a parent is often enough to disturb your focus. Throw you off your game.'

'You probably dealt with quite a few of the mothers when making dresses,' Kim said.

'Well, of course. They were my bread and butter.'

'Any strike you as particularly troublesome?'

'Officer, I worked in the industry for twelve years and made, on average, fifty dresses per year. You're going to have to narrow it down a bit.'

'Do you remember working for a woman named Sheryl Hawne?'

'Hell yes.'

Kim sat up straight. Those two words told her a lot. Of all the parents he'd dealt with, he recalled this one immediately.

'Care to elaborate?'

'She was an absolute terror. Wouldn't even let me design the dresses. She'd bring me a photo with her own amendments and wanted them followed to the letter. If even one rhinestone was out of place, she knew about it.'

'And her daughter Katie?'

'Oh, Katie was adorable. A real cutie. Must have got her looks from her dad's side. Bless her, she was terrified of the woman. I don't mean physically – there was no violence that I know of – but Sheryl was a very intimidating presence. Hell, even I was scared of her, and I didn't have to go home with her.'

'But you kept working for her?' Kim asked.

He laughed. 'If I'd refused to work for every difficult mother, I wouldn't have lasted very long.'

'Did Sheryl put a lot of people's backs up?' Kim asked.

'I'd imagine so. If she was demanding with me, I'd assume she was the same with other service providers.'

'Any particular incidents you recall?'

'May I ask what this is about?'

'Sheryl Hawne was murdered yesterday.'

His hand flew to his mouth. 'Oh my God, how awful, how terrible. Oh my. I don't know what to say. I feel terrible about all the things I just said. God rest her soul.'

'No need to feel bad about the truth. That's exactly what we need right now.'

'How's little Katie?'

'Not so little, but to answer your question I think struggling is a fair assessment,' Kim said honestly.

'Poor girl,' he said, looking genuinely concerned.

'Do you remember a woman named Andrea Shaw?'

'Toyah's mom?' he asked as the colour began to drain from his face.

Kim nodded.

'Don't tell me she's... No, you can't be...'

Kim nodded.

'Jesus Christ, sorry Lord,' he said, glancing upwards. 'What the devil is going on?'

'That's what we're hoping to find out. Were the two of them close?'

'None of the mothers were close. They didn't go for coffee or the occasional night out. These women don't really make friendships; it's more like they form alliances against a common enemy.'

'And did they?'

'N-Not that I can recall specifically. To be fair, they were very different people.'

'Is there anything you can remember that might have linked them?' Kim asked.

'They used the same make-up woman, I think, but then so did many other moms.'

'Got it,' she said, standing. 'You've been a great help.'

He stood and moved towards the door.

'Last thing,' Kim said as a thought occurred to her. 'You clearly enjoyed the pageant world, so why did you leave it?'

'It was just time to move on,' he said, unlocking the door.

She would swear she saw a slight tension tighten his jaw.

'There must have been something,' she pushed, stepping over the threshold and onto the pavement.

The face looking at her now was completely different to the

affable one they'd seen inside the store. His expression was wary and guarded.

'Nothing I care to share, Inspector. Safe travels and have a good night.'

Before she had the chance to ask anything further, the door had been closed in her face.

Two minutes ago, Kelvin had been candid and informative, offering insight and background. He'd been a co-operative helper, and now she had to wonder if he was something more.

'Strange,' Bryant observed.

'Which particular part?' Kim asked as they approached the car.

'The part where he said the mothers formed alliances against a common enemy but was unable to give us anything further.'

Yes, what the hell was that all about?

THIRTY-SEVEN

The welcome from the Denches' next-door neighbour couldn't have been more different to the one they'd received from Logan and his mum.

Within minutes of knocking the door, Tiff and Penn were seated at the kitchen table with a cup of tea and a plate full of digestives.

'Now, tell me how I can help,' Doris Winslow said, pushing the plate towards Tiff.

After wondering if she particularly looked like she needed feeding, Tiff took a biscuit but held it in her hand. 'Not sure if you've seen the news, Mrs Winslow, but we recovered a body from one of the Dudley fishing lakes. The man was James Nixon, a very good friend of your neighbours.'

'Oh no, poor man.'

'Did you know him?' Tiff asked before taking a nibble of her biscuit.

'Not really, but he seemed nice enough. He'd smile and wave if he saw me. He pulled my bin back down the path a few times, even cleared the slabs of snow one time. Ahh, that's a shame. Heart attack, was it?'

'We're not sure yet,' Tiff said. It was the response she'd expected, but that wasn't the reason for the visit.

Mrs Winslow continued. 'My Derek died of a heart attack. Fitter than a butcher's dog, he was, but it still got him; buying a loaf of bread, he was. All we wanted was a bit of toast, but right there in the supermarket he keeled over and died. They ker-chunked him,' she said, making a motion with her hands that Tiff guessed was meant to be a defibrillator. 'But it was no good. That was Derek. Once he made his mind up, that was it.'

Tiff wasn't sure how much control the man had had, but the woman's chatting had given her time to eat her biscuit.

'Olivia seems to have thought the world of James,' Tiff said, bringing the conversation back.

'Oh, I think she did in her own way. She'd been through the mill with her husband. Lost him to cancer, but it wasn't for the want of trying. If anyone could have prevented his death through passion and commitment, it would have been Olivia. She refused to take a break, wouldn't leave his bedside. She even set up a mattress next to his sick bed so that he wouldn't be alone.'

'It must have hit her hard when he died,' Penn offered.

'It's no easier when you know it's coming. There's still that point where one minute they're there and the next they're not. The boy was a big help to her, though I think he was relieved when James came around. Took some of the pressure off him. James made her laugh. They were good friends, and he was helping her heal.'

Tiff realised that with a woman like Doris Winslow, she didn't really need to ask questions.

'It was none of my business, but I think it was a bit soon for anything serious. Her heart was still with her husband. James going away was the final straw, and now poor Logan has to deal with it all on his own.'

'Deal with what?' Tiff asked, taking another biscuit as Penn sipped his tea.

'Well, I don't think she's very well,' Doris said, tapping her temple. 'Completely understandable. The stress of her husband dying and then the disappearance. You can understand how a few marbles might have come loose.'

Tiff looked past the woman's questionable description of mental health issues to probe further. 'She's been unwell?'

'Oh yes. Poor Logan has no real life of his own due to taking care of his mom.'

'He's told you this?' Penn asked.

'Oh, not in so many words. He's very loyal to her. He asked me to collect a prescription for him, well, for his mom. I didn't mean to be nosey. The bag was open. They were antidepressants. I didn't say anything. I just told him if he ever needed anything to give me a shout. He was so grateful for the kind words he almost burst into tears.' She shook her head sadly. 'And much to his shame, I saw what he was dealing with myself.'

'How so?' Tiff asked, growing more confused. Olivia hadn't struck her as someone on the edge, but could she really judge, having spent no more than a total of half an hour with her and having heard no more than a few sentences come out of her mouth?

'One night, oh, about a year ago now, I glanced out of the back bedroom window before closing the curtains. Olivia was out there in her nightie, no shoes, just her nightie, trying to climb the back fence. Logan was trying to talk her down, but she wouldn't listen. She was frantic, manic, scraping her hands and feet on the wooden slats. In the end, Logan had no choice but to yank her down by force. She put up a good fight, but luckily Logan is a strong boy and managed to get her back inside. He saw me watching, and I felt so sorry for the poor lad.

'He popped round for a cuppa the next morning and

explained she'd been forgetting to take her tablets. I offered my help, and he asked me for two things,' she said before taking a sip of her tea.

They waited.

'He asked me not to share what I'd seen with anyone. He was scared the doctor would insist on sending her to an institution and it would kill her being away from all the memories of his dad. He really felt she could do better on her own with more time. The boy was beside himself with worry. Of course I was happy to keep it to myself. No one else's business.'

'And the other thing?' Penn asked, finishing his tea.

'He asked if he could pop round now and again when she was sleeping, just for a bit of a break and a chat. Of course, I told him he was welcome any time.'

'And does he?'

'Oh yes. He comes round every couple of weeks. Tells me about the jobs he's doing next door and apologises for the noise he makes sometimes. He's a good boy and doesn't complain about how much care his mom needs.'

The woman continued waxing lyrical about Logan's numerous good qualities. For a few minutes, they listened politely before thanking her for her time.

As she headed for the car, Tiff took one last look at the home of Logan and Olivia Dench. She had one question.

What the hell was going on in that house?

THIRTY-EIGHT

Olivia stared at the road long after the car had pulled away.

She'd seen the police officer glance back at the house with a question in her eyes, but she hadn't dared pull back the heavy net curtain. Logan had used rolls of thin Velcro to secure the curtains down both sides and along the bottom. If she broke the seal and was not able to reattach it exactly, he would know.

Part of her was praying that the constable had realised there was something wrong, but why would she? No one would ever believe what her life had become.

The young constable could never have guessed that Logan had put her in the single chair so she couldn't touch or nudge anyone to give them a signal. He had then seated himself directly opposite so he could see her expression at all times.

And she had complied. She'd had two police officers within feet of her and she hadn't said a word. She knew they'd never believe her. They'd never just take her away and protect her from her son for the rest of her life. She had no proof of the things he'd done and no witnesses to any of it.

She'd hoped that Doris might have put it together when she'd managed to get out into the garden that night. He'd forgotten to lock the back door, and she'd made a run for it, trying to scale the fence. Logan had caught her and dragged her back to the house. She'd been trying to mouth the word *Help* up at the neighbour's window, but Doris's gaze had been firmly on her son, compassion in her eyes.

He had taken great delight in regaling her with their conversation the following day, telling her Doris was now totally aware of her emotional breakdown.

And that was the problem, she thought as the tears stung her eyes. Everyone would believe Logan. Even she had believed him in the early days when he'd said she needed to see a doctor. He had assured her that if she got some medication, they'd be able to get back to normality, that he'd be able to trust her to make her own decisions.

And so, she had told the doctor about her mood swings, her feelings of rage and her occasional suicidal thoughts. Things that Logan had told her to say to get the drugs that would bring back normality.

It had worked. She'd been prescribed antidepressants and sleeping tablets. All of which Logan had controlled for over a year.

For two months, he had dispensed the antidepressants daily, but then he'd started to miss a day here and there. Her moods had become erratic, her emotions all over the place, her thoughts of eternal peace more frequent. And then he'd level her out again.

Her stomach jumped into her mouth as the bolt on the outside of her bedroom door slid across.

Logan stepped inside with a plate and a cup.

'No family time tonight,' he said, placing the refreshments on her bedside cabinet. 'Not until I work out what you did.'

'I didn't do anything,' she protested.

Family time consisted of her being allowed to watch some television in the lounge. She hated the programmes Logan chose, but it was a distraction from her own head. Up here, she had no TV or radio, and even her books had been removed after she'd asked to go to the supermarket with him.

'Then why would that little bitch try and get you alone?' he asked, eyeing her suspiciously and moving closer. 'What did you communicate to her?'

'N-Nothing, I swear,' she said as he flexed his right hand into a fist.

Her mind screamed silently as her body readied itself for the onslaught.

'I don't believe you,' he said, towering over her. 'I really wish you'd learn to understand that I'm in charge now. I'll be going round to see Doris to find out what they asked her. I'll be laying it on thick so she stays on my side. You've got to remember that no one is going to believe you. I've done nothing except take care of my sick mother. If you try anything stupid, I'll have you back here in no time, and things will be a whole lot worse, got it?'

She nodded, still looking down.

He moved back towards the door. The threat of violence was gone.

'Logan?' she said, holding out her hand.

'No, I don't think so. Not tonight. You need your mind clear of drugs to think about what you've done.'

As the door closed, she felt the terror steal over her. It was more potent than any fear of violence. She knew what was coming. The mood swings, the irrational thoughts, the darkness. As soon as the medication started to fade from her system, the anxiety would overwhelm her. She'd be incapable of stringing coherent thoughts together. Eventually she would be begging him to end the misery of her forced sudden withdrawal. And then she'd be so damn grateful when he gave her the next pill.

Unable to stop herself, the tears came and rolled over her cheeks.

How had she allowed this to happen? Had she invited it? What had she done to make Logan think she could be treated like this? And how easily had her links to the past been erased? There was a time when she'd had a job, colleagues, friends, a social life. She'd made a life with branches that reached out into the lives of other people, yet somehow Logan had amputated them, leaving her adrift, invisible, forgotten.

She'd wondered whether at some stage a part of her had craved a break from her own autonomy, a part that had welcomed someone taking away her independence, that wanted to hand over control of when she ate, slept, went out. But then she realised that in thinking those thoughts, she was doing what every good mother does: she was taking responsibility for her child's actions. It was easier for her to believe that she was somehow to blame than accept he was a monster. A monster she had raised, of course, so however she chose to look at it, it was her fault.

Throughout the last two years, she had held on to the vaguest hope that he would snap out of it. That he would somehow realise what he'd done to her and beg her forgiveness. Despite everything, she ached to go back to the way things had been before. Somehow, she would try and forget about the last two years and start fresh.

A small voice in her head knew that was never going to happen. She knew somewhere deep inside her that he had crossed a line. But now she also had to wonder if he had taken a life.

Had her son committed murder, and, if so, what the hell was she supposed to do about it?

THIRTY-NINE

'Okay, guys, it's show and tell time. I'll start,' Kim said, taking a position at the head of the room as she did whenever the spare desk was occupied. 'We know a lot more about beauty pageants and just how seriously they're taken, especially by the parents.'

'It's not just a bit of fun?' Penn asked.

'Are you kidding?' Stacey said. 'Even in our enlightened times, child pageants still focus on beauty. Apparently they're evolving to include inner beauty, personality, intelligence, but children shouldn't be concerned about the size of their thighs or their stomachs. As a girl who was a chubby kid, I can tell you that such a huge focus on body image at a young age just isn't healthy.'

Kim took a sip of her coffee which Stacey read as permission to continue.

'From what I've read today, toddlers are expected to perform as perfect Barbie dolls. It's an unrealistic standard that's gonna follow you your whole life. The whole thing makes it normal for a two-year-old to walk around stage in tiny, tight bikinis,' Stacey said, shuddering. 'How is it healthy to instil in kids that appearance is everything?'

'I think we can guess your opinion on the subject,' Kim said, unsure if she completely disagreed. But then she thought of Toyah, who had loved every minute of the experience; were it not for the murder of her mother, she would have presented as a grounded, confident young woman.

'I met a representative of a group you might like to join today,' Kim said with a raised eyebrow.

Stacey laughed. 'Nah, they seem a bit extreme for my taste. Sorry, it just boils my blood.'

'They certainly do have a hatred of the pageant world,' Bryant offered.

Kim nodded her agreement. 'And we have two victims seemingly bound only by the pageant world. We wondered whether Carly Spencer's mom was a third victim, but she died of natural causes.

'The dressmaker who worked with them both says they were very different, so it's hard to think what they might have in common outside of the circuit. Sticking with you, Stace, anything more jumping out from your matrix?'

'Still working on it, but I've got the name of a make-up artist who seemed to be in demand.'

'Get me an address by tomorrow,' Kim said, glancing at her watch. It was almost seven and she wasn't planning on going straight home.

She moved her gaze between Penn and Tiff. 'Progress from you two?'

Tiff looked to Penn to speak.

'Something not right, boss. The post-mortem is being rushed through cos no one is making any noise. He ain't Keats, that's a fact.'

Kim said nothing and waited for the question to come. Penn didn't like people doing half a job.

'Boss, what are your thoughts on asking for a second opinion?'

And there it was.

'It's not gonna be a popular request with our Sandwell colleagues, but if you think stuff is being missed, it's an option. What about suspects?'

'Weird dynamic between the victim's girlfriend and her son, for sure,' Penn said, echoing the sentiment that had caused Tiff to question it in the first place.

'Okay, stay with it, but keep me updated,' she said, folding her arms. 'And on to other matters. Do we have a viable talent for Sunday night?' As inconsequential as the subject might seem to her team in the face of the cases they were working, Woody wasn't going to budge on them coming up with something.

No answer.

'Are we seriously saying that there's not one talent amongst us?'

'You don't think Woody might give us a pass?' Stacey asked hopefully. 'I mean, double murder and all that.'

'You don't think every other department is just as busy as we are?' Kim asked, dashing her hopes.

'Couldn't you train Barney to do a few tricks?' Bryant asked.

'Have you met my dog?'

'Not even for an apple?' Bryant pushed.

'He just about tolerates my presence for an apple so you can forget anything more.'

Still nothing from the rest of her team.

'Ideas, people. We're running out of time. Now get lost and I'll see you all tomorrow. Except you, Tink – you can stay.'

Everyone else filtered out of the room, leaving the young constable with a pensive look on her face.

'Jeez, Tink, you've done nothing wrong. Now tell me what's up.'

'Nothing. I'm fine,' she said, adopting what Kim had come to know as the too-bright smile.

'You didn't talk once in the catch-up. You've been in our briefings before, and you usually have no trouble speaking up. You're not out of your depth here. You brought this case to us, and now you get to run with it. Understand?'

'I do, but how do you do this every day? How do you switch off? It's so intense and so... important.'

Kim smiled. 'We all have our ways. It is a pressurised job, Tink. You work for the victim, you work for the family, people are grieving, they're looking to you. You have to find a way to let the pressure out. Many a detective has succumbed to alcohol or drugs to ease the pressure. It doesn't help and just gives you a whole new set of problems. Some of us go home and mess with motorcycles; some of us run around a rugby field when we really have no business doing so. Stacey immerses herself in *World of Warcraft*, and Penn does God only knows what. You have to find an outlet that works for you.'

'Got it,' Tiff said, standing up.

'One more thing,' Kim said as she got to the door. 'You rely on your team. You use their strengths and weaknesses, and you share your frustrations. You lean on each other, clear?'

Now the genuine smile showed itself.

Tiff waved and headed out the door, and Kim readied herself to leave.

Unlike her team, she wasn't heading straight home to unwind.

There was another lost soul she wanted to check on.

FORTY

Kim pulled up outside the building in Pedmore as the landlord was exiting the property.

He smiled and held the door open for her. 'Hope this isn't some kind of party.'

'Excuse me?' Kim said, moving past him.

'She already has a visitor, so just mind the noise.'

'Understood,' she said, while thinking three people hardly constituted a nuisance level of noise. Kim was interested to see who else was visiting Katie Hawne, and if they were doing so for the same reasons she was.

The door was opened on the first knock and not by the person she was expecting.

'Are you fucking kidding me?' she exploded.

'Hey, Inspector, fancy seeing you here,' Tracy Frost said with a wide smile.

'Frost, get your arse out of here right now.'

'Well, I would, but Katie's making me a cuppa. Wouldn't want to appear rude. You joining us?'

Kim barged past her and headed straight for the kitchen.

Katie's face registered her surprise. 'Inspector, what are you—?'

'Katie, I suggest you ask this woman to leave. You do know who she is?'

Katie nodded. 'She's a reporter for the *Dudley Star*.'

'And you're happy to talk to her?'

'I have nothing to hide. You confirmed that.'

'All the same, you don't want to offer any details to this poor excuse of a—'

'I can hear you,' Frost said from behind.

Kim ignored her. 'Katie, she has a habit of twisting whatever you say to suit her own—'

'Still hearing you,' Frost said with amusement in her voice.

Many people were now savvy to the promises journalists made. Phrases like 'get your side of the story out there' or 'I can help you control the narrative' were nothing more than ploys to get across the threshold and exploit someone's unfortunate circumstances.

'I haven't said anything to her yet, and she promised there'd be no tricky questions.'

'I bet she did,' Kim said, removing her jacket and nodding towards the kettle. 'And yes, I'd love one. I'm sure no one will object to me sticking around.'

'Of course,' Katie said, turning back to the kettle.

If she hadn't known Frost so well, she wouldn't have noted the flash of annoyance that passed over her features as she sat down.

'I have nothing to hide,' Frost said, taking out her notebook.

Except ethics and a conscience, Kim thought as Katie placed three drinks on the table. Although the more objective part of her mind did know that wasn't strictly true. There had been occasions over the years where Frost's moral compass had got the better of her and she'd behaved like a decent human being. But finding her here like this just confirmed to Kim that she was still prepared to act a certain way to get a good story. No wonder the reporter was irritated that Kim had turned up, and she was glad her visit had been so well timed.

Kim took a moment to assess both Katie and her surroundings. The woman looked pale and tired and like she was wearing clothes a size too big for her. There was no lingering aroma of cooked food and no plates or utensils scattered around.

Kim felt her reservations grow. Katie wasn't up to this meeting. She was barely awake, certainly not alert, and she had no fuel to power either her body or her mind.

Kim sat back and folded her arms as Frost switched on her Dictaphone.

'Okay, Katie, first I'd like to say I'm sorry for your loss and if there's anything you need, just let me know. If you want to stop or if there's a question you don't want to answer, just let me know that too.'

Kim groaned internally at the sincerity in her voice. She was very good, but Kim knew that if Katie refused a question, Frost would just find another way to ask it.

She was pleased that she'd taken the time to stop by. She crossed her ankles beneath the table and settled in for the long haul.

Half an hour and three empty cups later, Kim realised that her focus had shifted from the reporter to Katie.

To be fair to Frost, she was questioning Katie with care and empathy. There were no leading or trick questions, and she had asked for little information on the gruesome scene.

Feeling that the reporter was behaving herself, she'd paid more attention to Katie. That was when she'd noticed the subtle stiffening of her body every time Frost referred to Sheryl as 'your mum'. Each question that contained those words was making Katie more and more uncomfortable.

And then, as if by magic, the real Frost put in an appearance.

'And were you treated okay by the police?'

Katie nodded.

'Any issues in the custody suite?'

'Okay, I think we're done,' Kim said, looking to Katie for confirmation.

She nodded wearily, and Kim could see how tired she was.

When all was said and done, she'd had a traumatic and exhausting forty-eight hours.

'You've got enough, Frost.'

The reporter shot daggers her way, but she was lucky to have what she did.

'You've got my number, Katie,' Frost said, putting her Dictaphone into her bag. 'Anything you need give me a call.'

'Thanks,' she offered weakly.

With a final side eye at Kim, Frost let herself out the front door.

'So, how are you really?' Kim asked, once they were alone.

'The honest answer is empty,' Katie said, rubbing at her head with her hands. 'It really feels that all this happened to someone else. A part of me is sure that if I go over there, she'll still be alive.'

'Katie, can I ask you a question?' Kim said.

'Of course.'

'Did you resent your mum for the pageant years?'

Katie didn't appear surprised by the question, but Kim had still detected that slight stiffening at the mention of her mum.

'Sometimes, but I resent her more for being a heartless, selfish bitch.'

'Katie...'

'I'm tired, Inspector.'

The wall was back up, and Katie was positioned safely behind it.

Kim stood and reached for her jacket.

'May I ask you one question before you go, Inspector?'

'Of course.'

'When can I have the house back?'

Kim hid her surprise. 'I'm not sure how much longer forensics will want it, but most likely just another few days.'

'Just time to pack,' she said, following Kim to the door.

'You want to move back in?'

'Of course. It's my home.'

'We'll let you know,' Kim said, stepping outside.

Katie thanked her and closed the door.

Despite Judith's advice, it looked as though Katie was unable to leave the past behind her. According to the neighbour, Katie had still visited Sheryl if not often, at least regularly. She had not been able to sever that tie with the only family member she had. Kim guessed that moving back into the family home reflected that same need for familiarity.

'So, what's going on, Stone?' Frost asked, appearing from behind a conifer tree.

'Jesus, are you trying to give me a heart attack? Why the hell are you still lurking around?'

'Figured you'd be out soon enough. So, what's the story?'

'About what?' Kim asked, heading for her car.

'Her mum. There's something more there.'

'You mean apart from her mother being brutally murdered and Katie being the one to find her? That not juicy enough for you?'

'Not when I know there's more.'

'Like trying to get details on something that happened at the station?' Kim asked, referring to the low blow.

'Hey, I wouldn't be doing my job if I didn't chance my arm a little bit.'

'Well, use your arm to write a decent piece and get out of my way.'

Frost stepped aside, and Kim got in the car.

She still hadn't started driving by the time Frost had hobbled out of sight.

The reporter's instinct wasn't wrong about Katie and her relationship with her mum. It appeared to be formed of many layers.

But that had nothing to do with the reasons for Kim paying her a surprise visit. Her concerns were twofold. On the one hand, she wanted to ensure the woman was okay. A part of her wished she could have kept Katie at Bushey Fields to get help, but she couldn't. She was an adult who could take care of herself. But there was something unnerving about being in Katie's presence. Subtle mood changes that happened frequently.

Every conversation left Kim feeling that the woman was one wrong question away from a meltdown.

She was also certain there was something about Katie and her mother that they didn't yet know.

FORTY-ONE

Kim refreshed her phone as her team started to file into the squad room.

It was three minutes to seven and she wanted to see Frost's article about Katie Hawne the second it landed. The time she'd spent with Katie the night before had unnerved her and got her thinking about mother and daughter relationships far more than she was comfortable with. She'd removed her own experience from the analysis. Having a schizophrenic mother who was hell-bent on killing both you and your twin brother was an exception and not the rule.

From what she knew of her team, Stacey had an incredibly close relationship with her mum and they talked about almost everything. Bryant had been raised by parents who had been hard-working but not overly demonstrative. Penn's mother had passed only a couple of years ago, but they too had been close.

Katie had wished her mother dead with such a deep passion that she had actually thought she was responsible for her murder when she'd found her body, yet despite that rage, she was eager to move back to the family home instead of forging ahead with the independent life she was starting to make for herself.

It just didn't make sense to her, but she had to let it go. Whatever her concerns about Katie's mental health, the woman was an adult and no longer in need of her attention.

She refreshed her phone once more before heading out to the squad room.

'Morning, people, and don't think I was joking last night. I expect you all to present your talent before the end of play tomorrow and someone will be chosen to represent us. I don't even care how bad you are. Anything has to be better than Penn and his poetry.'

'Actually, boss, I've been thinking,' Penn said, reaching into his bag. 'I had a pretty cool skill when I was a kid. I was a record holder.'

Kim allowed her hopes to rise.

'Look,' he said with a very proud smile.

'A Rubik's cube?' she asked, folding her arms.

'Yeah, here,' he said, passing it to her. 'Mess it up. As much as you like. I won't look.'

She tossed it to Tiff when Penn turned his back. Her time was better spent getting a refill from the coffee machine.

There was an air of expectation by the time she had fresh coffee and Tiff handed the cube back to Penn. It looked pretty well messed up.

'Want me to time you?' Stacey asked, taking out her phone.

'Oh yes,' Penn said.

'Okay, start,' she instructed.

He began twisting and turning the three rows of random colours. They watched, and watched, and watched.

'Two minutes,' Stacey called.

'That I'll never get back,' Kim said. 'Give it up, Penn.'

'I can do it, honest,' he said, still turning the colours. It looked no better than it had when Tiff had passed it back to him.

'Yeah, but even if you do it, no one will be impressed. If you finish right now, most kids under ten could match you.'

'Honest, boss, I used to hold the record,' he insisted.

'What record – world record? National record? Regional?'

'Well, no, just amongst my mates, but I was still the quickest.'

'Put it away. Your audition is done and you ain't through to the next round.' She turned and cast a glance between Stacey and Bryant. 'Next one better be an improvement on that.'

She paused to let that thought sink in.

'Okay, day three and we still have more questions than answers. Theories?'

'Jealousy?' Bryant offered.

'Of what though?' Stacey asked. 'It was the girls that were competing, not the moms.'

'And why now?' Kim asked. 'No one we've spoken to has competed in years. Both girls have been living totally different lives.'

'Yeah, but Kelvin Hobbs raised an interesting idea – perhaps the best way to hurt the girls is through their moms.'

Kim nodded her acceptance of the point. 'Still doesn't answer the question of why now.'

'Revenge?' Bryant tried. 'Could it be punishment for something either the girls did or the moms were part of?'

'I think we're getting closer, but that still doesn't help narrow it down if we're looking at pageant participants or someone associated with the industry,' Kim said. 'We still have no specific people to focus on. The families didn't associate with each other. The daughters weren't in touch. All we know is that Kelvin Hobbs is lying about his reason for leaving the circuit, claiming he'd suddenly decided he'd had enough even though he loved it. His words were believable but his body language was all over the place.'

'Boss, what are your thoughts on the flipper and the eyelashes?' Stacey asked.

'That our murderer is mightily pissed off about something to do with pageants, but that still doesn't help us much,' Kim said, turning to Penn. 'You ever heard of anything similar?'

Asking him was quicker than searching the internet.

'There was a case a few years back where a woman killed her daughter by forcing a wooden crucifix down her throat.'

'Really?' Bryant asked.

'Yeah, but I think it was cos she thought she was possessed and was trying to drive the devil out of her, or so her lawyer claimed. There was another case in Ireland, back in the—'

'Okay, Penn, thanks,' Kim said. There was nothing there to help them right now.

'Perhaps the make-up artist I've found knows something,' Stacey offered. 'She was present at the majority of the pageants over an eight-year period and would have known the girls, their mothers and the other tradespeople.'

Kim nodded her agreement.

'Already texted the address,' Stacey said, nodding towards Bryant.

'Okay, Stace, as well as interrogating your spreadsheet, I want you to get cracking on the origin of the stuff found in our victims' throats. Not sure what you might get from the eyelashes, but see what you can find out about the flipper.'

'On it, boss.'

Kim turned to Penn. 'You and Tink are off to see Keats, yes?'

'We are, boss, but I've been thinking about something else. What are our chances of getting the dive team back out?'

'You think there's something else to find down there?'

'No, that's the whole point,' he answered. 'I don't think there is.'

'Hmm, let me think. You want to throw funding at a specialist dive team for a case that no one is claiming, to look for stuff you don't even think is down there?'

'Pretty much,' Penn answered.

'I'm so sure that Woody will authorise that, I'm gonna let you go ask him yourself.'

Penn looked doubtful.

'His stuff was never found,' Tiff said. 'If he fell in, either his rods and stuff went in with him or most likely his killer took it away to remove any trace of his presence.'

'Or it was left, and somebody nicked it,' Kim answered. Not everyone needed to know the provenance of something, especially if it was just lying around free of charge.

'We need to know,' Penn pushed.

'Leave it with me. Go make nice with Keats and I'll see what I can do.'

'Thanks, boss.'

Kim headed into the Bowl to grab her jacket. This case was beginning to feel like a ball of string, rolled so tightly it was impossible to find the end. But with two murders in two days, she just prayed that she could unravel it before anyone else lost their life.

FORTY-TWO

Stacey was still thinking about the talent show once the office had emptied around her. Penn's effort had been a dud so the pressure was on her and Bryant.

There was no time in her life when she had done anything to perform or seek out attention. She'd had enough scrutiny as one of the only two black kids in her class. When the time had come for school plays or concerts, she'd been sure to scrunch herself up to near invisibility to avoid being chosen. Even on holiday, at Pontins in Rhyl, she had refused to get on stage or take part in anything that drew the attention of an audience.

Added to that, she had absolutely no skill or talent to showcase. She'd spent the night watching old auditions of *Britain's Got Talent* and even then, after watching a guy make portraits from toast and a woman knitting to music, she'd come up empty.

There had been no subject at school she had excelled at.

'Ooh, hang on,' she said to an empty room.

There had been one thing at which she'd beaten every other girl in her street. Whether or not she could still do it remained to be seen. But she had something to demonstrate, which was all the boss had demanded of her. A quick trip out at lunchtime and she'd be good to go.

'Okay, flipper, where are you?'

She opened the folder holding the pictures Mitch had sent to her. He had photographed the fake teeth from every angle and circled a tiny emblem on the underside of the upper-right molar.

Zooming in, she could make out a P and an S.

She turned to Google and told it exactly what she wanted.

Her search for 'baby false teeth manufacturers' brought up a dozen or so names. Her attention was instantly grabbed by a company called Perfect Smile, which featured a crown-wearing pageant child on its first page.

She scrolled down to the contact details to find they were based in Rotherham. No quick visit then, she thought, dialling the number.

The phone was answered by a polite female by the name of Donna, offering to help.

'Hello, there, this is Detective Constable Stacey Wood at West Mids police. I wonder if you can help me.'

'I'll certainly try,' Donna said brightly, as though she received calls from the police every day.

'I have a denture for a child – I think you call it a flipper. I need to try and confirm the identity of the child it was made for.'

'Okay, if you can just give me the serial number?'

Stacey had seen no such number on the photos.

'Where might I find that?'

'It's underneath at the back.'

Stacey went through every photo she had. 'There's no number.'

'Ah, then we have a problem.'

'Could the serial number have worn off?' Stacey asked,

wondering if there was some kind of forensic procedure Mitch could employ to make it visible.

'Unlikely. It would take an excessive amount of wear for that to happen. Most likely it predates 2019.'

'Go on,' Stacey said.

'We only started engraving and recording numbers a few years ago. All those records are computerised and searchable.'

'And do you have records for ones you made before that year?'

'Well, kind of. We have paper records in the basement.'

Stacey was trying to hang on to the last shred of hope. 'But there are records?'

'Officer, we produce thousands of flippers every year. Our records prior to 2019 would number somewhere around twenty to twenty-five thousand. Even if you had dental records, you'd still have to search to find a match.'

Stacey thanked her for her time and ended the call.

When trying to match up the glass slipper, Prince Charming had at least had a place to start.

FORTY-THREE

'Is this your first?' Penn asked Tiff as they headed to the morgue.

She nodded. 'I've obviously seen bodies, but never a live post-mortem.'

'You'll be fine,' he reassured her. 'Keats is a legend.'

Even more so because he had made the request for the transfer of the body and had also been in contact with Esther Nixon for permission to investigate further.

Penn had taken the opportunity of Lynne being on a late shift to educate himself on what happened in a digital post-mortem. He now knew that it was a non-invasive process using CT and MRI scans to develop three-dimensional images that allowed a virtual exploration of the body.

One of the first documented studies had been conducted at the department of neuroradiology in Germany in 1980, where stillborn and live-birth infants had been studied. The technology had advanced since the eighties to include multiplanar reconstructions and high-definition 3D rendering. These days, digital autopsies tried to answer the same investigative questions without actual dissection.

Taking everything into account, it was a shift he supported.

'Hey, Jimmy,' Penn greeted Keats's assistant as he passed through the first set of doors.

Jimmy nodded towards the counter and two piles of protective equipment. They worked silently to put the gear on until Jimmy indicated that they were suitable for entry.

'Ahh, Penn,' Keats greeted them, turning towards the door. 'What a strange choice you've made for a first date.'

'I'm Tiff. I'm—'

'He knows,' Penn said. 'He's just messing. No one gets in here without Keats knowing who they are.'

'Oh, okay.'

'So, Penn, care to explain why you found it necessary to add to my already considerable workload?'

'Trust,' Penn answered.

'In the pathologist or the process?' Keats asked as Jimmy wheeled in the gurney.

'Don't really want to answer that.'

'Wrong answer. It's the process you should distrust the most.'

'Doesn't digital autopsy have many benefits?' Penn asked, hoping to put his recent research to good use.

'Name them.'

Not sure if he was being led into a trap or if Keats was actually inviting healthy debate, he decided to proceed with caution.

'It's impossible to preserve the body after dissection. This method lets you gather the findings with non-destructive and contamination-free procedures.'

'Spoken by a man who crammed on the subject last night. I don't disagree, so please continue.'

'It makes it easier to see some areas of the body.'

'Agreed. Data acquisition from some areas is problematic. Continue.'

Penn now knew for sure that he was being led somewhere.

'Keats, you're scaring me now.'

'Have you made all your points?'

'I think so.'

'You forgot to mention that it can speed up data acquisition in disasters, but I'll forgive you that one. It's true that bodies can be examined digitally multiple times. However.'

Penn groaned. Here it came.

'However, a very obvious difference is the real colour of internal body organs and their changes in the deceased, in comparison to what is simulated in the visualisation software. Even vague colour changes in organs can offer clues on the cause of death. Plus this novel technology hasn't been given enough time in action to be sure of its findings. In addition—'

'Okay, Keats, you got me,' Penn said, holding up his hands in defeat.

'Oh no, young Penn, a little information is a dangerous thing. You wanted to learn, but you failed to realise the most important fact.'

'Which is?' he asked resignedly.

'That there aren't many justice systems around the world who accept digital autopsies in court, so to put it in a nutshell, without dissection, you have no case.' He sighed heavily. 'And unfortunately that may be the situation we find ourselves in with this poor fellow too.'

Penn waited but sensed it was not going to be good news.

'I'm happy to carry out a full post-mortem, but on first inspection, there is nothing obvious to tell us how this man ended up in the water.'

'But the marks...'

'Could very easily have been made by the body moving around in the water after death. I'm sorry, Penn, but— Oh, hang on one little minute.' He peered down at the man's right hand.

'Hmm... out you go for a second,' he said, ushering them towards the door.

They stood in the anteroom silently and watched as Keats wheeled over the portable X-Ray machine. He positioned it over the right hand.

Both he and Tiff watched as Keats pressed a few buttons on the machine and then beckoned them back in.

The screen on the wall sparked into life and a skeletal hand appeared. Before Penn had a chance to try and make sense of it, Keats was already pointing.

'That's the right thumb, and you'll see we have a fracture of the second phalanx.'

'The middle one,' Penn offered. As far as he knew, fingers had three phalanges.

Keats offered him a withering glance. 'Basic biology, my boy. Unlike fingers, the thumb has only two and one of them is broken.'

Every day was a school day, especially with Keats, but Penn was unsure why the pathologist was looking so pleased with himself.

'Could have been an existing injury,' Penn said.

'Said a man who has never fished,' Keats scoffed. 'You try operating a fishing rod with a broken thumb. Never gonna happ —' Keats stopped speaking as his phone rang.

He listened, frowned and ended the call.

'Jimmy. Please put our friend back to bed.'

As though they were invisible, Keats rushed back to his anteroom and began to disrobe.

Penn had a feeling his boss was about to get a call.

FORTY-FOUR

'Nobody seems to have done particularly well out of the pageant business,' Bryant observed as they headed towards an unremarkable area of Dudley.

Kim understood his point. The dressmaker to the baby stars lived in a flat above his shop in Bewdley, and a sought-after make-up artist lived in a shoddy-looking end terrace with a walk-through meadow for a front garden.

Bryant shook his head as he pulled up outside the house. They all had their little pet peeves and one of Bryant's was the state of people's front gardens. He hated being badgered into doing his own, but he did understand Jenny's insistence on keeping it tidy.

'One sec,' Kim said as her phone tinged a notification. It was the one she'd been waiting for. Frost's article was live on the *Dudley Star* website.

She clicked in and began to read.

Bryant peered over and seeing what had her attention sat back and waited in silence.

Kim read the piece quickly, looking for sensationalism or the inclusion of unnecessary gruesome details. She found none.

She read it again, slowly, to ensure that nothing had been printed that could adversely affect Katie in any way. There was nothing.

'She's not done a bad job,' Kim grudgingly admitted, putting her phone away. The piece was interesting but factual, sympathetic without sentimentality, and made no mention of any activity in the custody suite.

'You gonna give her a break then?' Bryant asked as they got out of the car.

'I'm gonna assume that question was rhetorical,' Kim answered, approaching the gate.

Bryant laughed as they traversed the weeds that had grown alongside and between the paving slabs. At the top of the path, he knocked the door.

It was answered hurriedly by a woman in her late thirties with tied-back brown hair and a tee shirt sporting the name of a local funeral director.

'I'm an atheist,' she said, trying to close the door just as swiftly as she'd opened it.

'Good for you,' Kim said, placing her foot in the way and producing her ID.

'Oh, sorry, thought you were Jehovah's. They love estates like this. Think we all need saving. What now?' she asked impatiently, looking up and down the street. 'Whatever it is, I didn't see nothing, and I didn't hear nothing.'

Kim was warmed by her community spirit and willingness to aid the police.

'Jenna Bond?' Kim asked.

The woman nodded.

'Then it's you we need to speak to.'

'About what?' she asked, folding her arms.

'May we come in?' Kim asked, trying to let her first impressions take a little time. One of the best lessons she'd learned from Bryant was not to act on her first wave of irritation.

'Not really. The place is a mess, and I've got to get to work.'

As though sensing her incoming second wave of irritation, Bryant stepped forward. 'We'll try not to keep you, Ms Bond, but we'd appreciate your help regarding a very serious matter.'

She sighed heavily and stepped aside. Okay, that took more words than if Kim had just knocked her out of the way to gain entry, but it was far less likely to result in a formal complaint. Go, Bryant.

'Look, I haven't got long,' Jenna said, walking through to the kitchen.

'Maybe you could call work and tell them you might be a bit late,' Bryant suggested pleasantly. 'We really do need your help, and we wouldn't keep you if it wasn't urgent.'

'Jesus, fine,' she said, grabbing her phone.

Bryant sometimes had that effect on people. There was something about him people liked immediately. Her, not so much.

Jenna typed out a quick text message and put her phone down.

'Thank you, Ms Bond,' Bryant said.

'Call me Jenna. You've got further through those doors than any man has in years.'

Kim gave him a brief nod to tell him to lead the questioning. It was still a mystery how some people just didn't warm to her immediately, but you had to make use of the tools you had available.

'Jenna, I'm not sure if you've seen the news, but we're working a major investigation that appears to be linked to the pageant world.'

'What? Some little brat got their flipper in a twist?' she said and then chuckled at her own joke.

Bryant smiled his appreciation. 'We have two victims. Both mothers of girls involved in events where you did hair and make-up back in your pageant days.'

'Wh-What?' she asked, taking a seat. All the amusement had slipped from her face. Her phone dinged a message which she ignored.

'Our first victim was named Sheryl Hawne. Our second victim was Andrea Shaw.'

She shook her head. 'Give me the kids' names. I knew them better.'

'Sheryl was mum to Katie, and Andrea was mum to Toyah.'

'Oh... Oooh,' Jenna said, frowning.

Kim's mouth wanted to open, but part of the point of letting Bryant lead sometimes was to get the best information. She had to trust that he'd ask the right questions.

'Two quite different reactions there. Not both were a surprise to you?'

'I suppose both should be cos, like, we're talking murder, but I can far easier understand someone being pissed off at Sheryl than Andrea.'

It seemed that now she had placed the girls, memories of the mums were coming back to her.

'Why's that?'

'Oh, well, I don't really want to say now I know she's—'

'Not being honest won't help her,' Bryant reassured her. 'Nor will it help us find the person responsible.'

Jenna nodded, accepting his permission to be candid.

'Sheryl was a bitter pill. Very driven, very focussed. Didn't even seem to enjoy it. Everything was about being the best, getting the best service, getting Katie done first. Lots of the other moms just gave in because it was easier than making her into an enemy. I'm sorry to say she was one of the least-popular moms on the circuit. Katie, bless her, was a sweetheart. Clearly embarrassed at times by her mother, but she wouldn't say boo to a goose. She'd just hang her head in shame when Sheryl started on her antics.'

'What sort of antics?' Bryant asked.

'Oh, making a show of herself if she didn't get her own way. She'd garner support from some of the other moms and make threats.'

'Against who?'

'Everyone: service people, organisers, announcers, judges. Anyone she felt wasn't giving Katie the attention she deserved.'

'Did she ever threaten you?'

She shrugged. 'Sometimes. Now and again, she'd bring in a photo of how she wanted Katie to look, and if I couldn't replicate it completely, she'd scream about it to anyone who'd listen. She'd threaten me with non-payment or getting me thrown off the circuit, of blackening my name, ruining my reputation.'

'And what about Andrea?' he asked.

'Chalk and cheese. Andrea was a laugh. She didn't take it too seriously. She didn't scold Toyah if she got stuff wrong, or ignore her, or drag her out by the arm. They had a chuckle, watched the other girls and then got a burger on the way home.'

The next question was burning on Kim's lips, but she held it in.

'If they were so different, can you imagine anything they had in common?'

That was the question she'd been waiting for Bryant to ask.

'Well, Andrea was lovely, but she was easily manipulated. When Sheryl decided to rally the troops, she'd get Andrea on side first, and cos a lot of moms trusted Andrea, they'd follow suit as well.'

'Anyone in particular spring to mind?' Bryant asked.

She thought about it for a good few minutes.

'There was a woman with a little blonde girl, Carol or something.'

'Carly?' Bryant offered hopefully.

Her face softened. 'Yeah, that's the one. Sweet girl, always helping other kids. Zipping them up or straightening their ruffles. Always friendly, always pleasant, but her mom...'

'Is already deceased,' Bryant said. 'Natural causes.'

'There may have been others who joined Sheryl's little gang now and again, but I can't recall for sure.'

'It sounds like you had a good time and were very much in demand, so why are you no longer in the business?' he asked.

'Kids,' she said too quickly. 'I wanted kids, and the travelling didn't work for me any more.'

It was only because Kim was watching her closely that she detected her explanation wasn't the truth. It might have been close to the truth, but it wasn't the whole of it.

Bryant looked her way to signal he was done.

'Just one last question, if you don't mind,' Kim said.

'Crack on. Boss will already have docked me half an hour.'

'Do you remember any particular incident where this little group might have really pissed someone off? Someone who might have been severely affected by their behaviour?'

'Not that I can— Oh, hang on. Of course, there was a dress-maker, Kevin or—'

'Kelvin Hobbs?' Kim interrupted sharply.

'Yes, yes, that's him. Made the most gorgeous dresses for those girls. Every one was a masterpiece.'

'And?' Bryant asked.

'There was an overcharge or something. If I remember correctly, Katie had put on a couple of pounds between fittings. The dress needed alterations which cost money. Sheryl didn't want to pay and accused him of not taking the correct measurements. Everyone knew he was right. She was hardly fat, but Katie had gained a little weight. Kelvin chose that hill to die on and wouldn't back down. He demanded payment up front or no dress.'

'What happened?'

'She paid for the dress, got it, and then pulled her little group together and complained to the organisers.'

'About pricing?' Bryant asked, frowning.

Yeah, Kim was pretty sure the organisers wouldn't have entered into such petty squabbles. It would have needed to be something bigger to get their attention.

'As if Sheryl was going to fight fair,' Jenna scoffed. 'She told them he'd touched her child inappropriately. They took him to the side and warned him there would be a full investigation and that the police would be called.'

'I'm sensing he was presented with another option?' Bryant asked.

'To step away from any events involving little girls and the matter would go no further.'

'Did he do anything wrong?' Bryant asked.

'Not to my knowledge. It was a revenge attack that forced him out of the business.'

'But other mums went along with it?' Kim asked.

'Of course. The best place to stand is behind a bully. That way they can't set their sights on you.'

Kim appreciated the analogy but felt a wave of compassion for Kelvin Hobbs, even though he hadn't been truthful with them.

They thanked Jenny for her time and saw themselves out.

Bryant sighed. 'I'm starting to realise that pageant moms are not all that popular with—' He stopped speaking as her phone rang.

'Hey, Keats, the kids aren't giving you too much trouble, are they?' she asked of Penn and Tiff.

'I'm not there,' he said gravely.

Her stomach flipped. She needed no further explanation.

'Okay, wherever you are, we're on our way.'

FORTY-FIVE

Bryant pulled into the car park of The Tenth Lock pub, which gave direct access to the stretch of canal at the bottom lock of a flight from Merry Hill to Stourbridge.

Kim stepped onto the towpath and assessed the scene quickly. To her left were a bunch of uniforms and Keats. Another sharp shower had accompanied them all the way from Dudley, and one of the two constables to her right had a small sausage dog tucked into his high-vis jacket.

Without speaking, Kim turned left and Bryant turned right towards the cyclist standing next to the two police officers.

Keats saw her approach and waved with a half-smile. Knowing that couldn't be for her, Kim turned to find Mitch right behind her.

'You know, one of these days you're gonna have to let me in on your secret,' she said.

'I just argue with him less,' Mitch replied, falling into step beside her.

'Ah, I'm stuffed then,' she said as they reached him.

'Sally-Ann Davis,' Keats told them. 'Fifty years of age and walks her dog here every morning.'

Keats stepped aside to reveal the body of a petite woman with short brown hair. She wore jeans, trainers and a short raincoat over a sweatshirt.

The first thing that struck Kim was the absence of knife wounds.

'Two,' Keats offered. 'In the back.'

He pointed to one between the shoulder blades and one lower, around the right kidney.

She surveyed the body again, taking a good look round. Nothing under the fingernails, clothing not in disarray. This was definitely a stealth attack from behind.

She looked closer at the face and frowned.

Unlike in the movies, dead people rarely maintained their last expressions on their faces; fear, horror, joy were all erased as the facial muscles relaxed for the final time. And yet there was something about this attack that had lingered.

'Her eyes are red,' Kim said, realising what looked out of place.

'Well spotted, Inspector. Neither of the stab wounds killed her. She choked to death.'

'Wh-What?'

'Given long enough without medical attention, she likely would have bled out from the knife wounds, but she didn't get the chance.'

'Foreign object?' she asked, remembering the flipper and the eyelashes.

'Yes, but I can't tell what yet. It's been pushed pretty far down.'

Kim was pondering whether she'd prefer the choking or bleeding-out option. Both probably brought unconsciousness first. At least for this woman's sake she hoped so.

'Guy on the bike found her. Sees her most mornings on his way to work,' Bryant offered, appearing beside her.

'Anything Keats hasn't already told me?'

'The dog's name is Banger.'

'I'll rephrase. Anything useful?'

'Nope.'

'Got an address for me?'

'Already on Bryant's phone,' Keats said.

Kim turned to leave the scene but paused to reflect. The first murder had been more brutal, the rage fully expended in multiple stab wounds. The killer had taken their time in the privacy of Sheryl's home. The second had taken place in Andrea's home. More violent stab wounds.

The third victim was out in the open and exposed. It was more risky, and yet the killer hadn't used the reduced time available to stab the woman to death. They'd used it to make sure they forced something down the victim's throat. What the hell was that about? And who was it for? Was the killer trying to tell the victim something, or the police? Was it a literal representation of forcing something down someone's throat, or was it more subtle? Did it mean anything if this particular victim had still been alive when it had been inserted?

Kim didn't yet know its purpose, but she was starting to wonder if the message was more important than the crime.

FORTY-SIX

My eyes open and the delicious aroma from downstairs finds me. My pleasure is short-lived as I realise what this means.

Mom is cooking.

I will get downstairs and the kitchen counter will be filling up with plates piled high with savoury snacks; little pizzas, mini burgers, sausage rolls, pork pies, Scotch eggs, all the things I love that make my mouth water. But I won't be allowed to touch them.

My weight has been stable since my last diet. I breathe a sigh of relief every week at the weigh-in when a smile lights up her face. I get to eat, but I don't get to eat food like this.

That's not even the reason for my misery. The food preparation means we're expecting company. It will most likely be Mrs Rushton, who lives in the next street with her three sons, all named after royalty. The eldest, Henry, has a permanent sneer; the middle one, Louis, loves to rile his older brother; and baby William just follows the pack. They will instantly dive into the goodies, will be allowed to eat whatever they want, gobbling and gorging.

A portioned plate will be put aside for me before they

arrive. I will nibble my meagre ration to make it last while Mom and Mrs Rushton ask questions about each other's lives.

'Rise and shine,' Mom calls out, bursting into my room. She bustles across the floor and throws open the curtains. 'Our visitors will be here soon and I want you to show off your new walk.' She claps her hands in delight.

The thought of having to perform for those three boys pushes away any appetite I had for the food downstairs.

I want to refuse. My mouth opens as she plucks clothes from my wardrobe and lays them on the bottom of the bed. No words come out, and the beating of my heart is deafening.

'Quick, do as you're told, and don't let me down,' she says, heading back out of the room.

The moment is gone and my mouth closes. I hate my own weakness, but I also fear her anger.

My heart sinks even further when I see that she has chosen a pink satin and taffeta dress embroidered with flowers, with a bodice formed of pink roses which is sure to secure further torment from those boys. There's a little bolero cardigan to be slipped over the top.

I dutifully put them on after washing my face and brushing my hair.

I head downstairs, all thoughts of food now gone as I start wishing the next few hours away.

'About time,' Mom says, sculpting foil lids over the plates of food. 'They'll be here any—'

A banging at the door proves her point. I don't even have to look to know the heavy knocking came from Henry.

'Go on then – open the door,' she says, nudging me towards the hallway.

I do so without question and catch a glimpse of myself in the mirror. I am almost ten and I look like a four-year-old going to a Disney party.

Henry laughs in my face as I open the door. His brothers follow him in and copy his ridicule.

'Oh, ignore them; they're just stupid boys,' Mrs Rushton says, putting her arm around my shoulders. It's a strange sensation as she draws me towards her, and although alien, I don't fight it. 'You look lovely, and they're just jealous.'

I don't believe the words; they don't even sound convincing, but I appreciate her saying it.

Mom removes the covers from the plates and invites the boys to dive in.

'Can I have a quiche?' I ask as the boys dive into the food. Mrs Rushton's presence makes me feel brave.

'Yours is here,' Mom says, sliding the covered plate across the table.

I remove the foil. A crustless square of bread containing a thin layer of egg mayonnaise, one mini pizza and one cocktail sausage roll. No quiche or any of the other goodies on offer to the boys. I bite back my dismay and take a seat in the corner.

'Stop sulking,' Mom barks.

I try to hide my feelings and attempt not to compare my plate to those of the boys. I am not successful.

'Leave it then and come and show Mrs Rushton your new walk.'

'There's no need...'

'Nonsense,' Mom protests, heading for the living room so that everyone else is compelled to follow. 'She's been dying to show you.'

I haven't, but I throw all the food on my plate into my mouth and chew as I follow them to the other room. It's inevitable, and if I get it over quickly, I won't have to think about it any more.

Everyone takes a seat; my mother stands at the top of the room so she can see me clearly.

'She's moved into a new age range so they're all new routines,' Mom explains.

I stand in place, still chewing my last mouthful. The boys are fighting over who gets the other armchair and who has to sit on the sofa. Mrs Rushton looks uncomfortable but smiles at me encouragingly.

I start my walk.

'Too fast,' Mom barks.

I start again.

'Too slow.'

I start again, and now all the boys are staring at me because of the tone in Mom's voice.

'Hahahaha, you're crap,' Henry sneers.

Mrs Rushton shushes him.

I can see by Mom's face that I'm letting her down. She wanted to show me off to her friend, and I've already messed it up.

My legs wobble as I see the rage building in her face. I feel sick. The food is threatening to come back up. I can't move, and I know she's getting angrier and angrier. Everyone in the room is just looking at me.

Louis goes to stand beside his mom. His small body nestles against her leg. Mrs Rushton's hand automatically rises and strokes his head. An unconscious, loving gesture.

Suddenly it's all too much and I burst into tears.

Mrs Rushton rises from the sofa.

'Leave her alone,' Mom snaps. 'She's got nothing to cry for. I'm the one who should be crying because she's useless. Ugly, fat, stupid and—'

'Get your things, boys,' Mrs Rushton says, heading towards the door.

I say nothing as they leave. I stay where I am in the middle of the room unable to stop the sobs. I gag and vomit and still I can't stop crying. The mucus is pouring from my nose over my lips.

'Well, what a clever girl you are,' Mom says from the doorway. 'Completely humiliated me in front of my friend. After everything I've done for you, this is how you repay me. You can't even walk in a straight line. You don't have one ounce of grace to make up for your looks. I'm expected to work miracles with a lump of dough. I don't even know why I'm wasting my time. You're never going to be good at anything.'

Every word stabs me in the heart. I cry harder. I want her to hold me. I want her to ask me if I'm okay. I want her to soothe me. I want her to stop saying these horrible words.

'Get upstairs until you can stop that snivelling. I can't even look at you right now. You disgust me.'

With the tears refusing to stop, I turn and run up to my room.

FORTY-SEVEN

The home of Sally-Ann Davis was less than a mile from where her body had been found.

Kim had barely had a chance to compose herself before Bryant pulled up behind the squad car outside the house. It didn't matter how many times she spoke to grieving families, it never got any easier.

A pair of shears and a lawnmower had been abandoned on the lawn. From the length of the grass, the job was a week or two overdue. It had probably been put off until it could be delayed no more. Something so mundane, so ordinary, and now it wouldn't get a second thought.

Inspector Plant met them at the door.

'He's not having it,' the inspector advised as another squad car turned up.

'He might now,' she said as a constable got out holding Banger.

Bryant took the dog from his arms. It was trembling like a leaf.

'Come on, buddy – let's get you home, eh?' Bryant said, carrying him up the path.

'Banger, Banger, come here,' said a man at the door. The dog scrabbled to be reunited with his owner.

'Mr Davis?' Kim asked, showing her ID.

He nodded, looking beyond her, waiting for his wife to return. Kim's throat constricted at the hope etched into his features.

'May we come inside?' she asked, eager to close the door so that he knew no one else was coming.

He choked back a sob as he turned away. 'I don't understand,' he said, taking a seat on the sofa.

The little sausage dog sat dutifully on his lap.

'Mr Davis, we are so sorry for your loss. I understand that you're in shock right now, but may we ask you some questions?'

'But how did she die? Was it a hit and run? Are you sure there's been no mistake and it wasn't Sally-Ann?'

Kim looked pointedly at the dog. 'I'm afraid there's no mistake. Banger was found just feet away from your wife.'

Acceptance seemed to be coming slowly to the man. He was likely to hold on to some shred of hope until he actually saw the proof for himself. An early identification was probably needed in this case.

'Mr Davis, had your wife been having any problems recently?'

'What kind of problems?'

'Strange phone calls, hang ups, messages, emails?'

'Nothing.'

'Any mention of being followed or strange people hanging around?'

He shook his head.

'Any late-night callers? Someone lost and looking for directions?'

'Nothing of the sort, Officer. Please explain why you're asking.'

Kim now understood why Sally-Ann had been killed out of the house. The first two victims had lived alone.

'Mr Davis, did your wife walk the dog at the same time every day?'

'Oh yes,' he said, smiling and patting Banger's head. 'She says that's the only time the dog feels like hers. He's like this the rest of the day.'

The dog was curled in his lap and appeared to be sleeping peacefully.

Not for the first time Kim found herself wishing that Doctor Doolittle wasn't a work of fiction. This small dog had witnessed the whole thing. Sally-Ann's regular habit had given the killer the perfect opportunity.

Now she had to try and establish a link between Sally-Ann and Sheryl and Andrea.

The question of children was on her lips as the front door burst open.

'Dad, what the hell?' The woman was mid-twenties with red hair tied back in a ponytail. She seemed not to notice them for a moment. 'This had better not be another one of your schemes to get me and Mom talking again.'

He looked to them, stricken, and then back at his daughter. 'Lottie... I...'

Normally, Kim would have considered helping him out and delivering the news herself, but this man needed to utter the words so that he might finally start accepting it.

'Lottie, please take a seat,' Kim said, standing. 'Your dad has something to tell you. We'll go and put the kettle on.'

'Dad, what's going on?' Lottie asked, sitting beside her father.

Bryant closed the door behind them.

Kim had barely got the water in the kettle when a high-pitched, tortured cry filled every room in the house.

FORTY-EIGHT

Penn had to hand it to the boss. If she said she was going to do something, she did.

By the time they arrived at Donkey Pool, the team were going in for their second dive.

Penn had witnessed the team in action on many occasions and was always in awe. People didn't always understand that they searched not only for submerged bodies, but were also involved in anti-drugs and anti-terrorism operations, as well as forensic evidence recovery.

Despite his admiration, it wasn't a role he'd ever coveted. They had to face a number of environmental hazards like underwater structures, debris, industrial pollution, shifting currents and poor visibility.

The service had evolved over the years. He'd even heard about the use of trained dogs who could detect human remains underwater at depths of 150 metres. Given how in demand they were now, it was hard to believe that at one time the police had called upon the skills of the British Sub-Aqua Club to find submerged bodies before starting their own diving branches.

'You know, one time I saw a dive team recover a five-centimetre hair slide that helped identify the body of an eighteen-year-old girl in an accidental drowning incident.'

'Wow,' Tiff said as they approached the dive captain.

Penn had met him on a previous case and knew the man went by the nickname of Ahab. Penn shook his hand before introducing Tiff.

'Nice to meet you. Now which one of you thinks we didn't do a good-enough job the first time?'

Although the jibe was good-natured, the man had a point.

'Not looking so closely at foul play then,' Penn said. 'Now we're trying to make a case.'

He shrugged. 'Happy to double charge you guys, but nothing has changed since Tuesday. We'll do one more dive and if you want any more after that, your department has got more money than sense.'

'Got it,' Penn said, spotting a familiar face on the other side of the lake. 'Come on,' he said to Tiff, heading over.

Harry Guestford from Lower Gornal was in his usual spot across the lake, watching proceedings.

'Hey, buddy, how are you doing?' Penn asked when they reached him.

'Better if I could get some bloody peaceful fishing in.'

'Yeah, sorry about that, but we're just trying to locate James's fishing gear. We're thinking it might have gone in with him.'

'Well, that ain't very likely, is it?' Harry asked, giving Penn a disgusted look. 'Call yourself a detective. How's he gonna fall in and take his chair, two rods, a rod stand, a bait box and a cooler in with him?'

'Blimey, you had a good idea of what he had with him,' Penn noted.

He shrugged. 'It's pretty much what we all have.'

'You don't think they'll find his stuff in there?' Tiff asked.

'I reckon they'd have found it by now. No, somebody had that stuff away.'

'You wouldn't happen to know anything about that, would you, Harry?'

'Hey, fella, what you accusing me of?'

'Pretty tempting,' Penn said, nodding across the lake. 'All that stuff just sitting there, unattended.'

'Bloody hell, stupid and untrusting. Listen, my missus nags the life out of me for the space my stuff already takes up. If I turned up with more, I'd be out on my ear.'

For some reason, Penn believed him.

'And you heard nothing on the grapevine about the stuff back then?' Tiff asked.

'Nah, the underworld fishing fencing ring has been a bit quiet lately.' He offered a smile to take the sting out of his words. 'But to tell the truth, if any locals had nicked it, somebody would have opened their big mouth about it.'

'Fair enough,' Tiff said as Penn glanced across the lake.

The second dive team were getting out of the water. Ahab waved across the lake and then shook his head.

Penn finally had his answer, and he was convinced that the equipment wasn't in the water. He was also sure that none of the locals had taken the abandoned stuff, which left only one reasonable option.

James's killer had taken it with them.

FORTY-NINE

Kim waited until the sound of the sobbing had died down before heading back into the room next door.

The tea that she and Bryant had made was probably cold, but she placed the tray on the table anyway. Lottie took her face out of her father's shoulder and met Kim's gaze.

'We're so sorry for your loss,' Kim said as both she and Bryant retook their seats.

Lottie nodded her acknowledgement, and Kim realised that few of the questions they'd asked the father would be relevant to the girl. Kim had gauged from Lottie's first words that she and her mother hadn't been close, so she was unlikely to know if there had been any recent events out of the ordinary.

'What you said when you came in seemed to indicate that you and your mum weren't on the best of terms,' Kim started.

A multitude of emotions passed over Lottie's face, including guilt and then regret. She opened her mouth to say something, but then just shook her head. If it hadn't already, the realisation would come that whatever the reason had been, it could now not be undone. It was too late.

'May I ask how long you'd been estranged?'

'Oh God, don't say that. It sounds so formal,' Lottie said. 'We're just not speaking at the minute.'

'For how long?' Kim asked gently. Present tense. It hadn't yet dawned on Lottie that whatever had transpired between them was now set in stone.

'Around two months.'

'I tried,' Mr Davis said. 'I tried to get them talking again, but they're both as stubborn as each other.'

'It's not your fault, Dad,' Lottie said, patting his hand. 'It wasn't up to you to mend us.'

Kim was reminded of a child caught up in the shrapnel of their parents' divorce. Only this time it was the father caught between his wife and their child.

'And was there something in particular that caused the rift?' Kim asked.

Lottie coughed. 'Dad, can you get me some water?'

'Of course, love,' he said, sitting forward. The movement prompted the dog to jump from his lap.

Banger stood and waited for a clue to his owner's direction of travel.

'I don't want him to hear,' Lottie said as the door closed behind her dad.

Kim nodded at Bryant, who got the message and headed to the kitchen to delay the man's return.

'He doesn't get it. He hates it when I tell the truth about our relationship.'

'Go on,' Kim urged.

'My dad only sees the time we spent together over the years. He thinks it was closeness, which I suppose it was, for a long time, until I came to know better.'

Kim waited.

'We were very close until I started to learn my own mind. It was only good when I just did what I was told.'

'Was this during your pageant years?' Kim asked, taking a wild guess.

'How do you know about that?'

Kim waved away the question. 'Please continue.'

'Well, yes, I mean, I had her whole attention. I'm an only child, and I'd get to spend loads of time with my mom. I was her world. We were having a great time until I wasn't any more. I was bored, I wanted to try other stuff, netball, hockey, athletics... but whatever I tried, Mom tried to attach herself to that too. She wanted everything to stay the same, even as I grew older.'

'Must have been hard,' Kim said.

'It was. She insisted on watching me practise for every sport I tried.'

Kim had been thinking more about how difficult it must have been for Sally-Ann, facing sudden exclusion from her daughter's life once puberty came along.

'It was just embarrassing. I told her hundreds of times to just stay home. I lied; I made stuff up. I gave her the wrong locations for some of my games.'

Kim tried not to picture the woman turning up to dark and empty venues.

'And then I'd have to lie and say I'd never told her that to get myself out of the shit.'

Great, gaslighting as well, Kim thought, trying her hardest not to dislike the girl. From the sound of it, she'd not been exactly sensitive to her mum's attachment.

'Anyway, to cut a long story short, she never gets the message. It doesn't matter how many times I tell her, she tries to involve herself in every part of my life. She just happens to be walking past Nando's when I'm due on my break or driving past the pub when I've been out with my mates.'

The ironic half-smile told Kim that Lottie didn't yet comprehend that that was never going to be a problem for her again. The concept of permanence didn't always land immediately with people in their mid-twenties.

'And did that lead to the two of you not talking?' Kim asked.

Lottie nodded. 'I told her I needed a boundary break.'

Something about the phrase felt off, but Kim couldn't work out what it was.

'What exactly did that entail?'

'No contact. No phone calls, emails or visits until she could learn to respect my boundaries.'

Kim opened her mouth to ask another question when two things happened.

Bryant appeared at the door with an apologetic look on his face, and every ounce of colour faded from Lottie's cheeks.

Mr Davis entered the room carrying his daughter's glass of water. 'Lottie... Lottie... what's happened?' he asked, seeing the stricken look on her face.

'Sh-She's gone?'

And there it was. The cold hard truth had landed and would be followed by some pretty ruthless emotions.

There was just one more question Kim needed to ask before she left this family to grieve in peace. She wanted to know who had suggested the boundary break in the first place.

She would ask it, but she was pretty sure she already knew the answer.

FIFTY

Olivia heard the key in the lock at 12.59 p.m. Logan always liked his lunch at dead on one. He never wanted anything fancy. Just a snack; one of his childhood favourites. It made him happy when she got it right.

'Ahh, cheese-and-bean toastie, thanks, Mom,' he said, grabbing the plate as if this was all perfectly normal, as if she had fixed the meal willingly, lovingly. As if she wasn't trembling with fear that she had got something wrong or that she'd done something to displease him, or that within an hour she'd be locked back inside her room.

'What the hell is this?' he asked in that low, calm voice which touched every nerve ending in her body.

'Wh-What?' she asked, without turning from the sink.

'The toast is burned.'

'Sorry, love, let me put some more bread in the—' She stopped speaking as his plate flew across the table and then crashed to the ground. Her body tensed in anticipation.

'Are you really so useless you can't even fix a decent snack?' he thundered, rising from the chair.

'Ju-Just g-give me a minute to—'

'Too late,' he said, grabbing her hair from behind.

'I'm sorry, love,' she said, walking backwards so he didn't hurt her too badly. 'I was just distracted by all this talk about James.'

He stopped dead. 'Why? He's been gone ages. What concern is it of yours?'

'H-He was a good man,' she said as Logan twisted her around to face him.

The fire leaped from his eyes. 'He wasn't a good man. He was a bastard who was trying to come between us,' he said, and his fist met with her ribs.

She cried out as the pain exploded on the left side of her body.

She gathered her breath back into her lungs. 'Wh-Whatever you say, you can't erase the time we h-had.'

His eyes widened. 'Oh, Mommy, that's fighting talk. I thought we agreed we weren't going to talk about him again,' he said, landing another punch in the exact same spot, knowing it was going to double her pain.

'H-He was a g-good man,' she repeated. 'And I loved him.'

The fire in his eyes intensified as he punched her on the other side. Her words were igniting his rage.

'It was going nowhere.'

'He loved me,' she insisted as the blows kept coming.

'Don't be stupid. He never loved you, and you just wanted company after Dad—'

'We talked about marriage,' she protested, swallowing down the pain and trying to separate herself from it.

'Then it's a good job I put a stop to it, isn't it?' he asked triumphantly.

'Wh-What?'

'Don't tell me it hasn't crossed your mind since the police came. I know you're not that dumb.'

'But how, when, where?' she spluttered in shock.

'Fucking hell, Mom, it wasn't even that hard. I knew where he fished. It happened the Sunday when he gave me that look.'

Olivia remembered it well. It was the last time she'd seen James. He'd stayed over, and they'd been enjoying a leisurely breakfast when Logan had come into the kitchen demanding she cook him a full English. James's look of disgust at her son's entitled tone had not gone unnoticed by either of them.

Within minutes, James had excused himself and left the house. Olivia had been able to feel her son's simmering resentment with every mouthful. He had left the house not long afterwards.

He had returned much happier; had even made her a cappuccino and run her a bath.

'You really thought I was going to accept being treated like that in my own home, a home that I've controlled since Dad died? Who the fuck did he think he was?'

Olivia said nothing as he pushed her to the ground and then stood over her.

'And that's how easy it was, Mommy,' he spat. 'I sat on a chopped-down log and bided my time. I hid from a fat guy walking his fat black Labrador, and I stayed out of sight until that old fart across the lake packed up. I thought he'd never finish his call and fuck off, but when he left at teatime, I just strode over to James, quietly, and pushed him in. He struggled so I held him down. He held out his hand for me to pull him out. I laughed. Like, what would be the point of that? I gave it a good stamp,' he said, mimicking the movement with his foot. 'He slid down the bank, and just like that he was gone.'

'Logan,' she coughed. Even now there was a part of her that wished it wasn't true, that he was saying it to hurt her, but she knew in her heart of hearts it was true. Deep down, she had always known that Logan was responsible.

'Are you happy now?' he asked, finally stepping away from her.

There was so much she wanted to scream at him. So many things she wanted to say. But her heart was heavy with the guilt that James had lost his life because of her. If they'd never met, he'd still be alive.

And now, along with everything else she knew about her violent, aggressive, controlling, abusive son, she also knew that he was a killer.

The burned toast had been intentional. She had wanted him to get so full of rage that he'd reveal his involvement in James's death. She'd known the level of beating she'd be forced to endure to get the details, and she'd been right.

Now she had the information, she just had to decide what she was going to do with it.

FIFTY-ONE

'How's about I tell her the reason we're here?' Bryant asked as they approached the doorway.

Kim hadn't expected to make a repeat visit to Oldbury, but Judith Palmer certainly needed to answer for her behaviour.

'You really think that's gonna calm me down?' she raged at her colleague.

'No, but it might get us in the house, which I'm pretty sure the sound of your voice will not do. You're just gonna scream at her the second you see her.'

He wasn't wrong. The drive hadn't calmed her down, and she definitely preferred the idea of laying into the woman face to face.

Kim turned away and fiddled with her phone once she heard footsteps approach. She'd always struggled to remove the anger from her expression and put it back in neutral.

'Thank you for seeing us, Judith,' Bryant said, establishing his role as good cop from the outset. 'We just have a couple more questions.'

'Of course. Come in,' she said, standing aside.

'Well, just the one question really,' Kim exploded, unable to keep quiet any longer. They were in the house now.

Judith regarded her with surprise, but Kim didn't care.

'What the hell do you think you're doing to all these girls?'

Her hand went to her throat. 'What girls?'

'The ones you're advising or supporting or whatever it is you do.'

Lottie had confirmed Kim's suspicions that she'd spent time with Judith Palmer.

'Excuse me?'

'You're not a qualified counsellor or therapist, yet you're advising women about boundary breaks and stuff that you have no business in—'

'Wait a minute, Inspector. As I told you the last time, I don't give advice. I recount my own journey at the hands of a narcissistic mother. If what I have experienced helps anyone to overcome a difficult relationship with their—'

'But what if you're wrong?' Kim challenged her. 'Not every mother is a narcissist. Some are just overprotective, others may be clingy, some may be struggling to adjust to life once their kids have grown up and left the home. Girls are coming to you and you're giving out the same advice. You're like a doctor dispensing paracetamol for brain cancer. Just because that pill worked for you doesn't mean it's going to work for everyone.'

Kim could feel the rage building again, but she didn't care.

'Not every mother is a monster, and your guidance is robbing people of opportunities to work out their problems, to talk, to get counselling. We've just left a girl who will be guilt-ridden for the rest of her life because of you and your advice. You're not a professional, and you're not helping.'

'If parents don't respect healthy boundaries, they have to be given consequences,' Judith said, completely unmoved. 'It is often a painful process to separate the idea of motherhood from your own experience with your mother.'

'What do you perceive as stepping over boundaries?' Kim asked, trying to understand this woman's motives.

'Wanting to keep you as their own forever, co-dependency, needing to feel needed, refusing to acknowledge your emotions, trying to tear you down, showing you off while also cutting you down, being threatened by your success.'

'And your own mother did all this to you?'

'And worse, Inspector. Much worse.'

'And the right thing for you was to cut ties with her?'

'Absolutely.'

'And do you advise that to everyone who seeks your help?'

'I think it's the best course of action. Not everyone listens, of course, to their own detriment. Some people continue to think there's hope to be—'

'Just how many girls have received your guidance?' Kim asked.

'My name gets passed around in certain circles, but I'm not prepared to give names.'

Around the pageant circle? Kim wondered.

'Have you ever advised Carly Spencer?'

She shook her head, but there was clearly a flicker of recognition at the name.

She knew that the woman was lying. What she didn't know was why.

FIFTY-TWO

'Bloody hell, you two, if the wind changes, you'll stick like that,' Stacey said, noting her colleagues' miserable faces.

Both Penn and Tiff were nursing a cuppa with pensive expressions.

'Dead end,' Penn said, and Tiff nodded her agreement.

Stacey put aside her matrix for a minute. She was looking for certain information the boss had requested, but these two looked like they needed some kind of life support.

'So, what's up?' she asked.

'No suspects; nothing,' Penn said. 'No witnesses, no forensics, no enemies, no evidence, no lines of enquiry.'

Tiff nodded again.

'And in the hands of lesser detectives that would be a problem, but not you, Penn,' Stacey offered.

'Not this time. All we've found is a weird dynamic between James's girlfriend and her son.'

Stacey felt for them. Trying to piece together the events of two years ago was difficult.

'So, what's with the family then?' Stacey asked.

Penn nodded for Tiff to expand.

'Nothing I can put my finger on. Neighbour says Olivia's got emotional problems and that the son is a saint for taking care of her. She went through a lot with her husband and his illness so it'd be understandable if she was unwell, but the mental breakdown happened long after he'd died. Timeline doesn't quite work.'

'Mental illness doesn't follow a script,' Stacey said. 'Have you asked her about it?'

'Can't get bloody close enough,' Penn said.

'But you've been there twice?' Stacey asked.

'Yeah, but Logan always finds a way to stay in the room,' Penn explained.

'Oh, come on, there's lots of tricks for—'

'Doesn't work, Stace. We've tried them. That kid will not leave his mother alone with us.'

'Can't you grab her at the front door?' Stacey asked. There had to be some way of having a private conversation with a grown adult.

'She doesn't answer. Logan always unlocks the door – eventually.'

'She doesn't even say a word without glancing his way,' Tiff said.

'He even answers some of the questions we ask on her behalf,' Penn offered.

Stacey felt herself growing uneasy. They were right. There was definitely something off there.

'Guys, you gotta do something. Can you get Logan out of the house so you can speak to her?'

'He won't fall for it. He follows her everywhere, and he's already cautious now that we've tried to exclude him from the conversation.'

'He can't follow her everywhere,' Stacey said as a slow smile spread over her face. 'He can't follow her here.'

Penn's expression brightened as it dawned on him what

Stacey was saying.

'Oh, Stace, I love you. No matter what everyone else says about you.'

'Why, what do they say?' she asked, feigning surprise.

'Okay, Tiff, we have a plan. James Nixon was reported missing by Olivia Dench, one of the last people to see him alive,' he said, standing.

'I know that, but where are we going?'

'We're going to place Olivia Dench under arrest.'

FIFTY-THREE

Kim hadn't intended on making a repeat trip to talk to Carly, but so far she seemed to be one of the most reasonable and well-balanced girls to have come out of the pageant world, especially ones who had also had contact with Judith Palmer.

According to Stacey's matrix, Carly had been totally average as a competitor. Given that they'd learned that the girl had been the typical Miss Congeniality, helpful to the other girls and remembered fondly by all, it was bemusing that she'd sought assistance for issues with her mother.

As they headed from the car to Carly's office, Kim's phone tinged receipt of a message. It was from Keats. No text, just photos, and they needed no explanation.

'Bloody hell,' she said, scrolling down through the images.

As they'd suspected, there had been a foreign body lodged in Sally-Ann's throat. Keats had retrieved it during the post-mortem, and she had to say this one produced the biggest physical reaction from her. It was a piece of a crown complete with fake glass stones and sharp pointy edges. Kim couldn't imagine the agony of having it forced down her throat.

She passed the phone to Bryant as she knocked on the door

of the premises in Hagley. Her colleague's eyes opened wide as he took a big swallow, as though it was currently lodged in his own throat.

The door was opened by Carly, who looked surprised to see them again.

'Any more trouble?' Kim asked, glancing to where the window was still boarded up.

She shook her head as she stood aside. 'I think they know I've wound down the business so there's not much point.'

She closed the door behind them, and Kim noted that the office was now almost empty.

'I know you haven't returned to check on my premises so... oh, hell no, don't say there's been another one?'

'Afraid so,' Kim said as Carly steadied herself on a pile of boxes.

'Who?'

'Sally-Ann Davis, mother of Lottie. Did you know them?'

Carly nodded. 'She and her mom were very close. Why is this happening?'

'We were kind of hoping you might be able to help us with that.'

'How would I know?' she asked doubtfully. 'I haven't seen any of them in years.'

Kim leaned against the filing cabinet in the absence of anywhere to sit. 'We understand that you were close with a lot of the girls, that you helped out a lot, that you didn't take yourself too seriously?' she asked with a smile.

Carly smiled back. 'You obviously know that I was never a contender for the top spot.'

'Why was that?' Kim asked.

'Well, my mom used to say I wasn't competitive enough, which was true.'

'What about the others?' Kim asked.

'Oh, Katie was a timid little thing, scared to death of her

mom, but then again, most people were. Sheryl ridiculed Katie in front of everyone when she got stuff wrong. She tried so hard, but it was never good enough. Sheryl wanted her to come first in every competition, which just wasn't possible. I remember one time when she froze on stage, completely forgot her routine. Deer in the headlights. Every second felt like an hour. It was awful to watch. Her mom was standing in the aisle, glaring at her and giving her prompts which just made her worse. She started to cry and ran off stage, and the poor thing had wet herself. She was eleven. I had a spare pair of panties. She was sobbing in the toilets, and I pushed them under the door and ran off so she wasn't embarrassed. It made no difference; as soon as she came out, her mom was screaming at her about losing control of herself like a big baby and threatening her with a nappy. Anyone who hadn't noticed got to hear about it after the screaming from her mother.'

Kim could feel the humiliation she must have endured. That one episode must have followed Katie to every pageant thereafter.

'What about Toyah's mum, Andrea?' Kim asked.

Carly shrugged. 'I think Toyah enjoyed it up to a point, and Andrea tried to keep them both happy, which wasn't—'

'Both?' Kim asked.

'Oh yeah, her poor brother always tagged along. Not by choice, I'd imagine, cos he was a grumpy little shit. Dad must have been at work or something. Her brother made no secret of the fact he'd rather be anywhere else.'

Kim had met Tony and sympathised. It couldn't have been much fun being dragged around the pageant circuit with your sister getting all the attention.

'And then it just stopped. She wasn't there any more. It was very sudden, and we never saw Andrea and Toyah again.'

Kim wondered if that was when the marriage had broken up and Tony had gone to live with his dad. If her marriage hadn't been worth fighting for, then the pageants must have been more important to Andrea than people had thought.

She was reminded again that she still didn't know the real reason Toyah had given up competing.

'What about Lottie and her mum?' Kim asked.

'Now you're bringing all these memories back, I remember that Lottie's mom was a clinger. Lottie seemed to enjoy the pageant part of it, but Sally-Ann wouldn't let the girl out of her sight, not even to go to the bathroom.'

Kim couldn't help but think about Lottie demanding a boundary break more than ten years later. Maybe Sally-Ann's habits had continued into adulthood.

'Can you think of any reason why these three moms, in particular, might have been targeted?'

'Not at all. I mean, it was years ago. Who holds a grudge for that long?'

'You'd be surprised,' Kim said. 'How about you? Did you and your mum have a good time?'

'I wasn't as competitive as my mom. She wanted me to win, and I wanted to be liked. My therapy sessions have taught me that I just wanted to fit in. I wanted a peer group not adversaries. I lacked the ruthlessness to want to be better than everyone else. I am your consummate people pleaser,' she said, opening her hands.

'But you stayed in the business?' Kim said, pointing to the last few boxes.

'Given what I've told you, I'd think you could answer that one for yourself.'

'Your mum loved all things pageant, and you were still trying to gain her approval?'

'Bang on, Inspector, and you have no idea how many therapy sessions I paid for to reach that conclusion.'

'And is that why you went to see Judith Palmer?'

Carly didn't hide her surprise. 'Goodness, that was ages back. How did you know about that?'

Kim shrugged, indicating she wasn't going to answer. 'Did she help?'

Carly didn't answer immediately but eventually shook her head. 'Not really. I think she helped Katie. I saw her in Kidderminster one day. We had a quick coffee, and she told me about the woman, gave me a card. I was curious enough to go once, but Judith only likes to talk about her mom – who appears to be the most evil woman to ever draw breath – and her suggestion didn't sit well with me.'

'Which was?' Kim asked, suspecting she already knew the answer.

'Cut all ties. That may have worked for her, but not me. How was I going to get my mom's approval if I had nothing to do with her?'

Carly had a good point.

'How are they, the girls?' she asked with concern.

Obviously the same old Carly, looking out for her friends.

'Shocked, distraught, grieving. As you would expect. Regardless of the issues, they've all lost their mothers.'

Carly nodded. 'I hear you.'

Kim had to remind herself that this young woman had only recently lost her own mother and although not in the same circumstances, she was grieving all the same.

Kim thanked her for her time and left her to finalise the end of her business.

As she headed back to the car, Kim had to wonder if there was anyone who had come out of the pageant world unscathed.

FIFTY-FOUR

Olivia tried to hear past the sound of blood rushing through her ears.

It had taken every ounce of energy she possessed to pretend that everything was normal when Logan was nearby. Well, what passed as her version of normal now. Different parts of her body seemed determined to foil her plan before she'd even had the chance to try and execute it.

Her heart was beating so hard she felt it might break out of her chest. Her legs were trembling beneath her plain black trousers, and she was keeping her hands busy washing the same two plates over and over again.

She had to try and listen for the tell-tale sound of the front door closing. She'd only noticed a couple of weeks ago that Logan didn't lock the front door behind him when he went to collect the wheelie bin from the kerb.

The bins lived around the side of the house, so for just a few seconds, he was out of sight of the unlocked front door. Was it enough for her to get to the end of the path and away without Logan seeing her, giving her an extra few seconds before he realised the house was empty?

Her footwear wasn't ideal. She only ever wore flip-flops now. Her outside shoes had been locked away a long time ago.

She briefly wondered if she should remove them altogether before she started running. But that wouldn't work. The gravel from the borders that had been blown onto the path would have her crying out in pain and slow her down. No, she just had to go as fast as she could with them on. She couldn't risk him hearing her before she even got out the gate.

Who was she kidding? She probably wouldn't even make it to the gate. She shook the doubts away. She had to make it.

She dared not think of the consequences if he caught her. Her life had become much worse after the last attempt. She was sure if it happened again, he'd likely beat her to death. But the end of her life wasn't even the worst thing that could happen. At least in death there would be an escape.

The worst thing was the fear. Every living minute was spent in fear of angering him or doing something to set him off. The worst thing was her life continuing exactly as it was now.

Her body tensed as she heard the front door open. She held her breath as the door closed behind him.

Closed but not locked.

She headed for the front door and stood to the side, sneaking a glance through the plain glass panel.

He walked up the path to retrieve the bin. She shot back behind the solid door. If he saw her standing there, he'd know she was up to something.

She heard voices so she snuck another glance. It was Martin, a widower in his early sixties from across the road. Although she couldn't hear the words being exchanged, she guessed from the body language and his occasional glance to the front door that Martin was enquiring after her.

Please, Martin, not today, she pleaded silently. Her courage was in danger of deserting her at any second. Any delay was increasing her fear of failure. Her fear of being caught. The courage to actually execute her plan was fading.

The voices raised in farewells, followed by the unmistakeable sound of the wheelie bin being pulled down the path.

She pressed herself against the wall as her trembling hand reached for the door handle.

His shadow passed the front window. He had reached the edge of the house. Just another couple of seconds until he was at the farthest point away from the gate and out of sight.

I can't do it, she thought as nausea rose inside her. Beads of sweat broke out on her forehead. She couldn't go back now.

She pushed down the handle and bolted out of the front door. Despite the trembling in her legs, she reached the gate and flew through it. She turned left and began to run. She had no plan except to keep moving until she found somewhere to hide.

She was out of the house; she was free.

She didn't stop. Maybe she should knock a door. But who would believe her? She was crying, shaking with fear.

She heard Logan call after her.

She didn't stop. She had to knock a door. She had to make someone understand what was going on. Vera at number ten would help her. Three more steps and she'd be at the gate. She could hear Logan behind her. Running, calling her. Just another couple of steps.

The front of her flip-flop caught on a raised slab. She staggered and fell.

She cried out as a strong hand grabbed the back of her neck.

'Nice try, Mom,' Logan said with amusement in his voice. 'Scream once and I'll break every bone in your body,' he continued as he lifted her from the ground.

She looked desperately around the street, but there wasn't a soul in sight.

'Come on now, Mom – let's get you back home,' he said,

pulling her right arm up behind her back to force her back to the house.

Her eyes stung, and more tears fell as she realised the futility of resisting. She was being returned to prison, and she knew it was only going to get worse.

As helplessness engulfed her, she just hoped that the inevitable beating would be bad enough to be her last.

FIFTY-FIVE

'What the hell?' Penn said as he turned the car into Sycamore Drive and saw Logan strong-arming his mother along the pavement.

On closer inspection, Logan appeared to be helping his mother back to the house. A limp in her left leg indicated she'd taken a fall. Yet there was something in his brain telling him that his glance back at the road had given Logan a chance to adjust his hold, and his first impression had been right.

'Tiff?'

'Yes, I saw it too.'

Penn stepped out of the car and approached the two of them. Logan's hand was now firmly on Olivia's elbow, offering support.

'Everything okay?' Penn asked, looking to Olivia, who wouldn't meet his gaze. Her whole body seemed drained and shrunken.

'We're fine. Mom just went out to post a letter and fell on the way back. Damn flip-flops. She will insist on wearing them all the time.'

Penn was growing more uneasy as Olivia nodded while

staring at the ground. She had the air of a woman twenty years older.

'Logan, may we speak to your mom alone?' he asked as Tiff moved forward to support Olivia on the other side.

'I'm afraid not. She's not up to it. She hasn't been well, and now with this fall... I'm sorry, but I just need to get her inside and make sure she's okay.'

Penn blocked his entry through the gate. 'I'm sorry, Logan, but I really must insist.'

Logan's expression changed in the face of an authoritative voice challenging him. The fire in his eyes showed how quick he was to anger. But Penn was not prepared to back down this time. Something about this woman was broken.

'You have no right to insist. She's done nothing wrong. She briefly knew some guy who fell in the lake. It's not a crime, so can you kindly get out of my way, so I can get her safely into the house?'

Despite talking to Logan, Penn had been watching Olivia's body language. Although she hadn't yet lifted her head, there was a new tension to her body, despite the trembling he could see in her legs. She was definitely listening.

'Step aside, Logan,' Tiff instructed in a voice Penn hadn't heard before.

'Absolutely not,' he raged, grabbing his mother's arm even tighter. 'And once I get Mom settled, I'm making a formal complaint about the conduct of—'

'Okay, Logan, you leave me no choice,' Penn said. 'Olivia Dench, I am arresting you on suspicion of the murder of James Nixon. You do not have to say anything, but it may harm your defence if you do not mention when questioned something which you later rely on in court. Anything you do say may be given in evidence.'

Olivia had finally raised her head, her eyes wide with shock.

'I'm sorry, Olivia, but you're going to have to come with us now,' Penn said. 'Logan can't come with you. Do you understand?'

Olivia's eyes rolled back in her head as she began to fall to the ground.

Penn was sure that before her body had given out, he'd seen one expression. It was the same look he'd seen on that little boy all those years ago.

He would swear he'd seen relief.

FIFTY-SIX

'And how is she now?' Kim asked, perching herself in front of the coffee machine.

'The doc is with her at the minute,' Penn said.

She glanced at the clock. 'You know you're getting nowhere near her tonight?'

It was almost seven and the doc wasn't even finished. Olivia would need a meal and a rest before being questioned.

'I know, but I don't think it'll do her any harm,' Penn said.

'You think she knows something?' Kim checked. They weren't in the habit of arresting people for no reason.

'There's something she's not telling us, and Logan won't give her the chance to speak. To be honest, boss, she's terrified of him.'

'What are you saying?' Kim asked, folding her arms. This case was changing shape in front of her eyes.

Penn took a breath. 'I think we may have a serious domestic violence situation between mother and son.'

Although rare, they all knew this happened. The signs were no different whatever the relationship.

'She becomes smaller when he's around, as though she's trying to turn in on herself, shrivel up, make herself invisible. He doesn't allow her to speak, and we've not managed one minute alone with her.'

Kim saw the glance between Penn and Tiff. 'There's more?'

'I don't think it's just domestic violence. I think he's been keeping her prisoner in the house.'

'Penn, are you…?'

'Logan unlocks the door every time. Always him. It takes him longer than it should, as though he's setting the stage. I don't think she has access to her own mobile phone; there's no landline, and the neighbour hasn't seen her outside the house in almost two years.'

'Go on,' Kim said, now understanding their suspicions.

'When we arrived, Logan was apparently helping her back to the house, except that's not how it looked initially. Looked more like he was strong-arming her back. And the story about posting a letter was rubbish.'

'How so?' Bryant asked.

'No post-box within a half mile. She had no jacket, no brolly, she was wearing flip-flops and she had no house keys to let herself back in. Coincidentally it was bin day.'

'You think she saw that as an opportunity to try and escape?' Kim said.

Penn nodded his agreement.

'Hang on,' Bryant said. 'If that's true, why didn't she say that when you turned up?'

'Probably thought we wouldn't believe her,' Tiff offered. 'If she had spoken out and we'd done nothing, what punishment would she have faced from Logan?'

'What about the search?' Stacey asked.

'The search team turned up right behind us. We left with Olivia while Logan was arguing the toss with Planty.'

Kim knew no kid was going to stop Inspector Plant from doing his job.

'What did you get on the warrant?' she asked. There was no way they were getting a full search on the information they had.

'Fishing equipment in external areas including garage,' Tiff answered.

'Not bad,' Kim said.

'Does anyone else wanna grab the kid by the throat and give him a taste of his own medicine?' Bryant asked through gritted teeth.

'I think this week is bringing up a lot of emotion for all of us,' Stacey said. 'I've phoned my mom every night just to tell her I love her. She's been my best friend my whole life, and I can't imagine it being any other way.'

'Never even once talked back to mine,' Penn offered. 'She had her hands full with Jasper, but I never felt like I got less from her because of it. I still don't know how she pulled that off, but the house was always full of love.'

'I was a little shitbag, to be honest,' Bryant said with a smile on his face. 'I was always up to something. My mum wasn't overly demonstrative so I don't know if I was trying to get a rise out of her most of the time. We found our groove when I hit my twenties. I sometimes think she wished I was a girl, cos Jenny had a totally different relationship with her.'

'My mom prefers all my brothers to me, but I've learned to live with it,' Tiff added. 'Her own mother was like a throwback to the Tudors and valued boys more highly, so I understand where it comes from. Anyway, I console myself with the fact that I'll probably be the one to choose her care home.'

Despite the jokey manner of delivery, Kim knew it had taken Tiff a long time and a lot of heartache to reach this stage of acceptance.

Everyone in her team seemed to have different relationships

with their mothers, and this case seemed to be provoking emotions in all of them. All except her.

She looked around the room. She'd intended to do a full debrief, but they all looked shattered. At this point, she had no clue if the killer was done and could only pray that there were no more victims to come, but running her team on empty wasn't going to help. 'Go home, guys. We'll regroup in the morning and—'

'Hang on, boss,' Stacey said, standing. 'I almost forgot. I've got something to show you.'

She reached behind her and produced a large colourful plastic ring.

'Hell, no,' Kim said as Stacey stepped into it.

Bryant laughed as Penn covered his face, and Tiff's eyes opened wide in excitement.

'Honestly, boss, I was dead good at it when I was a kid,' Stacey insisted.

She marched to the centre of the room and pulled the hoop up above her waist. She let go of the hoop and thrust her hips to the side. The hoop fell dolefully to the ground.

'Just out of practice,' she said, picking it up.

She tried again – same result.

'What am I doing wrong?' she asked as she tried for a third time.

'Not sure,' Bryant said, wiping at his eyes. 'But that thrust is becoming a little bit disturbing.'

As the laughter from all of them, including Stacey, increased, Kim felt her will to live ebbing away.

'Honestly, boss, I know I can—'

'Put it away, Stace,' Kim advised. 'You can't manage to fill two seconds never mind a couple of minutes.'

She turned to Bryant. 'Hope you've got something for tomorrow.'

'Guv, I've already told you—' Bryant stopped speaking as Penn's phone rang.

He answered, listened and thanked the caller while punching the air.

They all waited.

'Fishing stuff. All of it tucked away in the back of the Denches' shed.'

FIFTY-SEVEN

Olivia leaned back against the coolness of the cell wall and tried to make sense of the feeling that was stealing over her.

She wasn't sure what time it was, but the doctor had finished with her a couple of hours ago.

With Logan's voice in her ear, she had told the doctor that she felt fine and that she'd simply passed out after having the fall. She'd assured him she had no blurred vision or headaches and that the nausea had passed. He had offered her a trip to hospital which she had quickly refused.

Hospital was out there. Logan would know. He'd find her and get her home somehow. She feared he'd kill her before the police even knew what was going on.

The doctor had been professional and kind, seeming not to judge her for having been arrested for murder. She supposed that wasn't his job. She really didn't know what had prompted the police to arrest her, but she did know they had saved her from being dragged back into the house by Logan.

Just the thought of her son brought somersaults to her stomach. She found herself looking around for him.

No, it was impossible. He couldn't get to her here. She was

in police custody. She was behind locked doors. There were police officers all around her.

A small voice still wondered if he could find a way.

That small voice caused her to wonder just how much power she'd given to her son, to believe he could overthrow the police force just to get to her.

The shame of what she'd become thickened her throat, but she pushed the tears away. She was sick to death of crying.

She had to make a plan. She knew the police would discover their mistake soon enough. There was nothing to tie her to James's death because she hadn't done anything wrong. And then what? She'd be set free, to go where? Back home?

Her heart flipped inside her chest at the thought. She couldn't go back, and she couldn't tell anyone that Logan had killed James. Who would believe her? He had everyone fooled; the neighbours, her doctor. He'd just convince everyone that she was delusional or having a breakdown.

Even if they did believe her, and they pressed charges, he'd probably be bailed. And if it even got to court, he'd likely get a suspended sentence because he'd never been in trouble in his life.

No, telling the truth wasn't an option, she realised, settling her breathing back down.

The unfamiliar feeling returned and worked its way through her body.

She tried to pin it down and put a name to it.

While being seen by the doctor, she had mentioned her medication. The doctor had nodded and assured her he would look into it.

Around an hour later, the flap on the cell door had opened and an officer had passed her a cup of water and her medication. She hadn't had to beg for it. He'd just given it to her and waited for her to give the plastic cup back.

An hour after that, the hatch had opened again and she'd

been offered a sandwich and a cup of tea. She knew the police had regulations to follow, but she had almost burst into tears at the kindness with which she'd been treated.

Despite her surroundings, she had eaten the sandwich and drunk the tea.

Safe.

The word darted into her mind. She felt safe. She'd been fed, watered and medicated without the threat of violence. In effect, she'd been transferred from one jail cell to another, but in this one she felt at peace.

Logan had given her all the details of the crime he'd committed, and the way ahead was now clear.

She knew exactly what she needed to do.

FIFTY-EIGHT

Kim hesitated as she thought about getting off the bike and knocking the door. Was this really such a good idea?

As was often the case with her visits here, it hadn't been a totally conscious decision. More like a gravitational pull that occurred when something was gnawing at the back of her mind.

The front door opened and Ted Morgan stood in the doorway. When she still didn't move, he headed down the path towards her.

'You're here now and the kettle's on,' he said before turning and walking back into the house.

Jesus, the man even understood her indecision.

She dismounted and followed him.

A vague frisson of comfort touched her as she moved through the hallway. The wallpaper might have changed, but the framed photos of Ted and his wife remained. They'd enjoyed little more than twenty years together before her early death from cancer, and Ted had never met a woman to match her.

The kitchen was much as she remembered it from her first visit when she'd been six years old. She had sat at the round table with a glass of pop, and there had been a plate of biscuits. She hadn't touched either and hadn't spoken a word. That had formed the pattern for many of their counselling sessions over the years, while he had tirelessly worked to gain her trust. And although there were things she'd never share with another living soul, he still knew her better than anyone else in the world.

She removed her jacket and took a seat.

'Jeez, Ted, how old are those mugs now?' she asked as he filled them with coffee. Another staple of her past were the cups with local football team logos on them.

'Nothing wrong with them,' he said proudly. 'Not even a chip.'

She smiled as he placed a mug before her and then grabbed a plate containing custard creams and bourbon biscuits.

'Ted, when have I ever?' she asked.

'I'm a dunker and I make no apology for it,' he said, sitting down on the opposite side of the table.

'How're the fish?' she asked, nodding towards the back door. The bench beside the small pond had been the location of many of their silent sessions.

'Still swimming in circles, as you'd expect,' he said, dipping a custard cream into his mug.

'And retirement?' she asked. The man hadn't fully quit until his early seventies and had now been totally work free for a couple of years.

'Busy. Not sure how I ever had the time to work,' he said, taking another custard cream.

He dunked, chewed and then pushed the plate away. 'So, my dear, what ails you?'

'Nothing; it's just a visit,' she said, taking a sip of her coffee.

'They tend to coincide with something playing on your mind.'

Retirement hadn't dulled his powers of perception.

'Come on – out with it. If you don't, I'll be tempted to busy myself with more biscuits, and two is enough.'

'We're working this case – well, two actually. They're both focussed heavily on maternal relationships.'

'Ouch, that must be tricky for you,' he said then took a good look at her face. 'Oh, I see. It's like that.'

'Just before I left the station, the team were all talking about their mothers, about the thoughts they've been having all week. I have nothing, not even anger or regret. The whole thing is evoking absolutely no emotion whatsoever.'

He nodded. 'Understandable really. You've closed that chapter. You knew that when you made the decision not to visit your mother before she passed.'

'I don't regret it,' she defended herself. She had known she had nothing to gain from it. Forgiveness had not been an option.

'I'm not saying you should regret it. It's a decision you made, and you'll stick with it as you always do. I'm saying that your pragmatic mind stuffed all thoughts and emotions on the subject into a box. That box was locked, sealed, wrapped in chains and dumped at the bottom of the sea in an unknown location. It will never be opened again.'

'But to feel nothing at all,' Kim pushed. 'How is that even normal?'

'Oh, my dear, can you recall a time when we've ever used that word in connection with you? I didn't say it was even close to normal behaviour, but it's normal for you.'

Ted reached for another biscuit, but she pulled the plate out of his reach. He'd said two was enough.

He rolled his eyes in response.

'Okay, you feel nothing because you can't identify with anyone else's experience. Not one person you know can understand your experience with your mother. Their tales of minor arguments, rebellions or groundings will never compare to you trying to keep yourself and your brother alive. Their enjoyable, positive memories will be met with not one happy memory for you. You can't connect with what they're saying. They might as well be talking about their experiences of flying to the moon. You have no reference.'

'But I had Erica,' she protested.

'Thank God for Erica. I've often felt that you wouldn't be sitting here today had it not been for the love of that lady. But that was only three years.'

'Quality not quantity,' Kim argued.

'Ah, it's not that easy. Mom is normally our history. She's a constant, like a diary, a journal. Her presence marks important events. She's there for your first day of school and your last day of college, not to mention everything in between. The relationship changes and adapts over the years and through the different stages of your life, but she's like a thread that leads from birth to wherever you are now.

'Mom is the person you can call and ask about that TV show you used to watch together. She'll know. Mom is the person you can call to check when you went to hospital for your tonsillectomy. She'll know. What was your favourite food, colour, book, subject at school? She'll know. You didn't have that.'

'So you're saying that my emotional response to the whole thing is normal, for me?' she asked, reaching for her jacket. It was all she had wanted to know.

'I am indeed saying that.'

'Okay, but you're wrong about one thing, Ted,' she said, looking around at the coffee mugs, the biscuit plate and beyond to the garden outside where the fish lived. 'I did have a constant. I just didn't know it at the time.'

FIFTY-NINE

'What the hell is that?' Kim asked, stepping into the squad room at 7 a.m. After her visit with Ted the night before, she felt energised. She hadn't realised how heavily her own lack of emotional involvement with the case had been weighing her down. And while she knew she'd never be normal, the fact that she was behaving to type had put her mind at rest.

Bryant turned to face her with a ridiculous grin on his face. 'It's my party piece, guv.'

'It's a six-year-old's magic kit.'

'Hey, it says for ages eight and up on the box,' he defended himself.

'Splendid,' she said, putting her coffee down. 'Go on then – amaze me.'

He picked up a deck of cards which looked tiny in his hands.

He splayed them out in a fan. 'Pick a card, any card.'

She did so, and he shuffled. She watched as he started placing the cards down one by one on his desk. The rest of the team watched in silent anticipation.

He stopped and held up the next card. 'Is this the card you chose?'

'No,' she said flatly.

He waited.

'It ain't the card,' she reiterated, picking up her drink.

'It's gotta be,' he protested.

'It's not the damn card.'

'Okay, let me try again.'

'Bryant, unless you can find me an eight-year-old who can actually perform these tricks, I suggest you use your little plastic wand to make yourself disappear.'

'Aw, guv, that hurt.'

'As will my ass when I go talk to Woody, but that's tomorrow's problem. All I can say for you lot is thank God the police force gave you a job.'

She took a sip of coffee, pushing aside the demon in her head wondering what she was going to tell her boss.

'Okay, laser focus today, guys. Three victims in three days. Our killer is fired up, and until we know why they're killing pageant moms, we won't know if they're done. Let's do a quick recap on our victims. Stacey, everything we know about our first victim, Sheryl Hawne.'

Stacey looked to the whiteboard to prompt the information that was primarily in her head. 'Sheryl was forty-eight years of age. One daughter, Katie, aged twenty-five. Katie's father is unclear and there's no other family. Several stab wounds sustained in her home and a pageant flipper forced into her throat, after death. By all accounts, she was not a warm and loving mother and quite ruthless on the circuit. Often belittled and humiliated Katie, who did reasonably well in local events but never entered the bigger ones. Sheryl was a stage mom on steroids, and the two of them didn't have a close relationship. In addition, we're pretty sure Katie sought advice from Judith Palmer.'

Kim nodded. That was a pretty good summary. She turned to her partner in crime. 'Bryant, same again for victim two.'

'Andrea Shaw was forty-seven years old and mother to twenty-two-year-old Toyah. Unlike Sheryl, she was divorced and mother to son Tony as well. Like Sheryl, she was attacked in her own home, but this time at night when Toyah was out. False eyelashes were forced into her throat. Andrea seemed to enjoy the pageants and so did Toyah, although the reasons for their exit are still unclear. Seems that Andrea had no enemies. It doesn't seem like she treated Toyah badly, and she wasn't rude to service people, but she was part of Sheryl's little group. There's no evidence to suggest Toyah had any contact with Judith Palmer.'

'Nicely done,' Kim acknowledged. 'And victim three, Sally-Ann Davis, was married and leaves behind twenty-six-year-old Lottie. Sally-Ann was killed out in the open, but despite the higher risk factor, our killer still took the time to force a sharp piece of tiara down her throat while she was still alive. Again, no current enemies that we know of; however we do know that she and her daughter were on a boundary break, most likely instigated by Judith Palmer. It's not clear whether Sally-Ann was a part of Sheryl's posse or not.'

'There's nothing that applies to all three of them,' Bryant noted, and he was right. There was no commonality on marital status, career choice or friends. Nothing to link them outside the pageant circuit.

'Anything at all on family members?' Kim asked.

Stacey shook her head. 'Lottie has a second cousin who has done time for theft, but he's not known to the police for anything else.'

However short of suspects they were, theft to multiple murder was a bit of a stretch.

'Okay, so we're absolutely sure it's pageant related. We've got that message loud and clear. It's safe to assume our killer is pretty angry about something, and given what we've learned this week about the pageant industry, it's pretty cutthroat. Excuse the pun, but the way I see it is, we're either looking for someone on the circuit who has been wronged in some way by all these women, or we're looking for a killer much closer to home.'

'You think one of the girls did it and is killing other mothers to cover her tracks?' Bryant asked. 'The reactions from all of them felt pretty genuine.'

She shrugged. 'A wise man recently explained to me that your mum is your oracle, your diary. She's entwined in every notable event you can recall. What if those notable events do not make for happy memories?'

'How is Ted these days?' Bryant asked, knowing exactly where she'd been.

'All I'm saying is that I'm not ruling out a damn thing at the minute,' she replied. 'Especially seeing as we found out yesterday that our affable dressmaker Kelvin Hobbs was pushed out of the industry by Sheryl and her buddies, although that doesn't explain why he's going on a murderous spree now. This happened over ten years ago after all.'

'He's going out of business, boss,' Stacey said. 'The lease on the shop is available from the end of next month.'

'Flat above as well?' Kim asked, knowing that he lived above the premises.

Stacey nodded. 'He loses the lot.'

'Okay, that deserves another chat. Stacey, I want you to focus on the girls and what they were all doing, except Katie. We know where she was during the murder of Andrea Shaw.'

'On it, boss.'

'Dig a bit deeper on Judith Palmer as well. She has an awful lot to say for someone who doesn't actually offer advice. I want to know if she has any ties to the pageant world at all.'

'Okay, boss.'

Kim turned to Penn. 'How's your prisoner this morning?'

'Doctor's report is in. Olivia's a bit undernourished and dehydrated. She has bruising to her stomach and back that she insists was sustained in the fall. There's no question she recently suffered a beating.'

'Jesus,' Kim whispered.

'Other than that she's fine for questioning. As a side note, she's taken advantage of every refreshment and meal she's been offered.'

'Okay, good to know she's—' Kim stopped speaking as Bryant's desk phone rang.

Seeing the caller, he picked it up and handed it straight to her.

'What's up, Jack?' she asked.

'Got a lady down here wants to talk to you.'

'About what?'

'Make-up tips. How should I know? Won't give me her name and won't talk to anyone else.'

She sighed. 'Okay, on my way,' she said before handing the phone back to Bryant.

'Okay, kiddies, talk amongst yourselves for a bit, and if you want to solve this case in my absence, have at it.'

She headed for the door and took the stairs at speed. She was eager to get the day started by having a more honest chat with Kelvin Hobbs about his reasons for leaving the pageant circuit.

She unlocked the door into the reception to find a woman in a full-length rain mac, looking back out of the glass doors to the car park.

Kim coughed.

The woman turned, and Kim noted two things immediately.

There was something in her features that was vaguely

familiar, and she had a port-wine-stain birthmark that covered a quarter of her face.

'May I help you?' Kim asked, stepping forward.

'Are you investigating the murder of the woman from that newspaper article by someone named Frost?'

She was referring to the piece on Sheryl Hawne and her daughter, Katie.

'I am.'

'Then there's something you need to know.'

'Go on.'

'I'm the real Katherine Hawne. Sheryl Hawne was my mother.'

SIXTY

Kim had all kinds of questions running through her head by the time she placed two coffees on the table in the interview room. She'd made a quick call upstairs to advise her team she'd be gone longer than she'd thought.

'Sorry to just come out with it like that, but I wanted you to know I wasn't here to waste your time.'

'What makes you think that Sheryl Hawne is your mother?'

'I don't think it, Inspector; I know it for sure. I wouldn't be wasting your time otherwise.'

Kim nodded for her to continue.

'Sheryl gave birth to me twenty-five years ago in a small town just north of Huddersfield. I was the result of a one-night stand, born to a woman who had been spoiled and overindulged. She was an only child, and both my grandparents gave in to her every whim. Whatever she wanted to do, they supported her, and Sheryl was happy as long as she was in the limelight.'

'Pageants?' Kim asked.

Katherine nodded. 'As well as singing competitions, danc-ing, gymnastics, modelling, acting, anything where she was getting attention. The only trouble was that she wanted to be the best, immediately, and if she wasn't, she quickly moved on to the next thing.

'By the time she hit twenty, she'd tried everything, and even though she was beautiful, she had no direction. She still wasn't particularly good at anything except getting male attention.'

Katherine took a sip of her coffee, and Kim decided to just let her talk. She didn't really need to pick holes in the woman's story. A simple DNA test would give her the truth if she had any doubt.

'When she found out she was having a girl, I became the focus of her world. Apparently we were going to do everything together, and I was going to be so beautiful. She spent nine months planning our future. We were going to be famous. I was going to be a child star. And then I was born, and she realised that was never going to happen.'

Katherine took a deep breath before continuing.

'She rejected me on sight. She told the nurse she didn't want to hold or touch me. Thinking it was some kind of post-natal depression, my gran stepped in immediately. She took us home, and she cared for me.

'I was six weeks old when Sheryl left. There was no note, no explanation. Gran woke up one morning and she was gone with one suitcase and a bag of Gran's good jewellery.'

'Was she reported missing?' Kim asked.

'Yes, but the police were honest enough to say there was little they could do. She was a grown adult, not vulnerable in any way, and able to make her own decisions. So, my gran did what any good gran would do: she raised me. I only learned the truth when I was twelve and Gran thought I could handle some of the facts. The rest I've teased out of her over the years.'

'And your childhood?' Kim asked.

'Was amazing. It's like my gran got a second chance to be a great mom, and I've never felt anything but love and support

from both her and my gramps. Life hasn't always been easy,' she
said, touching the birthmark on her face, 'but they taught me to
be strong and to never hide. It was that strength that enabled me
to want to meet Sheryl. I grew up in her childhood home. I
wasn't abandoned to strangers or put in care. I had the love and
support of my family. I've seen her past, her clothes, her schoolwork, her certificates, her recitals, videos, photos. I don't hate
her, and I wanted her to know that. I put a Google alert on for
her name, and I finally got a result from that article published
yesterday.'

Kim sat back in her chair. 'You'll excuse me for not warming
to this immediately.'

'Of course, and I'm happy to submit DNA to prove my
identity,' she said, reaching for her bag. She took out a piece of
paper and slid it across the table. 'My birth certificate.'

Kim took a look and saw nothing suspicious, just one added
detail of which she'd been unaware.

Sheryl had a middle name, and it was an unusual one.

'Octavia?'

'After my great-grandmother apparently. I never knew her.'

'And what is it that you want?' Kim asked, thinking of the
house Katie was planning on returning to.

'To take Sheryl home. I know that's not possible yet, but
when she's ready, I'd like to make the necessary arrangements.
It would help my grandparents grieve.'

Kim nodded her understanding but felt there was more.

'And?'

'The other Katie. I want to meet her. I want to understand
what she is to me. Obviously, I have no other siblings.'

Kim shook her head. 'I don't know. There's a lot to unpack
here.'

'I understand, but I'm not going anywhere.' She pushed a
card across the table, which offered her contact details below a
logo for her own website design business.

'I'm staying at the Village Hotel in Dudley. I'm happy to wait here while you arrange for a DNA sample to be taken, and then I'll return to my hotel and await your call.'

Kim thanked her and left the room. She'd get a sample. At this point, she really had nothing to lose.

It was an outlandish story she'd just heard, but it wasn't impossible. To give it credence she would have to believe, after what she'd learned, that Sheryl Hawne had been capable of walking out on her own six-week-old child without a backwards glance.

Damn it. It wasn't that much of a stretch.

But what about the other Katie, the pageant queen and the one left holding the knife? Had Sheryl become pregnant very quickly and named her second daughter Katie too, or were they looking at something a little more sinister?

SIXTY-ONE

Stacey found herself not wanting to believe what they all suspected to be true.

The boss had taken just a minute to update them and rearrange Stacey's priorities before heading off at speed to talk to the first Katie Hawne.

Penn and Tiff had left shortly afterwards to prepare for their interview with Olivia Dench.

Stacey had contacted Sheryl's doctor, who had confirmed that she had registered with the practice just five months after leaving Huddersfield, and that she had registered six-and-a-half-month-old Katie at the same time.

If Katherine and her dates were correct, then there was no way Sheryl was Katie's mom. Begging the question, who the hell was?

Stacey did what she always did when faced with a challenge. She turned to Google. She entered a search for missing children within a twenty-five-mile radius of Huddersfield from the alleged date of Sheryl's disappearance to the date she registered with the doctor.

Having a clear idea of when would enable her to increase the radius with each new search.

Google presented her with seventy-nine results.

It took her a further minute or two to remove the boys.

52 results.

She removed the children that were older than a year.

21 results.

She removed the children who had been found safe and well.

13 results.

She removed the children who hadn't been found safe and well.

3 results.

Stacey made a note of the parents' names.

Lorna and Yin Wong.

Trisha and Danny Lewis.

Viv and Karl Anderson.

She searched for the first couple and ruled them out immediately. As the name suggested, the father was Chinese, and the photo of the baby they held definitely had some of her father's facial characteristics.

She searched the second couple. News articles informed

her that the abductor was the child's father, who had taken his child to the Isle of Wight to start a new life.

That left one couple to check before Stacey increased the area radius of her search parameters.

Viv and Karl Anderson.

With the search refined, Stacey could note the details. Their daughter, Rebecca, had been abducted when she was three and a half months old. It had happened at a park in Ilkley where Viv had been with her two children, five-year-old Justin and baby Rebecca. Justin had fallen over, and Viv had instinctively run over to her son, leaving the pram unattended for a couple of minutes.

No one had seen a thing, and the baby, pink blanket and teddy bear had all vanished. The teddy had been found a quarter mile away. The distraught parents had issued heartfelt pleas to the public for the safe return of their daughter. They held a vigil on her birthday, 14 August, every year. Karl Anderson hadn't been present in the last five photos, but Viv had been there, supported by her son, at every one.

Stacey took a screenshot of the photo that had been held up to the television cameras when the child had first been abducted.

She sent it over to the boss. She knew it was unlikely that she'd hit gold on her first attempt, but oh my God, what if she had?

SIXTY-TWO

It was surreal walking back into the murder scene with Katie now the woman of the house. Although this time a lot of things made more sense to her. After learning more about Katie's childhood, Kim understood the complex reactions to her mother's death.

Katie guided them to the kitchen where Sheryl had lain brutally murdered just days earlier. She showed no reaction as she headed towards the kettle.

'Not for us, thanks,' Kim said, taking a seat.

'How can I help?' Katie asked, turning.

'It's going to sound like a weird question, but did your mum have a middle name?'

'Octavia,' Katie said, leaning against the counter. 'She hated it. After her grandmother.'

The art of successful deceit lay in staying as close to the truth as you could.

'Katie, do you have a copy of your birth certificate?'

'Of course. Why?' she asked, colouring.

'I'd like to see it if you don't mind.'

'It's upstairs,' she said, heading out of the room.

'Oh, and a couple of baby photos while you're at it,' Kim called after her.

'You gonna tell her what Stacey turned up?' Bryant whispered. The text had come through as he'd been parking the car.

Regardless of the dates, which meant that Sheryl couldn't have had another child, Kim wanted to see the birth certificate for herself.

'Not yet. We don't know anything for certain about where she came from.'

'Here it is,' Katie said, placing the document before her. In her other hand was a small photo album.

Kim knew immediately that the birth certificate was the same one that she'd already seen. There was no doubt now. Katie wasn't biologically Sheryl's child.

'You knew, didn't you?' Kim asked.

Katie hesitated, then nodded.

'Why didn't you tell us?'

'I only found out that morning. I'd sent off a DNA kit months ago. Took hair from her brush. It cost a fortune, but I had to know. I didn't tell you in case you changed your mind and decided I'd killed her. I wanted to. I thought I had. I wasn't going to give you any reason to doubt me again.'

'Your alibi was solid. You were in police custody when our second victim was killed.'

She shrugged. 'I suppose I was still in shock.'

'What made you wonder about Sheryl being your mum?' Kim asked.

'I don't know. It's just a feeling I'd get sometimes, like a distant homesickness or like I was in the wrong place, living the wrong life. I'd always had it, but I just pushed it aside. I also felt very little emotional connection to her. I didn't know that wasn't normal. We were nothing alike, had no similar qualities. I pushed those thoughts away too, but then both the feelings started to come together, and I decided to make sure.'

'And how did you feel when you found out you weren't related?'

'Initially I was relieved. I didn't want to be her daughter. I didn't want those same traits in my genes. After that I was angry. All those years of humiliation, of forcing me into pageants, the scolding, the claims of self-sacrifice for my happiness, the loneliness. Everything I endured... and I wasn't even her daughter.'

'And you never got the chance to ask her?'

'That's why I came over, to confront her, to get details of the adoption and answers as to why she'd never told me.'

'Do you want to know where you came from?' Kim asked.

'Of course. I've never fitted here, with her. It was all lies. But I don't see how I'll ever find out now. There's no paperwork here. I've checked everywhere.'

A part of Kim ached to tell her what they suspected, but on more than one occasion, she'd seen evidence of Katie's fragile psyche. She had to be sure.

'May I?' Kim asked, reaching for the album.

'Carry on.'

Kim opened the album to the first photo, a faded polaroid. It looked to be the earliest photo of Katie but was still a few months after the Anderson baby had been taken. She could see similarities, but growth meant she couldn't be sure.

Kim continued to leaf through the pages until she reached toddler stage. Her eyes searched every photo until she came to one where Katie was around six or seven years old.

'My first pageant dress,' Katie noted.

The sequinned gown had a full skirt and a satin bodice. The photo was taken from behind with Katie turning her head to look at the camera.

'Ah, there's something on the lens there,' Kim said, brushing at the picture around the left shoulder.

'That's a mole,' Katie said with a smile. 'There's no brushing that away.'

Kim continued to leaf through another couple of pages, for appearance's sake, but she needed nothing further.

She'd found what she'd been looking for.

SIXTY-THREE

Penn reread the caution to Olivia to ensure that she understood.

'To be clear, you've waived your right to legal representation?'

'I have,' Olivia said.

'And you've had sufficient refreshment and rest?' Tiff asked.

'I've been treated very well, thank you.'

Penn couldn't remember a time they'd ever been thanked for a night in the cells.

'Olivia, when we arrived yesterday, it seemed like Logan was forcing you back into the house,' Penn said.

Horror appeared on her face. 'Why would he be forcing me? I fell over. I hurt my ankle. He was helping me back home. I went to post a letter. It was those flip-flops.'

Penn hid his surprise at her response and also at her demeanour. He knew she was lying, but apart from that, he felt he was looking at a different woman. She seemed taller than he'd first thought, and her face was relaxed and open. This was not the woman they'd been seeing all week, and she didn't look like someone under arrest for murder.

'It's been difficult to get a moment alone with you. Logan seems very protective.'

'I think you mean supportive. Logan is a wonderful son who takes excellent care of me. Ask the neighbours.'

'We have. We were told about an incident where you were trying to escape over the back fence.'

'Escape?' she asked as her face contorted in confusion. 'Why would I be trying to escape my own home? I think there was a time when I saw a cat stranded in a tree, but I'd just started my antidepressants so it could have been anything.'

Every word caused him to believe her less. Her body language was completely at odds with her statements. Whenever she spoke, her eyes darted everywhere except meeting his gaze. She was squeezing her hands together tightly with every new sentence. Lying didn't sit easy with her.

'Olivia, we believe your son has been keeping you prisoner in your own home.'

Pause.

'Ridiculous. Absolute nonsense,' she said, forcing a light laugh from her lips. 'Why on earth would you think that? Logan does everything for me. I'm sorry but you have it completely wrong. Please move on to the reason for my arrest.'

'Olivia, we wanted an opportunity to speak to you alone. What you say about Logan isn't convincing us—'

'I did it,' Olivia blurted out.

'Did what?'

'Killed James. It was me. I did it.'

'Wh-What?' Penn spluttered.

'He was cheating on me. I found out. I was angry. I killed him.'

Penn recovered quickly, despite a confession from Olivia not even being in his top ten of possibilities during this interview.

'Okay, Olivia. I'm probably going to need a bit more detail.'

'I followed him that day. I pretended there was nothing wrong. I knew roughly where he fished. There were trees that I could easily hide behind. There was a chopped-down log. I sat and waited.'

'For what?'

'For the guy fishing over the other side to go. He talked on the phone, and then he packed up and left. There was a man with a black Labrador too. I waited for him to leave and then I did it.'

He himself had seen a man with a black Labrador at the fishing pool the day before when he'd been talking to Ahab. Presumably he was a regular there. But how could Olivia have known that?

'What did you do?' he asked.

'I sneaked forward a bit at a time and then I pushed him in. I pushed him hard. He struggled, and I kept my hand on his head. He tried to reach out. I stamped on his hand. He went limp and then just disappeared. I went home and reported him missing a few hours later.'

The level of detail in her story was compelling, given what they already knew to be true. But could Olivia really have held James's head underwater? Pushing someone was one thing, but this was someone she professed to have loved. Could she really have held him down until the breath left his body? Could she have stamped on a hand that was reaching out for help?

Despite the questions in his mind, she was offering a convincing account of what had happened.

Except for one thing.

'What did you do with his stuff?'

'His wh-what?'

'The fishing equipment. What did you do with it?'

Panic flashed across her features. 'I threw it in. I picked it all up and threw it in after he'd disappeared from view.'

'I'm sorry, Olivia, but I don't think that's what happened at all,' Penn said. Why would she be admitting to something that they knew was totally incorrect? Only the murderer knew where the fishing gear had really gone.

'It is. I've told you the truth. I've confessed. I'm not going to change my story, and now I'd like to speak to my lawyer.'

SIXTY-FOUR

Stacey had sent the details she'd uncovered about the abduction to the boss and was awaiting further instruction. She knew the boss was with Katie, and in the meantime, she was focussed on ensuring all the alibis for the girls were solid.

The boss had told her to disregard Katie, so her name had been officially crossed off the list, leaving Lottie and Toyah. She supposed she only needed to prove the whereabouts of each girl for one of the murders and that would rule them out of all three... but then again, would it?

She remembered watching a TV crime drama a few years earlier where a group of three adults, who had met as abused children, had killed each other's abuser so that they could each have an airtight alibi. Was it possible that Toyah's night out was designed to keep her away from the house? They already knew that Judith's information had been passed between Katie and Lottie. What if Toyah was lying and she too had been in touch with Judith, who clearly had a hatred of all mothers?

Even in her own mind, the theory was outlandish and something that belonged on the television, but she'd be happier if she could rule out all the girls for all the murders.

She began by sending an email to the Fox and Hounds pub in Dudley where Toyah had been on the night her mom was killed. From experience, she knew they had a good CCTV system. Confirming Toyah's presence and when she left would rule her out of the murder of her own mother.

Twenty minutes later, she sat back and reviewed what she'd learned. With information gathered from the police statements, social media and conversations the boss had had, she could deduce the following about Lottie's movements, thanks to the fact she enjoyed sharing her daily running achievements through her Fitbit.

Sheryl Hawne – Tuesday morning – at the gym – tagged by a friend.

Andrea Shaw – Tuesday night – late shift at work – to be checked.

Sally-Ann Davis – Thursday morning – running a 5-mile circuit that went nowhere near her mother's crime scene.

Only one alibi needed to be confirmed for Lottie, but pinning down any of Toyah's movements was not as straightforward.

The ringing of her phone disturbed her from the next part of her task.

'Yeah, boss,' Stacey said, answering the call.

'Track down the Anderson family. Speak to the mother. We need to find out if she recalls any distinguishing marks on the baby's body.'

'Do we have one to check against?'

'A mole on the left shoulder, but don't lead her. She has to state that without any prompting. If so, without giving anything away, invite her to come and talk to us at her earliest convenience.'

'Even if she confirms the mole, you don't want me to tell her that her child is alive?' Stacey asked.

'No way. We've got to get our ducks in a row on this one. It's growing more complex by the hour. Got it?'

'On it,' Stacey said before ending the call. She'd considered updating the boss on the progress of her alibi checking, but she needed one last piece of data.

From the information she had, she couldn't account for the whereabouts of Toyah either during the murders of Sheryl Hawne or Sally-Ann Davis.

Her final search would be the CCTV for the night of Andrea's murder, and the footage had just come into her inbox.

She opened the file that matched the search parameters she'd given, the period from 10.45 p.m. to 11.15 p.m. Toyah's statement read that she left the pub around eleven. Evidence of her leaving then would certainly rule her out. By that time, her mother had already been dead.

The pub was an old-fashioned establishment, and the camera above the exit looked down a corridor leading to the toilets, a main bar and a smaller room often called a snug. The corridor was the route to everywhere as well as the fire exit at the end of the hallway, meaning you couldn't leave the place without being caught on this camera.

Stacey allowed the video to play and saw people going in and out of the toilets, crossing rooms carrying pints of beer, others heading out front for a quick smoke with their last half before closing time.

Around ten minutes into the footage, the mass exodus began as people streamed into the corridor, shrugging them-selves into their jackets, reaching into pockets for their car keys. A steady throng of people passed beneath the camera to head home, but so far Toyah Shaw wasn't one of them.

A couple of minutes of nothing passed before the owner appeared with his keys behind two men. He was nodding and agreeing with whatever they were saying as he shepherded the stragglers to the front door, which he locked and bolted behind them.

No sign of Toyah on any of the footage she'd viewed, which brought one question to the front of Stacey's mind.

Had they overlooked the person who had been their poster child for pageants all week?

SIXTY-FIVE

Kim was still thinking about the photos she'd seen of Katie when Bryant pulled up in front of the dress shop in Bewdley.

'If we're right, it explains why Sheryl never took Katie to nationals,' Bryant said, revealing that it had been on his mind too.

'Yep, she'd have been avoiding any national press,' Kim said, wondering how deeply that must have niggled Sheryl, being unable to step into the spotlight for fear of being discovered.

She'd passed the info on to Stacey, and at this point there was no more she could do. She had a murderer to catch, and she couldn't help wondering if she was about to have a second conversation with him.

The expression on the face of Kelvin Hobbs was guarded when they walked through the door. With good reason.

'Officers,' he said.

She noted that today his sewing machine was empty.

'You don't appear to have been totally honest with us, Mr Hobbs,' she offered as a greeting.

'About what?' he asked like a man with more than one secret, who didn't want to fess up to the wrong one.

'Well, let's start with your reasons for leaving the pageant circuit. We understand that you didn't have a lot of choice.'

'Who told you that?'

'Doesn't matter.'

'It was Jenna, wasn't it?'

'Was she lying?'

He waited a good ten seconds before answering. 'I didn't do anything wrong. I didn't do what they said.'

'So why didn't you stand up for yourself?' Bryant asked.

'Because Sheryl hit me where it hurt. My sexuality.'

'Go on,' Kim urged.

'It's fair to say I've never had any interest in little girls, not even when I was a little boy. I'm gay and have struggled with it my whole life. Actually, saying the words out loud is something I've only mastered in the last five years.'

'But why has it been such a...?'

'Don't,' he said, holding up his hand. 'Public acceptance makes no difference to my own struggle. I could have defended myself against Sheryl's witch hunt, but that would have meant saying those words, and I was nowhere near ready. Even if I had been prepared to publicly utter the truth, the outraged cries would have changed from "he's a pervert" to "oh, he's just a different kind of pervert". Sheryl and her gang hit my weak spot. I couldn't fight back so I chose to leave.'

'Must have been hard.'

'I loved my work, and I loved those girls, even the difficult ones. They were all little princesses in my gowns. But it wasn't meant to be. I adjusted.'

'And now you've lost this as well, which is something else you failed to mention.'

'You're just a ray of fucking sunshine, aren't you?' he snapped as his jaw tensed. He appeared to be operating on a short fuse.

'But it is true, isn't it?' she pushed. 'You are losing your business and your home?'

'Yes, Inspector, I am. Thank you for the reminder of all my failures in one conversation, so now you've kicked a man when he's already down, please feel free to let yourself out.'

'Not quite, Mr Hobbs. I would imagine that the little group who ousted you have been on your mind recently.'

'Oh no you don't. I can see what you're trying to do and it's not going to work,' he said, pointing towards the door.

'You have to admit that it's a bit of a coincidence that a group of women who negatively affected your life to a huge degree are winding up dead at the same time your life is falling apart.'

'Inspector, do you get paid extra for being this rude?'

'I wish,' she answered.

'Maybe I would find it strange if I'd been the only person in the crosshairs of that group, but I was simply one of many.'

'Who else?'

'Oh, now you want my help?'

'Yes, if you'd like me to cross you off my list and go harass someone else.'

'Haven't you asked yourself why someone who had a lucrative career in hair and make-up is now beautifying the dead? You really think that's an aspirational career choice?'

'Is there something you want to share with us?'

He shook his head. 'Not a chance. I'm not like Jenna. It's not my story to tell. But I'm pretty sure it's a story that you're going to want to hear.'

SIXTY-SIX

'You can't see her,' Penn said for the seventh time. Each time he said it, Logan Dench grew more agitated.

'You have no right to keep me away from her.'

'We have every right. Your mom is helping us with our enquiries, and if you don't settle down, you're going to have to leave.'

He'd been called through by Jack after finishing the interview with Olivia because Logan was refusing to take no for an answer from the desk sergeant.

Penn was still trying to get his head around Olivia's admission of guilt and her all-out lies about her relationship with her son.

'You can't stop me from seeing her. She's my mom,' Logan said with an air of possession.

'Actually, I can. Your mom is in our care and under our protection, and you're not going to see her for a while yet.'

'But she's done nothing wrong. I'm going to call a solicitor.'

'For yourself?' Penn asked.

'Of course not for me, you idiot,' he hissed.

Penn let the insult and the derision in his voice pass. For

now. As much as he would have liked to give the guy a taste of his own medicine, it did no one any favours to reveal what they suspected about this warped relationship.

'Your mom has had access to a solicitor and she has chosen to speak to us without one.'

Logan looked horrified. 'She's done what? How could you have allowed that to happen?'

'She's a grown adult. She can make her own decisions.' He paused. 'She can, can't she, Logan?'

His face darkened. 'Of course she can. What did she say about me?'

'Your name came up,' Penn said and wasn't lying. 'But the content of our interview is confidential.'

'Just wait—'

'Until what, Logan? Who has to wait? Who are you threatening?' Penn asked, stepping into the man's space.

Their eyes met and held, but Penn would grow old before backing down. He sensed that even without words the truth was passing between them.

Logan eventually stepped back. 'I'm going to get coffee, but I'll be back to wait for her.'

Penn didn't doubt it. Logan was terrified to move too far away from the action. It was almost as though he felt he could control his mother's silence by being in close proximity.

Trouble was, if they didn't work out what was going on soon, they'd have no choice but to release her. Confession or not, they knew she hadn't killed James Nixon.

And once they let her go, Logan would be waiting for her, ready to take her back to her prison, and the violence would be worse than it was before.

Without any confirmation from her about his abuse, there was absolutely nothing they could do about it.

SIXTY-SEVEN

Stacey took a deep breath before picking up the phone.

This one conversation had the power to start a journey that could lead to heartbreak or jubilation, and she had to force herself to tread carefully. The phone was answered on the second ring with a simple hello.

'Mrs Anderson?'

'Speaking...'

'Hi, I'm Detective Constable Wood from the West Midlands Police.'

'Okay,' she said in a voice that had turned wary.

'Mrs Anderson, I understand that your daughter, Rebecca, has been missing for twenty-five years.'

'Correct.'

'Do you mind if I ask you some questions?'

'Are you a reporter?'

'No. I am who I say I am, and I'm happy for you to ring Halesowen police station and check before you speak to me.'

'Okay, I believe you, but do you mind telling me where Halesowen is?'

'We're a few miles south of Birmingham.'

'How could you know anything about Rebecca?'

Stacey left the question unanswered and posed one of her own. 'I understand Rebecca was just a few months old when she was abducted.'

'That's correct. She was almost four months.'

Stacey heard the crack in her voice. This woman felt the pain as if it had happened yesterday.

Her heart ached.

'And you've had no contact, no calls, no ransom demands in that time?'

'Nothing. We don't know a thing about what happened to her.'

Stacey could tell that she was fighting back the tears and felt awful for resurrecting her pain, especially if it was for nothing.

'Officer, please end my misery and tell me what's going on. There's no scenario you can give me that hasn't gone through my mind, and it would be a blessing just to know.'

'We have an incident down here that might shed light on what happened to your daughter.'

The sharp intake of breath was followed by a sob. 'Please, tell me anything. Whatever it is, tell me.'

'Mrs Anderson, I have one final question. Did Rebecca have any distinguishing features on her body like a birthmark or something identifiable?' Stacey crossed her fingers and closed her eyes, praying for the right answer.

'A mole,' the woman said, and Stacey almost gasped with relief, but she kept herself in check.

'Where?'

'Her left shoulder. I'd kiss it every time I bathed her.'

Stacey desperately wanted to blurt out the truth. She opened her mouth, but the woman beat her to it.

'You've found her, haven't you? You've found my little girl. You're telling me she's dead. Just tell me.'

'I don't want to say any more over the phone.'

'Just tell me what happened to her. Did she suffer? Please, just give me that. I've waited twenty-five years.'

'I think it's best if we speak in person. The situation isn't that simple. Is there anyone that can bring you here to see us?'

'My son. He'll bring me. But can I ask one thing? Will we need to identify the body?'

'That won't be necessary, Mrs Anderson.'

'I'm going to get closure, aren't I? It's over.'

'Yes, Mrs Anderson. The wait is definitely over,' Stacey said before ending the call.

She would have loved to say more, but right now they had no idea how Katie was going to react to the news.

Mrs Anderson would soon be on her way, and Stacey had no clue if they were giving her a daughter or a stranger who wanted nothing to do with her.

She took a moment to compose herself before making her next call.

Toyah answered the call on the second ring. Her voice was thick and gruff, as though she'd just finished having a good old cry. Stacey instantly felt guilty for her suspicions and would make this as painless as possible. The girl was barely two days into the loss of her mother.

'Hi, Toyah, I'm DC Stacey Wood, a member of DI Stone's team. Have you got a minute to talk?'

'Have you found him?' she asked hopefully. 'Have you caught the murderer?'

'Not yet, but we will. In the meantime, I'm just clarifying all the information we've gathered, and I just wanted to check a couple of details with you about Tuesday night.'

'Of course,' she said, covering the microphone and saying something to the side.

'You told my colleague that you were at the Fox and Hounds?'

'Y-Yes, that's correct.'

'And you left around eleven?'

'I th-think so, but...'

The line went silent for a second before another voice sounded on the phone. A male voice.

'Who the hell is this?'

Stacey reintroduced herself while wondering what was going on.

'How dare you harass my sister in such a way. Do you have no sensitivity?'

Stacey felt the heat burn her cheeks. She would hate to think she'd upset the girl badly enough for her brother, Tony, to have to take the phone from her.

'I just—'

'What exactly do you need to know?' he barked. 'What could my sister possibly be able to tell you to help your investigation?'

Stacey was no longer stunned, and she still needed to ask the question. 'If I can check the details of Tuesday night—'

'Are you kidding, or are you just a fucking moron? Why the hell would you need to check that? Is she a suspect? You think she butchered her own mother?'

'Mr Shaw, if you could just hand me back to—'

'I absolutely will not. Her mother was savagely murdered barely more than forty-eight hours ago and you want to check where she was when it was happening. You are despicable, and you're not getting anywhere near my sister,' he shouted before ending the call.

Despite being stunned at the man's attitude, Stacey couldn't help but notice his odd turn of phrase. He'd referred to Andrea as 'her' mother twice during the call. Shouldn't he have been saying 'our' mother? Because Stacey was pretty sure that Andrea had been Tony's mother as well.

SIXTY-EIGHT

'Feeling a bit like a bloody tennis ball at the minute,' Bryant said as they pulled up outside Horton's Funeral Home in Sedgley.

Kim could understand his point. They were being volleyed between the dressmaker and the stylist to get the truth that should have been available from the start. For all she knew, the killer had another victim in their crosshairs and they were chasing other people's tails.

After trying Jenna Bond's home first, they'd surmised her absence meant she was at work. Stacey's digging had unearthed a disturbing rumour that had been circulating right before Jenna had left the circuit for 'family reasons'.

A bell above the door announced their arrival into a small foyer with a wall that bore the company name and framed photos of floral arrangements. With no reception desk, they had no choice but to wait to be discovered.

Kim shook her head as her colleague shuddered. The man could process the most horrific crime scenes, interrogate the most evil villains, but anything to do with the process after death disturbed him.

'May I help you?' asked a slim woman who appeared from around the corner.

Kim guessed her to be early sixties. Her grey hair was short and stylish, and her expression was already filled with compassion.

'May we speak to Jenna Bond? We assume she's at work today.'

The woman didn't hide her surprise as they both produced their IDs. 'Is everything okay?'

'It's fine. We just need to ask her a couple of questions.'

'Of course. If you give me a minute, I'll go get—'

'That's okay. If you take us to her, we can get out of your way. We won't keep her for long.'

Kim heard Bryant curse under his breath as the woman led the way.

He would have preferred to question Jenna away from the dead, and she would have preferred him to have performed a better magic trick, but hey ho, such was life.

They followed the woman along a corridor with display rooms on either side: coffins, flower arrangements and cards. They passed a couple of small offices before reaching a set of stairs that led to the lower level. Kim could imagine the expletives running through Bryant's head.

The woman tapped lightly on a door before opening it. Kim could already smell the formalin from the embalming process.

Jenna Bond was standing to the right of a trolley, leaning over the body of a woman who looked to have been in her eighties. The grey hair had been washed, dried and brushed. Kim could see immediately that she had not been subject to a forensic post-mortem, so no effort would be needed to hide the incisions that would have stretched from the neck up to behind the ears. Incisions for a routine post-mortem were on the chest only and easily covered by clothing.

'Sorry to visit you at work, Jenna, but we have a couple of follow-up questions.'

'Shoot,' she said. 'But I can't stop working. It's a busy day.'

'We're not sure you were completely honest about your reasons for leaving the pageant circuit.'

Jenna's hand stilled above the aged face. Kim could see that she was applying theatrical style make-up as a first layer. She knew that the skin turned many shades during the early stages of decomposition and the thicker, waxier substance covered the blemishes better.

'I haven't lied about anything,' she said.

Technically not, but her exit from the circuit had not been as drama free as she'd had them believe.

'There were rumours that you actually struck one of the girls.'

'Rumours,' she said with a level of conviction not befitting a false allegation, although the passion in that one word caused her to rub harder on the woman's lower jaw. The lips didn't move, indicating they had likely been stitched closed to avoid the mouth gaping open during viewing.

'Gossip normally starts somewhere,' Kim said, pulling her eyes away, waiting to hear Jenna's account of the story.

'It was nothing.'

'It was clearly something, so we'd like to know about it.'

'I was looking for something, and Lottie accused me of stealing. I was doing no such thing. I was the one always looking after other people's stuff. I would never have stolen from them. Lottie was screaming thief in my face, and I pushed her to shut her up. That's all.'

Lottie, the child of Sally-Ann, the latest woman to lose her life.

Kim took a minute to unpack what she'd just been told as Jenna reached for a tray of normal cosmetics to build the next coat of make-up. She pictured the scene: a hotel room, mothers taking their daughters to and from the stage. Leaving all their belongings in a safe place while they performed, ready to come back and change for the next category.

Knowing how much some of these moms spent on pageants, could she have been tempted by all those unattended handbags and purses while earning a pittance wrangling kids for hair and make-up all day?

Kim didn't want to brand her a thief, but the opportunity had been there.

'So, what happened next?'

'Oh, Lottie went off crying and brought back a whole army of mothers demanding to know about the red mark on her face.'

'From a push?' Kim queried.

'I might have accidentally caught her chin or something as I moved her out of the way. Trust me, that's nothing to how some of those moms push their kids around.'

Jenna's story was becoming less plausible by the second, and Kim questioned her own reticence at not branding her a thief.

'And?'

'I denied it of course. I was completely innocent. They checked their purses, and Andrea claimed she had a ten-pound note missing. Swore it was her emergency tenner and it had a small pen mark on it.'

'And?'

'They asked me to empty my purse and pockets to prove my innocence.'

'And did you?'

'Hell no. You really think I'm going to be bullied into that by a group of privileged, superficial woman? Not a chance. I knew they'd tell the others and no one would use me again. After being totally humiliated, I just packed up my things and left.'

Or you made good your escape before your guilt could be

uncovered, Kim thought. Innocent people didn't need to run for the hills.

'Why didn't you give us the whole story when we spoke last time?' Kim asked.

'Because, Inspector, every one of your victims was in that room.'

'And now you're here doing this,' Kim observed. Before, she had been part of the vibrant colour, light and excitement of the pageant world. Now she was in a windowless room face-painting a dead body.

'And all the better I am for it.'

'Really?' Kim asked.

Jenna put down the lipstick and faced her. 'You still have no idea how toxic that environment is?'

'Some kids enjoyed it,' Kim offered, feeling a need to defend at least one of the girls she'd spoken to this week.

'Perhaps, but not many from the lot you're talking about.'

'Toyah had a great time,' Kim said.

Jenna shrugged. 'Yeah, and look at the cost of that.'

'What cost?'

Jenna opened her mouth and closed it again. 'No. It's not my story to tell. There's been enough tittle-tattling already. But if you think that their family came out of it unscathed, you can think again.' She looked pointedly at the woman on the trolley. 'Now if you don't mind, this lady's family will be here any minute.'

Unable to keep her any longer, Kim thanked her for her time and opened the door to leave. The woman who had brought them downstairs materialised before them. An eerie gift given their location.

She guided them back to the front door, and Kim left with an uneasy feeling in her stomach.

'Wouldn't do that job if my life depended on it,' Bryant said as they headed to the car.

Kim considered where Jenna had once been, where she was now and the events that had led her there. Despite what the woman claimed about being better off, Kim had to wonder if she was looking at a motive for murder.

Before she had the chance to consider what Jenna had been implying about Toyah, her phone rang.

'Go ahead, Stace.'

'Seriously, boss, I've got no idea what's going on over at that house,' Stacey said.

'What house?'

'Toyah's. Just been chewed up and spat out by her brother, Tony.'

Kim's stomach lurched. It was the second time the girl's name had been mentioned in as many minutes. 'What happened?'

'I was working on the alibis like you said. Lottie's whereabouts are all accounted for, independently verified, but so far I can't place Toyah anywhere for any of the murders. No CCTV footage of her when she allegedly left the pub on Tuesday night, so I tried to get clarification and that Tony guy really gave me the business. Gotta say, the bloke is a total wanker who refers to Andrea as Toyah's mother alone. He seems to have disassociated himself from the whole thing.'

'Okay, Stace, go take a breather and leave it with us. We're on our way,' she said as the feeling of unease began to build.

SIXTY-NINE

'It's that party, isn't it?' Mom asks from across the table as I push the food around my plate, although the boiled chicken and plain rice is hardly tantalising. I heard a girl at school say that's what they fed their dog when it wasn't very well.

I nod. Yes, the party is on my mind. I hadn't expected to be invited to Sadie's eleventh birthday party. My first term at high school was only one week old and I'd barely spoken to any of my new classmates.

For a moment, I'd been excited and had eagerly accepted the invitation to a local pizza place rented by her parents. I'd thought it might be an opportunity to fit in in a way I hadn't been able to do in the past.

I'd spent the walk home from school working up the courage to ask Mom.

'Are you out of your mind?' she'd asked. 'Even you're not stupid enough to think you can go to a party two weeks before pageant season starts.'

My heart had plummeted. Of course I had known, but for just a few minutes, it had been fun to hope.

She'd laughed raucously and no more had been said about it.

But now the day is here and I can't get it off my mind. My whole class will be meeting up to have fun, and as usual I'll be the odd one out.

Mom frowns as she taps her nails on the table. 'You really want to go?'

I can't believe she's actually asking the question.

I nod vigorously. 'Of course.'

'Okay, you can go.'

'I can?' I ask, wanting to get up from the table to hug her, but there's never been a time when that was acceptable behaviour.

'I don't see how a couple of hours will hurt, and I know how much you want to make friends at your new school.'

'I do. I do,' I say, willing to agree with anything she says.

'Just one problem,' she says, her frown deepening. 'I heard one of the moms talking the other day. It's been changed to a fancy dress.'

My heart sinks. I don't have any kind of costume. I can't go.

Mom's expression turns thoughtful. 'Unless... no... I don't think...'

'What?' I ask, knowing she has an idea. I'm so close to going.

'That dress you had last year for the Little Miss Walsall pageant. The yellow striped one where the judges said you looked like a doll. We could actually make you look like a doll.'

'Okay,' I say, shooting out of my chair.

Going as a doll isn't my first choice, but I don't have anything else I can wear for a costume.

Mom follows me upstairs and grabs the dress from the wardrobe. 'Here, see if you can still get in it while I grab some make-up.'

I take off my clothes and pull the dress over my head. It sticks a bit around the ribcage, but I can just about pull it down.

'Okay, I've found these shoes,' Mom says, handing me some flat white patent shoes with a strap that goes across the foot.

'Um... I'm not sure...'

'It's not a fashion show. We're trying to make you look like a doll. They'll be perfect with some of your old frilly ankle socks.'

It's the first time I've seen her so animated about anything that's not to do with pageants. I didn't think she wanted me to go, but she seems as excited about it as I am.

'Right, sit down. I'm going to draw on some long eyelashes and apply some lipstick. I'll even put two red circles on your face. If we've got time, I'll plait your hair, and you'll be the best doll in the world.'

Half an hour later, we are rushing to the car. I catch a glimpse of myself in the glass of the door window. I'm not sure if I look like a doll or one of those drag queens I've seen on the telly. Mom has definitely put her all into making me a costume, and everyone else will be wearing one too. I won't be the odd one out.

'We'll only be a few minutes late,' Mom says as she drives towards the high street. The minutes stretch. I'm impatient. She's finally letting me go to a party, and I can't wait to see what the rest of my class looks like.

'Here we go,' she says, pulling into a space. 'Always good to make an entrance.'

She opens the door to the pizza parlour and pushes me inside.

Instantly I think we've made a mistake and we're at the wrong place, but then Sadie emerges from the crowd and spots me. Her face freezes in shock. So does mine. Her expression breaks down into amusement. Mine is still frozen in horror.

The room is full. There are more people here than are in my class. And not one of them is in fancy dress. The space is awash with jeans, leggings, tee shirts, hoodies and trainers.

A sea of people turn to stare as my cheeks flame hot. I am

rooted to the spot as the pointing and laughing starts. People step forward, in front of others, to get a better look. Mobile phones and cameras start to appear.

My humiliation is absolute.

'Oops,' Mom says with laughter in her voice.

How could she have made such a mistake?

And then I realise. In my eagerness to attend, I'd missed the logic of it all. If the theme of the party had changed, Sadie would have told me. I never told her I wasn't going to come.

I turn and see the amusement on my mother's face and all doubt about her deceit disappears.

She leans down, close to my ear. 'I wonder how many will want to be friends with you now.'

I turn away before the threatening tears add to my humiliation.

I already know that I will never forget this day as long as I live.

SEVENTY

'Go easy, guv,' Bryant said as they knocked the door of the house that belonged to Toyah's father.

'I'm fine,' she growled.

'Not really. Your face has been stuck on that expression since Stacey called.'

She ignored him, but he wasn't wrong. It took a lot to get Stacey worked up, so she could only imagine the level of Tony's rant, and no one got away with treating her team like that except her.

Thankfully it was Toyah who answered the door.

'May we have a minute?' Kim asked, stepping forward.

Toyah nodded, moving out of the way. 'Look, I'm sorry about—'

'Through here?' Kim asked, heading towards the kitchen.

She appreciated Toyah's effort in offering an apology, but it wasn't her manners at fault. She would go easy, give Tony the benefit of the doubt and assume he'd thought better of his behaviour.

Kim entered the kitchen, but before taking a seat, she

focussed her attention on Tony, who was reading the paper at the table. 'Mr Shaw, I understand that this is a stressful time for you all, but please don't ever speak to any member of my team in that manner again.'

A multitude of emotions passed over his face: irritation, rage, disgust. Kim could see that he wasn't the slightest bit sorry and in fact was ready and waiting for round two.

She held his gaze and tipped her head. She was happy to take the next bout.

Mr Shaw senior entered the room, and Tony glanced away. It appeared they now understood each other.

'Inspector, do you have an update?' he asked.

'Not as yet, Mr Shaw. We just need to clarify a couple of things with Toyah.'

'You couldn't have called?' he asked with a smile.

'We tried,' she said, looking pointedly at Tony, who pushed back his chair and headed for the kettle.

Mr Shaw beckoned for them to sit. 'Do you want us to leave?' he asked, looking over at his son.

Toyah immediately looked uncomfortable, and Kim shook her head as she sat down.

'It's minor details. We'll only take a minute,' she said before turning towards the young woman.

'Toyah, we just need clarification about the time you left the pub on Tuesday night.' She saw the look of horror that passed over Mr Shaw's features. 'It's procedure,' she reassured him. 'We have to be sure of everyone's whereabouts. One small detail can ruin an entire case in the courtroom.'

Mr Shaw nodded his understanding, even though his son muttered something under his breath over at the sink.

Kim ignored him and prepared to continue. She hadn't lied. That was exactly the reason they checked the accuracy of all timings. Defence lawyers were becoming increasingly focussed on attempting to discredit police investigations to get their clients off the hook. She chose to omit the fact that Toyah was the only daughter who didn't currently have an alibi for any of the murders.

'You said you left at eleven?' Kim clarified as Bryant took out his notebook.

'Did I?' she asked, frowning. 'Sorry, I think it might have been closer to ten. Then we went to the Cantonese place just down the road. I think we left there around eleven.'

A little bit different to what she'd originally said, Kim thought.

As though reading her mind, Toyah continued, 'Sorry, I didn't realise when I was asked that I needed to detail everything I'd done that night. I thought it was a general question.'

'Okay, no problem,' Kim said. It was checkable with receipts and further CCTV.

'And may I ask where you were on Tuesday morning?'

Mr Shaw frowned but said nothing.

'I was at home, with Mom,' she said as her eyes filled with tears.

Hmm... not so easily checkable.

'And finally, yesterday morning?' Kim continued.

'Here, with me,' Tony spat from the other side of the room.

Bryant was recording her responses for checking later. It wasn't something Kim was comfortable with pursuing further right now. Not least because there was another question she wanted to ask before she totally outstayed her welcome.

'Thanks for that. That's all we need. But while I'm here, can I just ask another question?'

'Of course,' Toyah said, but Kim could tell that her guard was up. She hadn't stopped chewing that thumbnail since she'd sat down at the table.

'When we spoke the other day, you told us that you loved doing pageants with your mom.'

'I did,' she said.

'And that when you'd had enough, you simply stopped and went on to other things.'

'That's right.'

'Are you sure about that, Toyah? Cos we're hearing otherwise.'

Panic registered on her face, and her stricken gaze immediately went to Tony.

'Inspector, is this really necessary?' Mr Shaw asked.

When she'd been asking his daughter where she'd been during three murders, he hadn't said a word, but he was speaking up when she was asking about pageants and Toyah's reason for quitting. Something wasn't right.

The air in the room had suddenly become charged. All three of them looked from one to the other.

'Of course it's fucking necessary,' Tony bellowed from the other side of the room. 'She won't be happy until she knows every last detail about us. Tell her whatever you want. I don't fucking care any more,' he said before storming out of the room.

His footsteps thundered up the stairs.

A distraught Toyah looked imploringly at her father.

'Go,' he said, waving her out of the room.

Mr Shaw took a seat as Kim wondered what the hell had just happened.

She waited.

Mr Shaw sighed heavily. 'I didn't tell you the whole truth the other day. I told you that Andrea got more and more into the whole thing and so did Toyah. She loved every minute of it. The events were always held at weekends, and I was normally working, so Tony had to tag along. Neither of us had any close relatives to babysit, and Tony didn't have many school friends.'

For some reason, Kim wasn't surprised.

'Tony hated every minute of it. He wasn't great with crowds of people, and he didn't like being the only boy around. Even some of the other moms used to tease him.

'As Andrea got more and more involved, she wouldn't even listen when I tried to tell her that Tony was suffering. She wouldn't hear it. She insisted that when Tony found something he was passionate about, she'd be just as enthusiastic. Over time things got worse. Not only did the pageants take over our weekends, but weekdays were taken up with learning and practising new routines. From that point on, Tony didn't get a look-in. He literally spent no time with his mom. He withdrew even more due to the arguments between me and her, but I couldn't make her see that he needed her.' He paused to take a breath. 'And then when he was fourteen years old, he tried to take his own life.'

Kim shook her head. The young man was far more troubled than she'd thought.

'I found him. He'd taken tablets. I'm still not sure if it was a serious attempt or a cry for help, but either way, it got everyone's attention, including Toyah, who has been plagued by guilt ever since. There was no question that the pageant days were over.'

'But the marriage ended anyway?' Kim asked, thinking that was something else the kid had had to deal with.

Mr Shaw nodded. 'Unfortunately it was too late. Much as I tried, I couldn't see Andrea the same way afterwards. Every time I looked at her, I pictured Tony lying unconscious on the sofa. I blamed her, which wasn't fair. I could have done more, and she never stopped trying to make it up to him.'

'He doesn't like to talk about it,' Kim stated, thinking about his earlier reaction.

'He has anger issues. He's very quick to react to stressful situations and has enough trouble trying to find work. If this comes out, it'll ruin his chances even further.'

'I'm sorry we had to raise it,' Kim said.

'It's not your fault. It can't be helped. It's just that the timing of all of this could not be worse for him.'

'Why so?' Kim asked.

'It's the ten-year anniversary this week.'

SEVENTY-ONE

Judith Palmer's childhood did not make for pleasant reading, Stacey thought. If she was using her own experience to guide others in her role as 'supporter', then goodness only knew what advice she was giving.

Stacey had learned that Judith Palmer had been born in Tipton to an alcoholic mother who was nineteen years old and had already done two stretches at Her Majesty's pleasure. Judith had spent the first seven months of her life in hospital suffering from alcohol withdrawal.

Her whole childhood had been horrific. She had been removed from school because her mom couldn't get up to take her. She was placed in and out of care her entire life, but her mom would always get clean and fool the authorities again. Her mom refused to do the decent thing and give up parental responsibility so that Judith would have the chance of adoption. Instead, she would fetch her out of care, and then the whole cycle would start again.

Judith had been sent around to the neighbours to beg for alcohol and had been forced to leave the house when her mom had entertained men for a cheap bottle of whisky. She'd been forced to eat the scraps from other people's bins when her mom forgot to feed her.

Her whole childhood had been a horrific litany of abuse and neglect at the hands of a woman who cared only for herself.

Stacey sat back and sighed, confused. Given what she'd learned, why the hell had she been able to read about such horrific mistreatment and yet remain unmoved?

Stacey was well aware that her emotions lived very close to the surface. Only the other day, Devon had read her an article about an elderly dog finally finding his forever home and the tears had gathered in her throat.

And yet here she was after a tale of prolonged suffering and heartbreak and she didn't feel a thing.

Her concerns about her own humanity were interrupted by the return of Penn and Tiff, who had chosen to take lunch in the cafeteria while discussing what to do about Olivia.

'Cheers, matey,' she said as Penn placed a ham-and-cheese panini on her desk. Betty was getting adventurous, and Stacey had developed a liking for this new addition to the menu.

She sat back to eat it while it was hot as the two of them sat down.

'Is her brief here?' Stacey asked, seeking a distraction from her own workload. A change was as good as a rest, her mom always said.

'Yeah, he's with her now.'

'Why so glum? She confessed,' Stacy said, taking a bite of the sandwich.

'Cos she didn't do it,' Penn answered. 'We just need to work out why she's saying she did.'

'So work it out,' Stacey said. 'She's not a puzzle, Penn; she's a human being, so why would she confess to a crime she didn't commit? What does she have to gain?'

'Maybe she's taking the blame to save her son?' he mused.

Stacey shrugged. It was possible.

Penn was not the most skilled interpreter of the workings of the female mind, but Tiff looked like something was beginning to germinate in her brain.

'Penn, is Logan still here?' she asked.

'I think so. He was fetching coffee, but he insisted he wasn't going home until he saw his mom.'

'Okay, sounds like a good idea,' she said, standing.

'She's under arrest,' Penn offered needlessly.

'Come on – I've got an idea,' Tiff said, heading out the room. Penn shook his head before following closely behind.

Stacey smiled as she pushed away her sandwich. Oh, how Tiff had grown since they'd first met her. There was still the natural effervescence and joy in life. She still whistled theme tunes and sang the wrong words to musicals, but there was a new solidity, a confidence that added balance. Stacey liked to think they'd all been a part of that growth.

She returned to the blogs written by Judith Palmer and started again from the beginning.

She'd been dipping in and out of the blogs to get to the core of Judith's issues, but this time she would read them in full and in the order they were written.

Something about them just wasn't making sense.

SEVENTY-TWO

Tiff unlocked the door to interview room one and placed her folder on the table. Her heart was beating hard in her chest, and she wondered again if she could pull this off.

Penn had convinced Olivia's brief to get a late lunch at the canteen while they finalised the paperwork with CPS to charge Olivia with her boyfriend's murder.

On the way back, Penn was bringing Logan to see his mother.

Tiff took a deep breath as the door opened and Olivia was brought into the room. Her eyes widened in panic as she realised what was missing.

'Where's my brief?' she asked, sitting down.

As instructed, the officer left the door open.

'It's not that kind of meeting, Olivia. We're not questioning you further. We can't charge you until we have the correct paperwork. We have your confession so there's nothing more for your solicitor to do.'

She visibly relaxed before her face turned pensive again. 'So why am I back in here?'

'Logan's been waiting to see you since we brought you in. He's very worried about you.'

Her face paled. 'I don't want him to see me like this.'

'He won't mind. He's just concerned. You've told us he takes such good care of you, and he just wants to check that you've not come to any harm. He's not going to think badly of you. He's your son and he loves you, whatever you've done.'

Tiff could see the torment that crossed her face. Olivia didn't know which particular lie she was going to get caught in.

'Can't he see me once I've been charged, once it's all final?' she said, biting her lip.

''Fraid not. Our protocols are much more stringent after that. But right now we can allow him a few minutes to say good-bye; we know how close you are. I'll have to remain present, and the door will be open, but don't worry, you won't even know I'm here.'

'I don't want to see him,' Olivia cried as panic contorted her face.

Tiff heard the door at the top of the corridor open, and Logan's voice found its way to his mother's ears.

The fear in the room was palpable.

'Please. I don't want to see him. I'm begging you...'

'Olivia, trust me,' Tiff whispered, squeezing her fingers across the table before Logan appeared at the door.

He stormed into the room and grabbed his mother's hands. 'Mom, are you okay?'

Olivia nodded.

'Logan, you can sit down beside your mom,' Tiff offered. 'She's fine, but she has something to tell you. We know you've been worried, and we appreciate your patience.' She paused. 'Because your mom is under arrest, I have to stay here, but we wanted you to hear the truth and say goodbye before we charge her.'

'Charge her with what?' he cried.

Tiff opened the folder to indicate she was no longer a part of the conversation. She began making notes and flicking through papers that had nothing to do with this case.

Logan gave her one final glance before dismissing her, but she was listening to every word with her head down.

'Mom, what's going on? I've been out of my mind with worry.'

He certainly sounded like the concerned son.

And there it was. Already Tiff was doubting her own suspicions because of how well Logan presented himself. No wonder Olivia probably felt that no one would believe her.

'I killed him, Logan,' she said shakily.

'What are you talking about?'

'I killed James because he was cheating on me. I followed him to the lake. I waited until the man opposite had gone, and then I pushed him in.'

Tiff didn't bother to look up to gauge Logan's response. His feelings didn't matter. It only mattered what came out of his mouth.

'Oh, Mom, you haven't told them this, have you?'

'Yes, Logan. I've confessed to everything. I'm being charged later.'

'Did they pressure you?'

'No. I just couldn't live with myself any more. The guilt was eating away at me.'

'But there must be something we can do to get you back home. Maybe it was the pills. If you were unstable at the time you did it, the judge—'

'I wasn't unstable. I knew exactly what I was doing. I thought about it, and I planned it. I'm going to prison for the rest of my life, and I deserve to.'

From the corner of her eye, Tiff saw Logan's head fall into his hands.

He had to accept that his mother had outplayed him. Their

life as he knew it was over. He was no longer her captor or her controller, but the big question remained. Would he own up and tell the truth about what had happened to James? Or would he reverse the bus his mother had thrown herself under and in effect get away with murder?

'Oh, Mom, I don't know what to say. You're not a murderer.'

Tiff held her breath. Was he really going to admit to it, or would he secure his mother's future behind bars?

Logan sighed. 'He must have really hurt you for you to do something like this. I suppose there was a part of you that must have wanted to get caught.'

Tiff held her breath tighter.

'I mean, why else would you keep all of his fishing stuff in the garage?'

Euphoria shot through her as Penn rushed into the room. Olivia had claimed to have pushed it all into the lake.

Only the real killer knew where the kit was.

'Logan Dench, I am arresting you for the murder of James Nixon...'

Tiff tuned out as she reached across the table and squeezed the hand of the bewildered woman.

'It's okay, Olivia. It's time to take your life back.'

SEVENTY-THREE

'Stace, are you sure about this?' Kim asked as Bryant pulled up at the address they'd been given by the constable.

'I know, boss, but that's where she lives. I'm telling you there's something weird here. I've read those blogs five times now, and every time Judith tells the story of her childhood, it all gets a little bit worse.'

'You think she's embellishing?'

'I dunno what it is, but I'm just not getting any raw emotion from her words. Unless she's able to recount the horror from a purely factual and objective viewpoint without any sentiment, then there's definitely something off.'

'Okay, Stace, we'll let you know,' Kim said before ending the call. Kim hadn't been able to shift the feeling that something wasn't right with Judith, and Stacey's instinct about the blogs had cemented the unease. The fact that she had links to two of the daughters warranted further investigation, and where better to start than hearing from her drunk and abusive mother?

The semi-detached home on the edge of Brockmoor didn't look like the dwelling of a barely functioning alcoholic who had been in and out of prison for a quarter of a century. They'd interviewed many alcoholic ex-cons over the years and very few of them lived like this.

'Could've got clean, guv,' Bryant offered as they approached the front door.

Yeah, wouldn't that be a convenient little detail for Judith to leave out of her monologues? Kim thought.

The door was opened by a slender woman in her early fifties. She wore a kitchen apron covered with pictures of baked beans. The smell of something delicious had followed her to the door.

'Mrs Pugh?' Kim asked, taking a good sniff. There was no obvious smell of alcohol.

'Close enough. Who's asking?'

Kim produced her ID.

'Oh, good Lord, what's happened?'

'Nothing,' Kim reassured quickly. 'May I just check that Judith Palmer is your daughter?'

A sigh. 'Would you like to come in?'

Kim nodded, taking the invitation as an affirmative answer to her question.

'Is she okay?' the woman asked, heading along a short hallway.

'Alive and well the last time we spoke to her,' Kim said, following her to the kitchen and the epicentre of the delicious aroma.

'Excuse me,' she said, opening the chest-high oven. 'Kids with lactose problems. I'm trying new recipes.'

Kim had already noted an assortment of kids' toys and wondered if she operated a day care facility. To Kim's knowledge, Judith was an only child. If her mother was taking in kids, she really had cleaned up her act.

'Mrs Pugh, we're—'

'It's not Mrs. It's my maiden name actually, but please call me Ellie.'

'Okay, Ellie, I'm not gonna lie. We're a bit confused.'

'Of course you are. As is every other police officer that comes here. I don't usually get CID, but there you go. Have at it,' she said, taking a pack of paperwork from a drawer. She reached for her phone and passed that to Kim as well.

Kim glanced at her partner to see if she had missed a vital part of the conversation. His expression said she had not.

'I'm sorry; I don't understand.'

'What's she accused me of this time? Last time it was abusive text messages; the time before that was threatening emails. Time before that it was—'

'Sorry,' Kim interrupted. 'We are talking about your daughter, Judith?'

Ellie Pugh nodded before seeming to realise they honestly had no clue what she was talking about.

'Oh dear, it's your first time,' she said, taking a seat.

They followed suit.

'I assume you've read her blogs.'

'We know of them,' Kim said. They hadn't read them all, but Stacey had given them a detailed summary, along with her opinion that something didn't seem right. Looked like the constable had called it right.

'So, you know her account of her childhood?'

Kim nodded as Ellie opened the document folder.

'This is her birth certificate, and this is the photo of me bringing her home two days later. Neither of us were addicted to alcohol, and her father took the photo.

'These are her school pictures from the age of five up to fifteen. She was never placed in care, and I haven't spent one minute in prison. I've lived in this house for twenty-seven years.'

Kim was actually looking at the house deeds. 'You keep all this close by?'

'Saves me searching around to prove my story every time you guys come to call.'

'So Judith is a liar?'

'My daughter is a fantasist.'

Kim sat back and waited for her to continue.

'Judith makes things up in her own head and then ends up believing them. She honestly doesn't feel she's lying and now truly believes that the history she's invented is actually the truth. Luckily, I always have the proof she's lying, and then she becomes the victim of some huge conspiracy theory.'

'So there's no truth to any of her accusations?' Kim asked.

'None, although it doesn't make this continued torture any less painful.'

Kim let out a puff of breath as she sat back in her chair. Her mind was truly blown.

'It's a lot to get your head round. I suppose I'm not easily shocked any more. I've been dealing with this a long time.'

'When did it start?' Kim asked.

'She was around seven. She didn't take well to having a sister, Laurie. When she came to the hospital, she sat in silence and wouldn't look at the baby. I thought it would pass, but it didn't. She would scream at me to take it back. One time when Laurie was just a few months old, we went to the park, the three of us. When we got back, I left Laurie in her pushchair while she slept.

'I came out from the kitchen to check on her and the pushchair was gone. I won't bore you with the details of my panic, but it transpired that Judith had wheeled her to the end of the road and left her there.'

So, Judith had had trouble sharing, Kim thought. Not uncommon in second siblings. Not so strange.

'I found disturbing pictures she'd drawn, and in every one there was a dead baby.'

'Did you take her for help?' Kim asked, noting they were definitely heading in the direction of strange.

'Of course. I was told that she'd grow out of it. That it was an adjustment at having to share my attention. I tried to believe the experts, but then one day I got a call from the school, saying Judith had spoken to one of the teachers and that as a consequence of that conversation, child services had been called.'

Ellie paused before continuing.

'Judith had bruises on her arms. She told the teacher it was where I'd grabbed her while smacking her. Obviously, I was horrified, but luckily, I knew where the bruises had come from. My friend had to sign an affidavit that her daughter had the same bruises from a bungee trampoline during a trip to the park a few days earlier.'

'What would have happened if you hadn't been able to prove it?' Kim asked.

'Who knows. I started keeping a journal of every activity, every accusation. I'm sorry but I'm not going to elaborate further. It's too painful.'

'Sexual abuse too?' Kim asked.

Ellie's face contorted in pain before nodding. They had now moved from strange to incredibly disturbed.

'Judith sought emancipation the day she turned sixteen, and I didn't fight it. Maybe I should have done, but by then she was like a stranger to me. It's easy to look back and wonder if I could have done more, but at that point I couldn't even allow myself to be in the same room as her without someone else present. I needed a witness to be around my own daughter. I lived in fear of the next accusation.'

Kim couldn't even imagine it. She suspected that legal emancipation was probably the best for all concerned.

'Was that when she changed her name?' Kim asked.

'No, Inspector, I changed mine. Pugh is my maiden name, but once she started writing those blogs...'

'And your other daughter – has she been affected?'

'You'll know from the blogs that in Judith's world, her sister doesn't even exist. Still, Laurie changed her name by marriage two years ago, and my grandson obviously has his father's name too.'

The smile that hovered at her lips at the mention of her grandson indicated that she still had family members who brought joy to her life.

She gave her bottom lip a good chew before she spoke again. 'Is she okay though? Is there anything she needs?' Obviously, a small pebble of hope existed inside her.

Kim thought of the hate and aggression that had emanated from Judith every time she'd mentioned her mother.

'No, I think she's perfectly fine as she is.' Kim hesitated before asking the next question. 'I'm sorry to ask this, but in your opinion, is Judith capable of murder?'

The woman instinctively began to shake her head, perhaps thinking of the child Judith had been before her sister had been born.

Then she shrugged as tears filled her eyes. 'You know, I honestly couldn't tell you any more. I really don't know the woman she is now.'

'Thank you for your honesty,' Kim said, not feeling at all reassured about the role Judith was playing in advising young women about their relationships with their mothers. Every event she'd used had been a lie, and yet her influence over vulnerable young women had been impressive.

'Is there anything else I can help with?' Ellie asked.

'No. We appreciate the time you've given us,' Kim said, rising from her seat as her phone began to ring.

She nodded at Bryant to say their goodbyes as she headed for the door.

'Go ahead, Stace.'

'It's Katie's mom, boss.'

It took a second for Kim to remember they were no longer talking about Sheryl Hawne, their first victim.

'What about her?'

'She's here, boss, and she wants to see her daughter's body.'

SEVENTY-FOUR

'Back up there, Stone,' Woody said, beckoning for her to sit down. Following Stacey's phone call, they'd taken one detour and then headed back to the station.

Oh, she really wished he'd caught everything she'd said the first time. She had a lot to do. Even so, she took a seat. When he rested his chin on his laced fingers like that, she knew she wasn't going anywhere.

'You're telling me that during your investigation, you've uncovered that the daughter of your first victim, who was initially a suspect, is now not her daughter and also not a suspect. In addition, her identity was stolen from the victim's real daughter, who is alive and well and currently staying at a local hotel. As if that's not enough, you now think that daughter one was abducted, and you have both daughter one and her real family downstairs.'

She nodded. Looked like he had got it after all. Although they hadn't really uncovered it. Much as it narked her, it was Frost's article that had hit the ignition switch on this one.

'You do realise that such a delicate situation needs to be handled with a great deal of care.'

'Of course.'

'If handled incorrectly this could cause a lot of damage.'

'I understand, sir,' she said, trying not to look at her watch.

'We need safeguards in place for both parties. Before this goes any further, we need DNA confirmation and counselling support available. We can't just throw them together and hope for the best.'

'Of course not.'

As if she'd reunite the parties if she wasn't sure.

'Can you imagine the damage we could do if this was some type of false alarm?' he asked.

'Absolutely, sir,' she agreed, knowing it was the quickest way to get her ass off this chair and back downstairs.

'Unbelievable,' he said, shaking his head.

'Yes, sir,' she said, standing.

'And I assume you're all sorted for the talent show?'

'Of course. You're not going to believe what we have to offer.'

'You don't have anything, do you?' he asked.

It wasn't often she'd lied to Woody and got away with it.

'Let's just say we're a work in progress.'

'And the investigation. Anything new since last night's update?'

Kim thought of her day so far. Where to begin? If only she had the time and they weren't trying to ensure their killer didn't strike again. She prayed that no more families were going to be destroyed.

'I feel we're getting close, sir. Now may I...?'

'Yes, go,' he said, waving her out. 'But remember what I said. Care and caution all the way.'

'Of course, sir, care and caution,' she repeated before heading out of the room.

SEVENTY-FIVE

'Inspector, will you please tell me what's going on?' Katie asked as she took a seat in interview room one. 'You come to my house for the second time in the same day and insist I come with you without offering me one word of explanation.'

Yeah, cos I'm still wondering where to start, Kim thought.

'Katie, a lot has happened since we spoke earlier. We have answers to many of your questions.'

'I don't understand. What answers? I only saw you a few hours ago.'

Kim took a deep breath. 'A woman appeared here earlier today claiming to be the real Katie Hawne.'

Katie's mouth opened in shock.

'She has the same birth certificate as you and has been living with her grandparents.'

'My family?'

Kim shook her head. Oh, this was going to get complicated. 'She is Sheryl's biological daughter and was abandoned when she was a few weeks old. She has no memory of Sheryl, and her life is good.'

'But that makes no sense. Why would Sheryl abandon her own child and then adopt me?'

And this was where it got even trickier. Kim hoped Katie was strong enough to take everything she was about to learn, but she was entitled to the truth. All of it.

'Katie, you weren't adopted. You were abducted,' she said, putting Woody's instructions out of her head.

'Wh-What?' she cried, pushing back her chair. She stood and then paced as though she could out-walk the truth. 'No, you're wrong. I must have been adopted. Sheryl would never have done that. No. I'm sorry. Oh God, I feel sick,' she said, sitting back down.

'It's true. You were stolen when you were just a few months old from a place called Ilkley. Sheryl abandoned her own baby and took you instead. She moved from Huddersfield with you and kept the secret for years.'

'But weren't the police looking for her?' Katie asked.

'Sheryl was an adult who had left of her own accord. There was no reason to link her name to the case of a missing baby twenty miles away. To be safe, she never let you do national pageants or anything where your name would appear in the press or bring unwanted attention. It was actually that article you did with Tracy Frost that brought Sheryl's real daughter here.'

'Oh my God, you're telling the truth, aren't you?'

Kim nodded. 'I wouldn't have told you if we weren't sure.'

Katie shook her head as though she could shake sense into what she was being told. Upon learning that she and Sheryl weren't related, her mind had instantly fixed on adoption. No way could she have prepared for this.

'What's she like?' Katie asked. 'The other Katie?'

'She's staying at a local hotel, and she'd like to meet you. Obviously, you're not related...'

'But it feels like we are,' Katie said, frowning, 'it feels like we're family. I've been Sheryl's daughter for twenty-five years. She'll have questions, and only I have the answers. I feel somehow like I just gained a sister.'

In a strange way, Kim could understand it. As if that wasn't enough, the next part was going to blow her mind. She was trying to think of a way to lead into the even bigger news when the woman opposite saved her the trouble.

'So we're both Katie Hawne?'

Kim shook her head. 'No, that was a borrowed identity. Your birth name was Rebecca. Rebecca Anderson.'

Katie allowed the name to register in her mind before puzzlement rested on her face. 'How do you know that?'

'I told you in the car we'd been busy. One of my colleagues has tracked down your real mom, who loved you very much and has never given up hope of finding you.'

A sob escaped from Katie's lips as the tears rolled over her cheeks. 'You mean it? I have a mother – a real one?'

Kim nodded.

'No, no. It's too much to process,' she said, dropping her head into her hands. 'So many emotions, and I don't know what to do with them.'

And that was exactly what Kim had been afraid of, but she couldn't stop now.

'Katie, we have counsellors available. It's a lot to take in, but we can offer you support in the next stage of—'

She shook her head. 'Where are they?'

Katie had to know it all so she could decide what was going to happen next.

Woody's words passed through her brain on a ticker tape: *DNA, safeguarding, disastrous.* But there was no doubt in Kim's mind. Having seen the Andersons, especially Katie's resemblance to her brother, she knew wholeheartedly that they were related.

'Your mum is in the room next door. Would you like to meet her?'

Katie raised her head from her hands. Kim had no idea what her answer was going to be.

SEVENTY-SIX

'Officer, will you please tell me what's happened to my daughter?' Viv Anderson asked while clutching her son, Justin, who looked equally as pensive as his mother.

The boss had instructed her to tell the Andersons the truth as gently as possible and also explain that the decision to meet would rest purely with Katie.

'Let me start from the beginning. It's going to be hard to believe, but your daughter was abducted by a woman named Sheryl Hawne. She abandoned her own child and took yours. She gave your child her own daughter's name, and she was raised as Katie Hawne. As that was the name we came to know her by, that's what I'll call her.'

Viv Anderson nodded, eager to know her daughter's fate.

'Sheryl was not an affectionate woman and craved attention either for herself or through Katie. As a child, Katie was entered into pageants and did very well. It wasn't an overly loving child-hood and she wasn't allowed friends, but she was not physically mistreated or harmed.'

Stacey could see the pain of hearing of the loveless childhood written over Viv's face. Stacey would imagine that every possible scenario had passed through her mind over time.

'In recent years, they became estranged following Katie's need to distance herself from Sheryl's overbearing and manipulative nature.' Stacey paused. 'On Tuesday morning, Sheryl was found brutally murdered, and Katie was our prime suspect.'

Viv cried out in anguish and clutched her son's arm.

'Had she not been a person of interest, none of this would have been uncovered. Within twenty-four hours, we knew Katie was no murderer. Katie had just found out that she and Sheryl weren't even related and was on her way to confront Sheryl. Sheryl had never indicated that Katie was anything other than her biological daughter. That's when Katie found the body.'

Viv was gobbling up every word as though it was her last meal. A multitude of emotions were passing over her face as she listened. The current one was hope.

'But she's alive?' Viv asked, clutching her son's hand harder.

'She is indeed, but she's learning all of this right now, and as you can imagine, it's a lot to take in. She's gone from natural child to adopted to abducted in a very short period of time.'

'You're saying she might not want to meet me?'

'It's a lot. My boss is currently—'

'She's h-here?' Viv asked.

'She's next door, but we have to respect her wishes. She might be completely overwhelmed and—'

A three-knock signal sounded on the door. The boss had told her how she would communicate Katie's wishes.

Stacey smiled. 'Or she might be about to come through that door right now. Are you ready?'

Viv sprang up from her seat. 'I've been ready since the day I lost her.'

'Come in,' Stacey called out.

The boss pushed open the door, and Katie stepped into the room.

The tears were rolling openly over Viv's cheeks as she looked deep into her daughter's eyes.

'Rebecca,' she breathed, opening her arms.

Katie flew into them as a cry escaped her lips.

A quick glance at Justin confirmed that he was eager to join in but was simply waiting his turn.

Stacey squeezed his arm before quietly leaving the room. Any longer and the tears building in her eyes would have been rolling freely over her cheeks.

SEVENTY-SEVEN

'My mind still hasn't caught up,' Olivia said as the car turned into the street of the house where she'd been a virtual prisoner for the last two years.

'It's been a crazy twenty-four hours,' Tiff said, having been tasked by the boss to get Olivia safely home.

'But how did you know what he was doing to me?' Olivia asked, turning her way.

'Some intuition at first, but it was your confession in the end. We knew you didn't do it. You didn't even know that the fishing equipment was hidden in your garage, but you still had enough detail to have known what happened, and you were so determined to go to prison for a murder you didn't commit. There could only be one reason for that. Preferring prison life had to mean that life out here was untenable. I even understand why you didn't hand him in. You thought he'd get away with it. You thought he'd find a way to beat it and then he'd most likely kill you for going to the police.'

'I thought my only chance of safety from him was behind bars,' Olivia said as the car parked outside her house.

'I'll walk you inside,' Tiff said, getting out to open the door for her.

'It feels strange,' Olivia said, looking at the key in her hand. 'I haven't touched this in almost two years.'

During the customary search, Logan had been relieved of his possessions, and the house key had been handed straight to his mom.

His first fifteen minutes of cell life had been spent shouting obscenities and insults about his mother and all the rest of them. Logan was no longer in control, and his frustration at that fact was being voiced loudly and continuously. She couldn't help thinking about Olivia's use of that same cell as a chance to reflect, relax and feel safe. However Logan decided to handle it, he wasn't going anywhere, and it was important that Olivia knew that.

'There are going to be a lot of things to get used to,' Tiff said. 'He's not coming back, but...'

There was one thing on her mind that Olivia hadn't yet mentioned, and it needed to be addressed, but she'd give the woman a chance to find her feet.

Tiff followed Olivia to the kitchen as she looked at things as though seeing them for the first time. That tension that had pervaded the air had now gone.

'I don't have to be frightened of them any more,' she said, touching the hob and then the kettle. 'They're just appliances.'

'Olivia, there's something—'

'I have to testify, don't I?' she asked quietly.

'To be absolutely sure of securing a conviction, we'll need you to recount what he told you. It's likely there'll be finger-prints or DNA on the equipment that will link him to it, but he could try and claim that he only moved it and that you put it there in the first place. Only your testimony can put him at the scene and secure that conviction.'

'He's still my son,' she whispered. 'I have to believe he didn't mean everything he did to me.'

Tiff went to stand beside her at the window. 'You're not giving testimony about his treatment of you or to punish him for that. He's not being tried for his despicable crimes against you. This is about telling the truth. He killed someone, Olivia. He admitted to you that he took the life of an innocent person, a very dear friend of yours. You know that can't go unpunished.'

'I know, and I'll do it. I have to do it.'

Tiff lay a reassuring hand on her shoulder. 'I'll let myself out, but you have my number, and if there's anything at all you need, give me a call, okay?'

'Okay,' she said, turning.

However improper it was, Tiff hugged her tightly.

'Thank you for saving my life,' Olivia said as they pulled apart.

'You're welcome, but I want you to promise me that you'll now live it. I know it's hard, but you deserve to be happy. Don't continue to live in the prison he constructed.'

Olivia chuckled, and it was music to Tiff's ears.

'That's a soundbite that's going to stay with me for a long time.'

Tiff was pleased to see that the smile forming on the woman's face was genuine and full of hope.

Tiff squeezed her hand before heading for the door.

She got back into the car and sighed heavily.

She felt like she'd aged ten years in the last few days. The images associated with the case had been with her every waking minute: the body at the lake, Logan's hostile and superior demeanour, Olivia's timid and cowering posture.

At no time had she been able to put the pictures out of her mind. It had been draining and exhilarating all at the same time.

Could she really maintain this level of commitment every day for the rest of her working life?

Olivia pulled back the net curtain and waved as she pulled away from the kerb.

She knew she had been instrumental in breaking Olivia out of her prison and had possibly helped save her life.

Yes, the commitment was huge, but so were the rewards.

Was she ready to do it all again?

You bet your bottom dollar she was.

SEVENTY-EIGHT

'Okay, folks, get yourselves together. It's been an emotional day and a lot of stuff got solved.' Kim turned to Penn. 'Just one question on the whole Logan-and-Olivia thing. Why the hell did he keep the fishing equipment?'

Penn and Tiff looked at each other and then back at her.

'Arrogance,' they said together.

Penn nodded for Tiff to continue. 'He couldn't leave it at the side of the lake, as that would have alerted police to James's location, and he couldn't throw it all in just in case it didn't sink. He had no choice but to take it away.'

'But to keep it?' Bryant said with disbelief.

Tiff went on, 'Because of his mother's acquiescence, Logan really thought he could control all events around him. He never considered that we might suspect him of murder, and even after admitting it to his mom, he never thought she'd tell on him – and he was right. She used the information to try and keep herself safe, but she was missing that last bit of detail that only the person who took James's kit would know.'

Kim nodded. 'Nice job, guys. Unfortunately, none of that helps with our main case and time's a ticking,' she said, tapping her watch. 'Thoughts?' She was mainly asking Stacey and Bryant. Penn was still on catch-up after working the Dench case.

Neither responded.

'Anything?' she prompted.

'Everything I've read or learned about the pageant world reeks of jealousy, rivalry, competitiveness and in some cases even corruption,' Stacey observed. 'But that's all to do with the contestants themselves. Why target the moms and why do it now?'

Stacey had voiced the questions running around in her head.

All of them turned their attention to the board.

Kim started thinking aloud. 'The daughters had varying levels of success, and some enjoyed it more than others. Katie hated every minute and was humiliated by Sheryl. Toyah had a great time but had to stop because of her brother. Lottie enjoyed it but needed to spend less time with her mother. Both Katie and Lottie have had problems with their moms in the years since, and we suspect both have spent time being advised by Judith Palmer, a complete fantasist who wouldn't know the truth if it slapped her around the face.

'Given the little mementoes found in the throats of all three victims, it's fair to say our killer is angry about something pageant related. We know the ERA detests the pageant world and will cross lines to get their point across. We have service people who have been forced from the industry for one reason or another and have every reason to bear a grudge against all of these women. That's only half of what we've uncovered this week, so tell me, folks, did I forget anything?'

'Nope, pretty good summing up there,' Bryant offered, nodding his approval.

'Okay, guys, there's nothing else for it. We go back to the beginning and start again. We're missing something. Penn, I want you looking at Stacey's matrix which lists everything about the girls, including what they had for tea last night. We need fresh eyes on that.'

Stacey pushed a paper copy of her matrix across the desk towards him.

'Stace, I want you going deeper on the backgrounds of everyone we've spoken to since Tuesday. We have to—' Kim stopped speaking as Penn sniggered.

'Well, that's a turnaround, isn't it? How did she explain that?' he asked.

They all waited.

'I mean the irony of Bobbi's attitude towards the pageant business in her role at the ERA.'

'Still drawing a blank, Penn,' Kim said.

'Well, surely Bobbi Carter is also Roberta Carter, the most popular pageant girl at the top of this list?'

Kim looked at Stacey, who looked at Bryant, who looked at her.

How the hell had they all missed that?

SEVENTY-NINE

Kim was still wondering how they hadn't connected those particular dots when Bryant pulled up outside the premises of the ERA.

Another question was why Bobbi hadn't mentioned it either. She'd had plenty of other stuff to say about the pageant world.

The lady herself answered the door. 'Ah, you again,' she said, stepping aside for them to enter.

This time there were another two women present, drinking beer and making use of the pool table.

Kim wondered if the place was for serious issues or just a hangout spot.

'Just wanna chat about some new information,' Kim said.

'Shoot,' Bobbi said, taking a seat and reaching into a bowl of popcorn.

'You were quite the little performer in the pageant world as a child.'

The absence of reaction from the other two women told Kim this was no secret.

'Oh, yeah. I did it, and I was bloody good at it.'

'You certainly were,' Kim acknowledged. 'You pretty much won everything you entered.'

'I did indeed. I won money, gift vouchers, holidays. It was a blast. I remember the days fondly.'

'You made friends?'

'It wasn't like that. You had to compete, be better than the rest. There were some girls that wanted to be liked, but that's not how you won the big bucks.'

'You must have been popular?' Kim asked, raising an eyebrow.

'There was a lot of jealousy, but you got used to it.'

'You speak so fondly of those times I wonder why you have such an aversion to them now.'

'I did pageants for six years, and it's taken double that to recover.'

'Go on,' Kim urged. Although prickly, Bobbi did seem to have it all together, and despite her passion-driven forays into vandalism, she presented as intelligent and educated.

She held up a piece of popcorn. 'See this little sucker? I can tell you the calories and fat content. I know how many steps I need to do on the treadmill to work it off. Each piece I eat triggers a battle not to run to the bathroom and vomit it back up so the calories don't register. I won't because I've made progress, but controlling the actions is much easier than controlling the thoughts.'

'And your relationship with your mother?' Kim asked.

She smiled ruefully. 'Part of my treatment has included accepting my mother for who she is and choosing to love her anyway.'

Kim had wondered if they were dealing with a twisted kind of jealousy, targeting the girls who had done well and making them suffer through the loss of their mothers. But there had been no girl more prominent and successful than this one right here.

'And how is your mom?' Kim asked.

'Very well when she was getting on the train a few hours ago.'

'Train?' Kim asked.

'Yeah, she's had a week away in Scotland. Loves it up there.' She checked her watch. 'Should be just off the train now. I promised to nip round later and listen to her tales of—'

'Call her,' Kim said as the pebble of worry formed in her stomach. Was Bobbi's mother safe only because she hadn't been in the area?

'Why?' Bobbi asked, frowning.

'Just do it,' Kim said.

Bobbi took out her phone and rang the number, on speaker.

Kim's heart quickened with every ring that wasn't answered.

The call went to voicemail.

Bobbi immediately tried again. Same result.

'What time does her train get in?' Kim asked.

'About ten minutes ago.'

'To where?'

'Cradley Heath.'

'Is your mom on social media?' Kim asked.

'Isn't everyone?' Bobbi asked.

'What platforms?'

'Facebook,' Bobbi said, rolling her eyes. 'Loves showing off where she's going and what she's doing.'

'Private or public?' Kim asked.

'Public... why?' Bobbi asked as it dawned on her that Kim wasn't making polite conversation.

'Show me,' Kim said.

With a few taps on her phone, Bobbi showed her the profile.

'Shit,' Kim said, barely needing to scroll. An innocent-enough post stated where she was leaving and what time she'd be getting back. It wouldn't take a genius to use Trainline and fill in the blanks.

'Who collects her?' Kim asked, handing the phone back.

'Sherwood Taxis. She calls them when she's a couple of stops away.'

'Ring them. See if they have her.'

'Inspector, I think you need to calm down. I'm sure my mom is perfectly fine. Her phone was probably in a black spot.'

'Feel free to try her again, but I've got three dead pageant moms, and it looks like the only thing that's saved your mom is that she was a few hundred miles away.'

Finally, Bobbi's expression took on some of the fear that was twisting Kim's stomach.

'Hey, Jim, it's Bobbi Carter, Leona's daughter. Did you get a call from my mom?'

Bobbi put the phone on loudspeaker.

'Yeah, we got her call.'

Bobbi's face began to relax.

'So what's she playing at?' Jim continued.

'Wh-What do you mean?'

'Messing us around. When we got there, she'd already gone.'

EIGHTY

'Penn, get someone to Leona's house. Two out of three murders have been committed at the victim's home. If our killer suspects we're onto them, it's unlikely they'd be that stupid, but we have to rule it out. Once you've done that, start thinking of other locations. Stace, start gathering CCTV from around the train station. We need to know what vehicle picked her up.'

'On it, boss,' they said together before she ended the call.

They'd hotfooted it out of the ERA premises with a promise to Bobbi they'd be in touch the minute they knew anything.

Bryant had started the journey towards Cradley Heath while she'd been talking to the team.

She had no chance of getting CCTV direct from the station, but there was a chance someone had seen something.

'Everybody is most likely gone by now, guv,' Bryant said, pulling up in front of the glass doors.

'Fingers crossed the ticket master saw something,' she said, clinging to any shred of hope.

She was pretty sure the kiosk looked out onto the road.

She was proven right about the kiosk as she entered. The

station appeared to be between arrivals and departures and was empty except for a man in his early sixties reading a book.

The ticket master was facing the other way. She tapped on the glass to get his attention. She didn't have time to wait.

'Hey there,' she said as the man and his frown approached the glass. 'There was a woman who came through here about an hour ago. Average build, brown hair, with a leopard-print suitcase.'

'Okay,' he answered, waiting for more. It wasn't until the description came out of her mouth that she realised how little she had.

She took out her phone and found Leona's profile. She held it up. 'This woman.'

The man's blank expression didn't change.

'She got into a car. Do you know what type?' she pushed.

He frowned as though wondering if he was being asked a serious question. Given the numbers of people that passed by him every day, she couldn't really fault him.

He shrugged.

She knew that no amount of strong-arming was going to produce an answer.

She stepped away from the glass. 'Okay, Bryant, if you have any bright ideas, now would be—'

'I saw her,' said the man with the book. 'Sorry, I couldn't help overhearing. It was the suitcase that got my attention.'

'You saw her outside?'

He nodded. 'I was running late and missed my train anyway, but my wife has the exact same case. I can't tell you what make of car or anything. She was putting it into a boot, if that helps.'

Kim showed him her phone. 'This woman?'

He nodded. 'Definitely her.'

'Did you see the driver of the car?'

He shook his head. 'No, but I'm sure she's not in any danger.'

'Why would you say that?'

'Because she was under no coercion. She had a wide smile plastered across her face.'

'Thank you,' Kim said, heading back towards the car.

They hadn't learned much about the vehicle, but they did now know that Leona Carter had been taken by someone she knew.

EIGHTY-ONE

Stacey pressed the refresh button on her email for the tenth time.

The train station had one camera on the front of the building, and Stacey was sure there'd be something of interest. If only they'd send the footage along, she seethed silently.

After giving them a fifteen-minute time slot to search and an explanation of the urgency, she'd expected to receive the footage in a couple of minutes.

It had been almost ten minutes, and she was considering a second call.

'Nothing at the house,' Penn said, ending the call he was on. 'An officer is going to wait there. Any ideas on locations?' he asked her.

'If the killer hasn't taken Leona home, it has to mean they know we're onto them. Somehow, somewhere this week, we've got close. So this one has to make a statement. It has to say something,' Stacey offered.

'It is absolutely no surprise that your best friend is a profiler,' Penn observed, tapping his keyboard.

'Yes,' she said in triumph as the footage landed in her inbox.

She clicked on the file which opened onto the road that passed the station. A car pulled up, and Stacey could tell it was a Nissan Juke. She had a great view of the passenger side of the car and the roof. Not a thing of the driver's side.

Before going further, she clicked back to the beginning. Damn, the pull-in angle didn't show any part of the registration number. She continued watching until Leona stepped out onto the pavement. Her head turned to the right as though looking for the taxi she'd booked. Stacey watched as Leona jumped slightly. From the similar reaction of a man walking past, Stacey guessed that the driver of the car had peeped their horn.

Leona's attention was attracted to the car. She leaned down to look through the passenger-side window, obscuring Stacey's view. There was around five seconds of interaction before Leona straightened. The window went up, the boot popped open and Leona lifted her case into the back of the car before coming back around.

There was no doubt in Stacey's mind that the expression on her face was delight.

Leona got into the car, and Stacey's last hope was for a glimpse of the number plate as it pulled away.

'Aaargh,' she growled as the car moved slowly out of shot but gave no view of the registration.

Although she'd been watching the back of the car, a movement up front caught her eye.

She played it back. Her eyes widened as she saw Leona's head smash against the window.

EIGHTY-TWO

'Where am I going, Penn?' Kim barked into the phone.

After what Stacey had just told her, they didn't have a minute to lose. The fact that their killer was foregoing any kind of preamble meant they were in a hurry. They wanted Leona dead as soon as possible.

'I've got two potential locations, boss. Following Stacey's suggestion that our killer will want to make a statement at a place that means something, we have two local sites associated with pageants during our time frame. There was a community hall in Netherton that hosted some of the smaller pageants. The building is gone, but the land is still vacant.'

'And the other?'

'A civic hall in Wordsley that hosted the bigger events. The building is still there but derelict.'

'Did they have to be in opposite directions?' Kim asked, knowing that wasn't Penn's fault. 'Okay, people, which one?'

'Wordsley,' they all said together.

'Agreed. Penn, get yourself to Netherton just in case and let me know when you get there,' she said before ending the call.

Bryant was already heading away from the kerb.

Even if they'd called it right that their killer was intent on using a meaningful location, she now had to wonder if they'd chosen the right one.

If not, Leona Carter was as good as dead.

EIGHTY-THREE

Bryant took a left at The Cat and headed away from Wordsley High Street. The remains of the civic hall were located on the edge of the town before it gave way to the countryside beyond. It was one of those forgotten buildings that had been sold to a developer, but the planning permission for seven houses had been denied.

The subject of the eyesore came up now and again in news-paper articles or local Facebook groups, but no one seemed to know of any further plans, and the building fell further into disrepair every year. The owner no longer valued it enough to add fencing or other prohibitive measures, and it had been subjected to abuse by squatters, homeless people and vermin.

They drove straight into the car park. Kim immediately spotted the back end of a vehicle tucked around the side of the building. Thank God they'd called it right. There was no reason for anyone else to be here.

They jumped out of the car as a second vehicle sped into the car park. The headlights temporarily blinded them.

'What the—?' Kim stopped speaking as the occupant got out. 'Bobbi, what the hell?'

'I followed you. Where's my mom?' she asked, heading towards the building.

Bryant grabbed her arm. 'You can't go in there.'

'Get your hands off me,' she growled.

'Shut up,' Kim hissed. 'They'll hear you.'

She didn't have time for this. 'Bryant, keep her out of the way.'

Bobbi's arrival meant that Bryant was now busy babysitting and she would be forced to go into the building alone.

'Oh, bloody great,' Kim said as the first spots of a shower began to fall. When the hell was it going to stop raining?

'Just let me go,' Bobbi cried.

'You're not helping this situation one bit,' Kim snapped.

Bobbi tried to pull away from Bryant, but he held her firm.

'It's my mom,' she cried as the tears rolled down her face. 'I just want to help.'

Kim regarded her for a further few seconds as something clicked into place in her brain.

Then she sprinted towards the door.

EIGHTY-FOUR

Most of the building exterior had been vandalised. Graffiti plastered the walls, and there was no clear path through it which avoided the debris of glass and brick underfoot. Kim knew this would once have been the foyer to the event space and that the double doors ahead led to a hall that had once had a dividing curtain for smaller events.

No matter how slowly she tried to traverse the space, the shards and gravel crunched underfoot. A scurrying noise to her right did nothing to ease her nerves. Approaching slowly to remain undiscovered wasn't working.

She took a deep breath, burst through the door and stopped dead at the sight that met her.

Leona Carter was tied to a chair, her head lolling backwards. A swollen bruise was evident on the left side of her face.

A figure towered over the seated figure, brandishing a knife in front of her.

'Wake up,' screamed Carly Spencer. 'I want you awake when I kill you!'

'Step away,' Kim called out, keeping her voice calmer than she felt.

During their two conversations, Carly had seemed to be the most together person they'd spoken to, and the one least affected by her time in the spotlight. She'd recently lost her mum to natural causes and closed down a lucrative business. Kim could now see the link between all of those events, and the timing had been staring her in the face.

'Don't come any closer,' Carly said, turning.

Kim didn't dare move closer. The distance between Carly and Leona was two feet. She was more than fifteen feet away.

On her best day, Kim had no chance of covering the ground before a fatal wound was delivered.

This wasn't a situation where she was in immediate danger. She wished it was: she'd swap places with Leona Carter in a heartbeat. But it didn't matter if there were a hundred officers in and around the building. Not one of them could have physically restrained or disarmed the woman before she made her last kill.

And Carly knew it. She knew it was over and that she wasn't leaving this building without handcuffs. The only question remaining was whether she would leave one more dead woman behind her.

'Why, Carly?' Kim asked, simply, even though she already knew the answer.

'Of course you need to ask that,' Carly spat. 'I can imagine it now, a loving mother who encouraged and guided you. A mother who only ever wanted the best for you. A mother who—'

'I was taken into care when I was six years old,' Kim said, giving as much detail as she was prepared to offer.

'Lucky you. I only wish that had been my fate.'

'But that—'

'Couldn't have been any worse than what I suffered. You already know that abuse doesn't have to be physical. That woman ruined my life.'

'What did she do, Carly?' Kim asked.

'You'll never understand. You'll never get the damage that

was done. Can you even contemplate what it was like to be put on a diet when you're eight years old? To be fed nothing but lettuce and tomato until your weight dropped off? To have your mother call you a little "fatty" or "porky", to insult your skin, your teeth, your nose, everything about you. All the time, every single day, remarks on your appearance. An endless cycle of practice, practice, practice. Nothing else. Not even schoolwork. Walking up and down until my heels blistered and my legs cramped, until I fainted with the effort, and even that wasn't enough. It was all about getting those trophies and being the best.

'You see, I wasn't a natural pageant child. I wasn't pretty enough; I wasn't thin enough; I wasn't personable enough to the judges. My mom tried to make a silk purse from a sow's ear. She wanted a beautiful, graceful child that she could show off as a representation of herself. She clicked her fingers and I had to perform, and God forbid I made a mistake. I hated every second of it, but I tried, my God I tried, just to get a kind word from her, just to get her approval.'

'But you look—'

'Oh yes, I look different now. I've made it so. I take any treatment I can to look good. It's what she always wanted.'

'You started the pageant business for your mother?' Kim asked.

'Of course. I was still seeking her approval until the minute she died. All I ever wanted was for her to be proud of me. It's shaped my entire life.

'At the pageants, they would tell us to just be ourselves, but then they taught us to be someone else with all the fakeness and trickery, so being yourself isn't enough, is it? It's not enough for the judges or for the people who are supposed to love you. So you tell me, Inspector, what are you supposed to do?'

'Make yourself perfect?' Kim asked.

'Exactly. And I did. I always said yes when I wanted to say

no. I never expressed how I truly felt. She made me settle for less than I deserved.

'I've spent my entire life trying to please others, allowing people to mistreat, criticise or ignore me just to get their affection. I let fear of my mother govern every decision, and I always put myself last. That's what she did to me.'

'But she's gone, Carly. She can't hurt you any more.'

'Oh, I know that. Her death has freed me from those constraints. The moment she took her last breath, I was euphoric. Every last bit of self-loathing, of feeling inferior fell away. I no longer had anything to prove to anyone. It was the best moment of my life.'

At that second, the door behind Kim burst open, startling them both.

Like a flash a figure shot past her.

'Bobbi, no,' Kim cried as the young woman ran towards the knife.

EIGHTY-FIVE

'Don't do it,' Carly said, pointing the knife Bobbi's way.

'Bobbi, no, stay back,' Leona breathed. The sound of her daughter's name appeared to have roused her back to consciousness.

Bobbi stopped running but didn't take her eyes from her mum.

The tension in the room was now charged. For a moment, Kim had been convinced that no flesh was going to see the end of that knife. Now she wasn't so sure.

At no point during their exchange had Carly looked like a crazed killer. But now her eyes were darting around. Her movements were fidgety and stilted. Her voice was no longer steady, calm, reasonable. There was a tremor in her voice and, more importantly, in the hand that held the knife.

The door behind her opened again and Bryant entered. His face was flushed, and he was rubbing at his right hand. She could see a small amount of blood and guessed that Bobbi had bit him to escape.

His arrival had done nothing to ease the tension as Carly looked around at them all.

'Does no one understand that I've been doing a good thing?' Carly asked, gesturing with the knife.

Realising the peril both she and Leona were in, Bobbi remained silent and looked to Kim. Kim shook her head, indicating that Bobbi should continue to keep her mouth shut. One wrong move and Leona was dead.

She had to try and salvage this situation before someone got hurt.

'You always were the nice girl, weren't you, Carly?' Kim asked.

'I still am,' Carly said, as though that much was obvious. 'I'm being a good friend. I'm taking care of my buddies. All I ever wanted was friends, but my mom ruined that for me. She humiliated me so that no one would ever be my friend. But now I'm free and they're all still suffering. I'm emancipating them, relieving them of the impossible pressure of trying to be good enough for someone who will never be satisfied. They deserve to feel how I feel, to get the opportunity to live their own lives. I'm helping...'

Bobbi gasped, and Kim took the opportunity to interrupt.

'Carly, they don't all feel like you,' Kim said, forcing herself into Carly's one-way conversation.

'Of course they do. I remember them all; sometimes they'd cry, or they were quiet, or they weren't allowed to play, to make friends. They were all the same as me; suffered the way I suffered. They all carry the scars from the monsters who were their mothers.'

'They weren't all monsters,' Kim insisted.

'Of course they were. Who other than monsters would subject their children to that kind of abuse?'

'They didn't all see it that way,' Kim said. 'Right, Bobbi?'

Bobbi looked her way, and Kim nodded for her to speak.

'Carly, I love my mom. I couldn't bear the thought of

anything happening to her. Sh-She's my rock,' Bobbi said before her voice cracked.

Carly looked genuinely confused. 'But she...'

'Of course there were times your friends were unhappy,' Kim said. 'Maybe they were bored, fed up, tired, hungry, miserable, spoiled, any number of things, but they weren't all suffering the things you imagine, the things that you were. I'm not saying they all had the perfect mother–daughter relationship, but does that even exist? I'm not sure I've ever seen it. Have you?'

For a moment, in order to talk to Carly in a measured, calm manner, Kim had to put the picture of three dead women out of her mind.

'Carly, I get it. You thought you were helping your friends, and maybe in some cases you were, but that's not true with Bobbi and Leona.'

The woman's head lifted, and she whispered her daughter's name.

'Can't you see that Bobbi is beside herself with fear for her mother?'

'That'll pass as soon as she's able to be herself,' Carly said, shaking her head. 'She is trapped by her mother's expectations, but she'll see as soon as I—'

'She's already herself,' Kim protested. 'Like many of the others, Bobbi enjoyed the pageants for a while. She enjoyed winning, but when she didn't want to do it any more, she told Leona and they stopped.'

Kim paused to give Carly time to digest what she'd said. Her words had registered somewhere.

'Is Leona perfect? Probably not,' Kim said. 'Do they have to work at their relationship? Probably. But that's what it's all about. All relationships are a work in progress. But I can promise you that Bobbi loves her mother very much, and if anything happens to her, it would break Bobbi's heart. The exact thing you're trying to avoid.'

For the first time, Carly seemed unsure of herself.

'I know you're trying to help your friends,' Kim said. 'I get it. But you won't be helping Bobbi. Look at how she ran in here because her mum was in danger. If you take that away, you'll ruin the rest of her life.'

'It's true, Carly,' Bobbi whispered.

Carly searched her old friend's face as though looking for signs of deceit. Bobbi was unable to look anywhere except at her mum.

Seeing the truth right in front of her, Carly took one more look at the knife before allowing it to fall from her hand.

Bobbi ran to her mother.

Bryant ran to the knife.

Kim ran to catch Carly before she crumpled to the ground.

EIGHTY-SIX

Kim took no pleasure in handcuffing Carly and leading her to the front of the building. She felt only satisfaction that no more innocent women would be brutally killed at Carly's hand.

She paused at the edge of the building.

More police cars had arrived. A precautionary ambulance was waiting to the left, and Bryant was speaking to the driver of the police van primed to transport their killer while a paramedic applied a dressing to his hand.

Bobbi and Leona were holding on to each other as though neither of them would ever let go.

'What have I done?' Carly breathed as her eyes rested on mother and daughter. Tears streamed over her cheeks.

'You took away hope,' Kim said as she moved Carly forward slowly. 'None of these relationships was perfect. They rarely are. But your actions mean that the girls you were trying to protect can never make things right.'

Kim had never felt the need to seek parental approval. In her case, she'd have had to kill her own brother to get her mother's approval. And yet there was a small voice inside her that said she wasn't immune.

Her foster mother, Erica, had been one of the most decent people she had ever met. The woman had had a strong sense of right and wrong, tempered with fairness and empathy. She had trusted authority and believed in justice. The three years Kim had spent with her had taught her a lot.

She rarely questioned what had fuelled her own desire to become a police officer, but was she seeking parental approval from one of the only people she'd ever truly cared about? Erica hadn't given birth to her. She hadn't fed or bathed her. She hadn't rocked her to sleep as a baby. Yet in those few years, the relationship had been formed. Was her career choice an effort to make her foster mother proud?

'I just wanted to be their friend,' Carly said.

'You didn't have any friends at school?' Kim asked.

Carly shook her head. 'I wanted some. When Mom had had enough of me trying to find ways to make friends, she allowed me to go to a party not long after I started high school.'

Kim waited.

'I believed her when she told me it was a costume party. She dressed me as a doll. I was the only person in a costume. I looked ridiculous in front of the people who I'd be spending the next five years with.'

'I'm sorry she did that to you,' Kim said honestly.

'The girls will all hate me now, won't they?' Carly asked in a voice that was broken and lost.

Carly had only ever wanted to be liked, to be special, to have her mother's approval and to fit in with her peers. She wasn't psychotic and she wasn't evil, but ultimately she had taken three innocent lives.

'Yes, Carly, I'm afraid they will.'

EIGHTY-SEVEN

The image of Carly Spencer had accompanied Kim home and followed her back to the station on this Saturday morning.

She and the rest of her team were busy completing the paperwork for the CPS prior to formal charges.

Tiff had brought them all coffee and pastries on the way in. A lovely gesture.

There was something different about Saturday morning overspills. Not that they normally worked your average eight-hour days, but they weren't officially on duty, so the dress code slipped a bit. For both Stacey and Penn that meant jeans and tee shirts, but for Bryant it was just the absence of a tie. The behaviour of the team altered a little too, as demonstrated by Penn, who was throwing scrunched-up paper balls at Stacey.

The case was over. They had their killer locked away, and no more innocent people would die at her hand. Job done, and yet Carly was still on Kim's mind.

Now and again, along came a killer that she just couldn't hate.

There was no denying that she had visited three horrific crime scenes, and not one of the women had deserved to die in such a brutal manner – although Katie's mother, Sheryl, was a close call. Kim had to wonder what kind of woman could abandon her own child because of an unsightly birthmark. That alone was heinous enough, but to then steal the child of another woman, knowing the heartbreak it would cause, just because she hadn't been satisfied with her own was beyond unforgiveable.

She'd updated all the girls last night before anything had hit the news and had received different reactions from all three. Although officially named Rebecca, the daughter of their first victim would always be Katie in Kim's mind, and she'd been the first to learn the news. Once the shock of the killer's identity had abated and the reasons had been explained, Kim had sensed an element of sympathy in the woman's tone. Katie remembered Carly fondly from the past and had voiced concern about the reactions of the others. Given her history with her mum and all that she'd learned since, Katie could be forgiven for wanting to close this chapter of her life.

Lottie had shouted and screamed and threatened all kinds of things to Carly if she ever got near her. Kim understood her reaction. The person who had stolen her opportunity to heal the relationship with her mother was someone who was known to her. Carly's reasons were lost on Lottie. She didn't care that the woman thought she was helping her friends. Nothing mattered except the fact that her mother was gone.

Toyah had cried her heart out, almost as though having confirmation of the killer made it all more real. And permanent.

They'd been difficult calls to make, but at least the girls all had closure. The process of releasing the bodies could begin, and the normal order of things could resume.

The week had raised many questions for all of them about beauty pageants. Of all the girls she'd met, Toyah seemed the least affected by her time in the pageant world and had just enjoyed the dressing up and the limelight. Initially, her mum hadn't taken it too seriously, but even Andrea had been caught up in the competition and rivalry of it all, to such a degree that her other child had attempted to take his own life, forcing them to stop. Even so, Toyah's memories of competing were positive and filled with joy.

Poor Lottie had been talked into an estrangement with her mother by Judith Palmer and would never get the chance to make things right. Their boundary break was now permanent, and she would have to live with her choices.

Kim's own feelings on pageants had clarified in her mind as the week had worn on. Her initial indifference to the whole process and her naïveté in thinking it was all innocent fun had been replaced by a belief that it would all be so much better without the parents. The kids themselves enjoyed much of the process, and the ruthless competitiveness and rivalry was only bred into them by the parents' own desire to win. Some had hated it, and some had enjoyed spending that time with their mums.

And then you had Judith – poor, bitter, twisted Judith – who had reinvented her whole childhood to get back at her mother for having a second child. The fact that she now believed the lies she'd formed from jealousy and hate was something Kim still had trouble understanding.

Now aware of the damage her daughter was doing to others by setting herself up as an unofficial expert, Ellie Pugh had instructed lawyers to get the blogs taken down and the self-help book removed from sale. Kim was glad of the action, as legally there had been nothing they could do to prevent Judith from spreading her lies.

Throughout the week, Kim had been presented with different mother-and-daughter relationships and every one of them had been unique.

She'd seen the toxicity between Katie and the woman who hadn't even been her mother. She'd learned of the lack of affection between the two despite having lived their whole lives together. In contrast, she'd seen an immediate connection between her and her real mum, despite having not seen each other for over two decades.

She'd seen a fun and loving bond between Toyah and Andrea, who, despite the pageant years, had remained close.

She'd seen estrangement between Sally-Ann and Lottie, a situation that surely could have been rectified if they'd been given the time to agree boundaries they could both live with.

And then there'd been Carly: a girl who had been shaped by her mother's obsession. A girl forced into the spotlight who felt neither physically nor mentally suited to parading in front of judges. A girl who had wanted a peer group that was more than opponents and rivals, friends she didn't have to compete against. A girl who had been so consumed by gaining the approval of a cold and distant mother that she'd allowed that hunger to shape every decision she'd ever made. And once free of that constraint, the landscape of her existence bore no resemblance to her past. She had been liberated by her mother's death, unbound from the shackles of trying to please and satisfy someone who would never be content. That release had prompted her to free her friends, certain they were suffering in the same way.

The brutality of the act had been excessive, and Kim wondered if Carly would ever realise that she had been killing her own mother over and over again.

Inevitably her thoughts turned to Patty, the woman who had given birth to her; the woman who had killed her twin and almost succeeded in killing her too.

Patricia Stone had not been a mother to her, but Kim had lied when she was trying to talk Carly down. She'd said the perfect mother didn't exist, but that wasn't true. She had existed, and Kim had had the honour of being in her care for just three short years.

She swallowed back the emotion that always accompanied her thoughts of her foster mother, Erica.

Keith had been a wonderful man, and she had learned countless lessons from him, but Erica had been the love, the nurture, the person who had been determined to reach her and instil a belief that she could be or do anything she chose. She would consider Erica to be her only mother until the day she died.

Another lesson she'd learned this week was the expectation put on women after childbirth. There was a pressure to become perfect, yet every woman possesses their own identity before becoming a mother.

They might be a little bit selfish, a little bit lazy, but once a mother, all unsaintly traits were expected to disappear. Annoying traits became despicable, and any misdeed was followed by 'but she's a mother' as though that erased all other aspects of her personality.

It was possible to love a child and still have bad traits.

On the flip side, two other members of her team had found a mother being subjected to horrific abuse at the hands of her son. Had it not been for their tenacity and their insistence on following their gut instincts, who knew how much longer Olivia would have been imprisoned.

Penn and Tiff had caught a murderer and saved a life at the same time.

She was proud of all of them, she realised as she took her cup into the squad room for a refill.

What she hadn't heard from inside the Bowl was Tiff quietly humming a tune from a Disney animation about building a snowman or something. Without warning, words started to come out of Tiff's mouth, refashioned to the popular tune.

'Do you wanna write a statement?'

Kim's head snapped around.

'Before you go outside to play.'

Stacey, Penn and Bryant followed her gaze, mouths open.

'Do you wanna get your work done?'

Tiff remained head down, oblivious to their stares of awe.

'On a rainy Saturday.'

Kim coughed, and Tiff finally became aware of their attention.

She coloured. 'Sorry, I can't help myself.'

Kim glanced around the room at Penn's Rubik's cube, Stacey's hula hoop and Bryant's magic set.

A slow, genuine smile started to creep onto her face.

'Err... Tiff, have you got a minute?'

A LETTER FROM ANGELA

First of all, I want to say a huge thank you for choosing to read *Guilty Mothers*, the twentieth instalment of the Kim Stone series, and to many of you for sticking with Kim Stone and her team since the very beginning.

Originally this was in my mind to write as book nineteen, however the sudden passing of my mum prevented me being able to write this book at that particular time.

As ever, the books are born from my own need to explore subjects, and two that had been on my mind for a while were narcissistic mothers and the world of child pageantry. It made perfect sense to explore these together, and I must admit there were some surprises along the way (not least the amount of money paid for a pageant dress).

In addition, I wanted to explore the theme of psychological/physical abuse within the family unit, and this idea worked well with the theme above.

I thoroughly enjoyed writing *Guilty Mothers*, and if you enjoyed it, I would be forever grateful if you'd write a review. I'd love to hear what you think, and it can also help other readers to discover one of my books for the first time. Or maybe you can recommend it to your friends and family...

I'd love to hear from you – so please get in touch on my Facebook or Goodreads page, X or through my website.

And if you'd like to keep up to date with all my latest releases, just sign up at the website link below. Your email address will never be shared, and you can unsubscribe at any time.

www.bookouture.com/angela-marsons

Thank you so much for your support; it is hugely appreciated.

Angela Marsons

www.angelamarsons-books.com

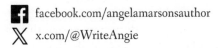 facebook.com/angelamarsonsauthor
x.com/@WriteAngie

ACKNOWLEDGEMENTS

Phew, this was a complicated one, and boy did Jules earn her cake and coffee with all the meetings we had about this one. From the outset, I knew the book that I wanted to write and, as ever, Julie was responsible for making sure that what was in my head translated to the written word. It's so easy to just repeat and to emphasise the great part that my partner in crime plays in the process, but I say again that these books would not exist without her tireless enthusiasm, support and belief in me even when I am full of doubt.

Although no longer with us, my eternal thanks goes to my mum, who would tirelessly spread the book news to anyone who would listen.

Thank you to my dad and to my sister Lyn, her husband Clive, and my nephews Matthew and Christopher for their support too.

Thank you to Amanda and Steve Nicol, who support us in so many ways, and to Kyle Nicol for book spotting my books everywhere he goes.

I would like to thank the awesome team at Bookouture for their continued enthusiasm for Kim Stone and her stories.

Special thanks to my editor, Ruth Tross, who was fiercely enthusiastic about the idea for this book from the moment I mentioned it. Without fail, my nails suffer every time I send her my work. This book was read within record time, and she was quick to put me out of my misery in a very timely manner. Her suggestions and input for improvement are both intuitive and accurate, and between us, we make the books the best they can possibly be.

To Kim Nash (Mama Bear) who works tirelessly to promote our books and protect us from the world and has offered a much appreciated helping hand through this one. To Noelle Holten who has limitless enthusiasm and passion for our work, and to Sarah Hardy and Jess Readett, who also champion our books at every opportunity.

A special thanks must go to Janette Currie, who has copy-edited the Kim Stone books from the very beginning. Her knowledge of the stories has ensured a continuity for which I'm extremely grateful.

Thank you to the fantastic Kim Slater who has been my writing buddy and an incredible support to me for many years now. Our friendship formed before either of us were published, and our writing journeys have been travelled together. Massive thanks to Catherine Thomson, who just gets me and my humour, and will happily assist me if I ever need to turn to OnlyFans! Also to the fabulous Renita D'Silva and Caroline Mitchell, both writers that I follow and read voraciously and without whom this journey would be impossible. Huge thanks to the growing family of Bookouture authors who continue to amuse, encourage and inspire me on a daily basis.

A special thanks to a lovely lady named Emma Jones who very kindly offers her advice and guidance on all morgue-related queries. Thanks for the make-up tips in this one, Emma!

My eternal gratitude goes to all the wonderful bloggers and reviewers who have taken the time to get to know Kim Stone and follow her story. These wonderful people shout loudly and share generously not because it is their job but because it is their passion. I will never tire of thanking this community for their support of both myself and my books. Thank you all so much.

Massive thanks to all my fabulous readers, especially the ones that have taken time out of their busy day to visit me on my website, Facebook page, Goodreads or X.

PUBLISHING TEAM

Turning a manuscript into a book requires the efforts of many people. The publishing team at Bookouture would like to acknowledge everyone who contributed to this publication.

Audio
Alba Proko
Melissa Tran
Sinead O'Connor

Commercial
Lauren Morrissette
Hannah Richmond
Imogen Allport

Data and analysis
Mark Alder
Mohamed Bussuri

Editorial
Ruth Tross
Melissa Tran

Copyeditor
Janette Currie